THE GHOSTED BRIDGE

D1493801

KRISTY ABBOTT

NORTH STAR PRESS OF ST. CLOUD, INC.
St. Cloud, Minnesota

First edition: August 1, 2013

Printed in the United States of America

Published by
North Star Press of St. Cloud, Inc.
P.O. Box 451
St. Cloud, MN 56302

www.northstarpress.com   Facebook - North Star Press Twitter - North Star Press

Life is a very narrow bridge between
Two eternities. Be not afraid.

—Rabbi Nachman of Braslav

PROLOGUE

THE SEDAN PULLED OUT of the residential street onto the main road. Inside the car, the windows were streaked with frozen moisture. Outside, above the sleepy streets, pointed peaks and rugged rocks towered in a circle of red.

The driver and her companion were quiet, each contemplating the words they'd just heard from a psychic reader with a soft, Scottish accent. Both sat stone-faced, neither knowing the thoughts in the other's head.

Highway 179 South was slippery with icy muck and as the sedan snaked past Sedona's restaurants and tourist shops, the mud sprayed along the bottom of the car.

"Hey," the driver said.

"What?"

"Look over there." She pointed to a purple building squatting in a sloppy parking lot next to another nearby building labeled ALIEN MUSEUM.

The passenger turned toward her with one eyebrow raised. "You want to go to the Alien Museum?"

"Naw, look at the other building. See what it says in that window?"

The woman read the neon words, PSYCHICS AVAILABLE. "Yeah?" she responded, curious.

"Let's go in. I've got this weird feeling to go check out one more psychic. After all, we came all this way . . ." She paused, measuring her words with a shake of her head. "Maybe I'm crazy but you never know what could happen. Besides, that last one, that Karisleena—"

"Was ridiculous. That's the truth," her friend agreed.

The car slid into the lot and pulled into a space in front of the building. Both women gingerly picked their way across the parking lot.

"Well, here goes nothing," the passenger said.

"No," the driver answered. "Here goes something." She opened the old wooden door and the two walked in.

1

CHAPTER
ONE

MADISON MORGAN STEPPED QUICKLY over the red rivulet of streaming mud. Everywhere, the streets and walkways were covered in the grimy stuff. The land in this part of the desert had not accepted the recent onslaught of winter gently. The clay makeup of the soil made the ground more of a glass-topped table than a sponge for moisture.

In the summer, the roads were layered with a fine, burnt dust that coated everything—shoes, clothes, skin, souls. People came from all over to bathe themselves in the healing properties of the bloody dirt. They hiked and climbed, looking for vortexes and magic. They tromped in meek groups through the pathways and narrow avenues of Sedona searching for someone to give them the answer. But the greasy streets were quiet this December afternoon.

Madison's temper was growing shorter. Psychics, like herself, weren't supposed to be late. They were supposed to be early or at least on time. Of all the professional rules she lived by, this was the first—a late psychic was an unemployed psychic. She quickened her pace.

Above her, the sun appeared beyond the austere cliffs. Finally some warmth might make its way down to this muddy mess. The cold stretch of the last few days irked her. Madison considered this low mood that had been seeping in for the last few weeks. She wasn't sure if it was the weather or the sharp pangs of disillusionment hammering at her these days. Twenty years as a carnival act was taking its toll. She had toyed with the notion of getting out of the business but had no idea who she would become next. Madison would have loved to take some quiet time to escape and never return, but her office had been filled nearly all day, every day for the past month. And she needed the money.

One last hop over a puddle and she landed onto the doorstep of the Enlightenment Center of Sedona. The purple building was rimmed with Christmas lights and crystals hanging from gutters and doorways. A collection of old rooms and porches served as a store and book room on the first floor and offices on the second. This ramshackle shelter looked as if it had been there forever, sprouted from the small grove of trees in which it sat, just yards from the highway. From the parking lot visitors could see glistening reflections of light bouncing off hanging fairies and transparent gems inside. Wind chimes sported multi-colored glass and floated beneath dragons, angels, and sunbursts.

Madison breathed deeply and shook her head. Maybe this would be the last reading. Maybe she'd just walk out of her office on the heels of this final client and never come back. The thought cheered her. She opened the tilted front door and bounded inside.

"Hello!" She bellowed in her New Jersey timbre. "I'm here, I'm heeere!"

She rounded the corner from the jewelry and gem display cases to the book room where she found two middle-aged women standing sheepishly next to Miriam, who sat at the concierge desk.

Miriam did little to hide her displeasure. "These two came in earlier and have been waiting for you." She accompanied the patronizing tone with a benevolent smile for the benefit of the two strangers.

Delightful as ever, thought Madison. She swung her sandwich bag around in the air and merrily faced her new clients.

"Wow," said the tall one to her blonde companion.

Madison looked intently at the inquisitive eyes. They were brown with pretty green specks set in a narrow face. The woman looked athletic, a good deal taller than both her companion and Madison. Her lean frame and long legs looked comfortable in her faded blue sweatshirt and jeans.

Madison cocked her head. "Have we met before?"

The woman laughed a quiet response and considered her in return. "I don't think so," she said.

"Hmm . . ." Madison brightly turned from the woman and announced, "You're lucky. I'm feeling the energy. I'm all here today!" She grinned.

"Wonderful," intoned Miriam, already intent again on the computer screen.

"So, what are we doing?" Madison looked between the two.

"Well," the tall one offered. "We found your picture in this book." She pointed to a binder loaded with the advertising pages of psychics, palm readers and clairvoyants. "We kinda thought, I don't know . . ." the woman looked at her friend for assistance.

Her friend remained silent, eyes fixed on Madison.

"We want to do a session together," the tall one continued uncomfortably. "Like, you talk to one, the other one sits by and—"

"Nope. Won't do it." Madison cut her off. "One at a time, that's the way I work," she sounded like a surgeon in the operating room.

"Oh, ok," the tall one replied, flummoxed. She looked at her companion, who merely shrugged. "Well, all right. Then who do you want to go first?"

Madison turned to the shorter woman, examining her for the first time. She, too, looked athletic, yet in a more compact, muscular way. Her thick blond hair was pulled back in a simple ponytail. She wore no makeup and was dressed similarly in jeans, sweatshirt, and worn tennis shoes. The woman flashed her an open-eyed look. "I'll take you," Madison said.

"Wow," the tall one said again. "Okay, I'll just wait for you guys on the stairs, I guess. There's no place else to sit?" She looked at Miriam, who clearly felt her responsibility toward them had expired.

"No, not really," Miriam shook her gray head and looked back at the screen dismissively.

"Off we go!" declared Madison. The short one followed her obediently around the corner and out the door, causing the wind chimes to tinkle their fragile limbs in discordant applause.

CHAPTER TWO

KATHERINE LOOKED AROUND the shop wondering what to do with herself. It was clear that the little lady behind the computer was going to be of no help at all, so she strolled out of the book room and made the rounds of the glass cases one more time.

She'd never seen so many strange knick knacks. Grant would probably lose his mind in a place like this. The thought of her husband brought a brief smile. Katherine hadn't seen him in three weeks—a long time for a life-sabbatical. This escape was supposed to give her a new perspective on things. It was a curious journey that had brought her here to frozen, spectacular Sedona.

Katherine Simon was awash in mixed emotions these days. She wanted desperately to get her life on track but couldn't get herself out of stuck mode. Maybe this Madison would push her in the right direction. The ceramic dragons glared at her, gemstone eyes glittering in the soft blue light under the glass.

Jesus, was she completely losing her mind? She walked into the fairy room and was entranced by just how many different colors and sizes of these mystical maidens existed. If someone had told her a year ago she'd be standing in a place like this, she would never have believed it. But here she was now, killing time while Barb and her dead people were sequestered with Madison. Katherine wondered idly, *would Barb's dead people be loud today?*

She peeked into a tiny porch overlooking a noisy creek below and caught a whiff of incense. The place had an inviting ambience. It felt like a tree house teetering on the edge of this hill.

After making another round, she settled onto the narrow staircase with a book she'd found about awakening a giant within. She snorted at the thought. First she'd have to find the damn thing before she worried about waking him up.

The jangling of the bell on the door startled her. Barb and Madison stomped inside.

"Well, how was it?" Katherine searched both of their faces. Had it already been thirty minutes?

"Good," Barb grinned.

"Did your dead people talk?"

"Ha. Yeah, some of them showed up. We can talk about it later."

"Yes, missy," Madison broke in. She pointed a finely manicured finger in Katherine's direction. "Your turn now!"

She dutifully got up, handed her book to Barb and followed the blonde head, about six inches shorter than her own.

"Have fun!" Barb's voice rang out behind them.

They walked outside to the next door. Inside was another steep stairway. At the top a tiny office overlooked the ice-rimmed creek. Madison led Katherine into the room and hummed absently along with Christmas music playing on a small CD player. She pointed to the chair opposite her desk.

Katherine sat down and studied the psychic. Madison looked to be about forty. She had flawless skin and meticulous make-up, but the most striking thing about her was her brilliant blue eyes. When they focused on Katherine she got the unsettling feeling that this woman could somehow see into her soul.

As Madison smoothed an errant bang back into place and eased into her chair Katherine surveyed the office. It was a pleasant space. Three of the walls were painted a soft cream color. The wall behind Madison was a gentle blue and decorated with photos of entertainers Katherine didn't recognize. Opposite the desk, a bookshelf beneath a large chart of playing cards held journals and some sort of Indian statue. On either side sat two wicker chairs with satin pillows. Through the slightly open window, Katherine could hear the creek bubbling. Although she was nervous about this whole experience, the room calmed and cheered her. She sighed, "Mmm, I love Christmas music."

"Really? Christmas music makes me sad." Madison glanced at her computer screen then proceeded to rifle through a pile of books next to it. "Where is it?" She mumbled to herself.

"How come?" Katherine asked.

"Because it reminds me of home and I haven't been there in a while." Madison's hand flew up and pointed at a bulletin board behind her covered with photos of people.

Katherine was somewhat surprised that Madison offered this information so easily. It made her wonder all the more about who this woman really was.

"Why don't you go home?"

"Can't."

"Oh, where is home?"

"Jersey." Madison squinted through her reading glasses and lifted a huge book off of the desk. From underneath it she dug out a well-worn, spiral-bound tablet. "Ah ha! Gottcha!" She then eyed Katherine. "I can't go back because I used to hang out with guys named Vinny and Zito." Katherine felt embarrassed by Madison's gaze.

"Oh, I see." Katherine didn't really see at all.

Then out of nowhere, Madison said something that produced a wave of goosebumps on Katherine's arms.

"You know, one time I had a lady in here and I saw bad things. You can't imagine how hard that is. It's only happened a couple of times." She leaned back in her chair and chewed on the end of her pen.

Katherine drew in a silent breath. Had Barb told Madison about the conversation they'd had driving up last night from Phoenix?

Now she was hooked. "What did you do?"

"It was terrible. I saw no color; I just saw a huge black space. I knew something was going to happen. I saw she was making herself sick, you know, like talking herself into it. I needed to tell her but I didn't know if I should. I mean, how do you tell people that kind of stuff?"

Katherine shook her head. It felt like Madison was asking her opinion, psychic to psychic. She was officially freaked out now.

"I said it in a way that meant if she didn't change something, bad things might happen. I can only suggest, you know, I can't change people's lives for them . . ."

Katherine shifted uneasily.

"Funny. Haven't thought about her 'til just now." Madison shook her head, instantaneously back to business.

"Let's get started," she commanded in her distinctly New Jersey accent. "After all, we've only got thirty minutes."

"Okay." Katherine's stomach tightened just a little bit. She sat straighter in the chair and waited.

"Full name, middle initial?"

"Katherine P. Simon."

"Birthday?"

"November 2, 1960."

"Address?"

Twelve-ten Brown Road, Orono, Minnesota . . ." She waited to see if Madison wanted the zip code.

"Zip?"

"Five five three nine one."

"Phone number, number of siblings, number of children?" Madison rattled off the commands and entered the numbers.

Katherine obligingly answered, all the while wondering why Madison needed all this stuff. Was this info for some future marketing thing? Katherine felt more uncomfortable.

"Okay." Madison looked at the numbers and began scribbling alongside of them. She quietly recited the figures to herself and created a series of formulas. She drew a circle, bigger and bigger until it contained all the numbers on the page.

Then, she put her pen down emphatically. "Give me your hands."

Katherine stretched them forward.

Madison grasped them. She looked intently into Katherine's eyes. Katherine was fascinated now. She felt like Madison was leading her somewhere else. Madison continued her stare and Katherine waited, her hands and soul linked to Madison.

This is crazy. It certainly is, the logical voice in her head said, but Katherine stubbornly put it aside, locked in the magnetic blue-eyed gaze pulling things out of her, summoning things around her. She felt exposed, yet wonderfully safe. It seemed that they weren't two separate people, more like they had bonded together in one space over the glass-topped desk.

Suddenly, Madison released her hands and sat back. "Have you been in an accident?"

"What?"

"An accident. Did you fall off of something or hit your head sometime in the last year or so?"

"Nooo, I don't think so."

Madison shook her head. "I see a strong, green aura around you. Somethingggg . . ." she drew the word out, "has happened to your head."

Katherine shook her offending, supposedly injured head.

"Well, just remember then." Madison looked down at the tablet. "You are stuck, you know."

Katherine nodded.

"Why can't you just move? You've got to be responsible for yourself. What's bothering you?"

Katherine licked her bottom lip, wondering how much information she should share. After all wasn't this "psychic" supposed to know everything?

Madison didn't give her time to answer. She pulled out a large, dog-eared book and began leafing through. "Let's see, you are a seven of hearts. That means you are open to love. You get love, you give lots of it. You do things for people. You like to do these things. Umm, you have a huge heart. And because of that," she paused, peering at Katherine. "You get hurt easily."

Tell me something I don't know, Katherine answered silently.

Madison looked up at the chart of playing cards on her wall. She pointed to the display and stood up. "See, you are a seven of hearts," she repeated, tapping the chart. "Hey, I know why we connected!" She turned to Katherine and smiled triumphantly. "I am your Venus card!"

Katherine stared back. "My Venus card?"

"Yeah. It means we are connected. Like, we could be best friends if we really knew each other. You know how great it is to have a Venus connection? It's really fantastic. Not everyone has one."

"Ah," Katherine replied, not really understanding but trying to appreciate the good news.

Madison continued. She told Katherine snippets of things to expect, ways to move forward. None of the information seemed especially clairvoyant but Katherine appreciated it nonetheless. She was, at the least, fascinated by this strange, captivating woman.

The half-hour seemed to blink by. Katherine was suddenly disappointed when Madison announced their time was up. It felt really strange experiencing a connection that seemed deep and then having it end with the stroke of a clock's hand.

"You know," Madison's voice was friendly and warm. "You can always call me. I can talk to you any time."

"Thanks." Katherine wondered how her unemployed husband would take to a new "friend" who cost $100 an hour to converse with.

"Here, take my card." Madison pushed her business card into Katherine's hand. The touch of her fingers sent a little shock into Katherine's system. She looked at Madison's photograph and was drawn again to the intense gaze. *Wow, losing that visual was going to take a while,* she figured.

They got up and walked out the door. Madison reached up and tapped her shoulder. "You remember how to get out? Just down those stairs."

"Yeah, and thanks again." Katherine headed down the steps.

"No problem. Have a great day." Madison turned and walked back into her office but stopped at the doorway. "Hey . . . hey?"

"Yup?" Katherine looked up at her. The light of the doorway below framed her in an outline of white. She looked expectantly at Madison and saw something on her face she couldn't quite define.

Madison just stared at her for a minute. "Hmm. I don't, I'm not sure. Oh hell, never mind. It's nothing." She shrugged. "Have a good one."

"You too." Katherine turned, puzzled. She trotted down the stairs and out the door into the muddy lot now gently lit by the sun.

She glanced around and saw Barb was waiting for her in the car. She gingerly stepped through the puddles of brown water.

"Well? How did it go?"

"That has to be one of the craziest things I have ever done!" Barb laughed. "I gotta say, it was cool."

"Yeah, did she get a hold of your dead people?"

"Yup, they were all over the place."

Katherine laughed at the image of Barb's deceased relatives jostling for position in the small room.

She maneuvered the car onto the road back to Phoenix.

As MADISON SAT BACK down into her chair, she considered the session. Katherine's hands had felt light in Madison's grip but the cascade of colors all around her body—brilliant purple and shards of red and yellow—indicated some strong cosmic energy around her. A halo of green had shrouded Katherine's head like a soft hood. The color told Madison this woman had hurt her head somehow. She'd liked doing this reading. She'd felt a peculiar connection with this stranger . . . and then there was something else.

Madison had felt a sudden urge to stop Katherine on the stairs. At the very moment she called to Katherine, one more picture wavered before her eyes. But it wasn't really a picture, it was a person. An older lady stood at the bottom of the stairs, directly in Katherine's path.

After a moment's consideration, Madison decided not to call attention to the apparition. After all, it had been a long day, the girl's thirty minutes were up, and mention of this probable trailing spirit from the reading before would definitely screw up getting her next appointment going in time.

As these thoughts had competed for Madison's attention and Katherine had turned back to go down the stairs, the old woman disappeared. Katherine went out the door never knowing that a ghost had been there, hovering just behind her.

Madison didn't have much time to think about it, as she had to retrieve her next client. She tidied up the room and looked at the chair where Katherine had sat. The vacant space still shimmered with a slight aura of green.

ON THE ROAD BACK to Phoenix, Katherine and Barb bounced their recollections back and forth recounting their separate meetings with Madison. They laughed loudly over Barb's dead people and the fact that Madison had talked to a few of them, and then made the rest go away.

They weren't so sure that Madison wasn't just a really good entertainer. But both agreed that the experience had been one they'd never forget—worth the fifty dollars each had spent.

Then Katherine remembered the other thing. "Did you say anything to her about what we talked about on the way up?"

"What do you mean? What did we talk about on the way up?"

"Remember how we wondered what a psychic does when they see that something bad is going to happen to someone?"

"Oh yeah." Barb shook her head. "Nope, never came up. Why?"

"It was really weird. Before we even started, she just randomly brought up this situation where a lady she had read was going to have something bad happen to her and Madison wasn't sure how to tell her."

"Wow, freaky."

"Don't you think it's strange that she starts by discussing the same subject we'd talked about the night before?"

"That definitely creeps me out," agreed Barb.

Behind them, the looming Sedona cliffs traced a scarlet outline in the shadowy winter sky.

"I'll tell you one thing," Katherine said quietly.

"What's that?"

"2007 definitely needs to be better than 2006."

"I'll drink to that," Barb answered.

CHAPTER THREE

MADISON DIDN'T NOTICE it at first. The psychic was having so many readings a day that her tablet pages covered with numbers were filling up fast. She made a note to go to the office supply store and get another. She looked at her watch and then contemplated the rest of the day. One more reading, and then off to yoga at five thirty. The phone rang.

"Yup, I'm coming." She told the perpetually crabby Miriam. As she trotted down the stairs she realized that the heaviness that had been hanging around her had lifted a bit. Mercury was leaving retrograde, she guessed.

Fifteen minutes later she was just warming up her new client (an eight of diamonds—business expertise extraordinaire) in a session on opportunities coming down the pike, when a peculiar vibration filled the room. Immediately, Madison's hands went cold and her hair stood on end, but she was so intent on the young woman in front of her that for a minute, she didn't even see the older woman standing in the corner. With the ghost's entrance, she got a stronger shiver that told her someone from the other side was around, and she lifted her eyes to meet the measured gray stare from the woman by the door.

"Uh oh," Madison squeaked.

"What?" The young woman sat up straight in her chair.

"Nothing, just, just . . . shut up for a minute."

The girl sat back quickly with a look of shock.

Madison turned her attention to the figure in the corner. She looked older and was dressed in a plain pastel dress. The ghost's skin shimmered as her visible molecules filled the space where she stood. Madison sat fascinated. She knew from experience that these people didn't typically speak in words. In fact, they rarely made themselves seen. They used pictures instead. The ability for this one to crystallize impressed her.

The ghost stood silently in the corner. Madison realized that this amount of energy was a huge effort. She whispered softly to the apparition.

"You have a word for this girl?" Madison pointed at the silent woman, whose face still registered confusion. The woman looked over her left shoulder. Seeing nothing, she looked back to Madison, eyes wider than before.

The apparition gave no trace of response. Madison tried again. "You need something from this girl?" Her quiet presence entranced Madison.

"Is your mother still alive?" Madison asked the client quietly.

"Yes."

"Grandmothers?"

"Yes." The woman was brimming with prickling curiosity. "Is there somebody here?"

Of course there is somebody here, Madison's internal dialog snapped. *What are you, an idiot? Do you think I'm making this up?* But the voice that left her lips was soft and gentle. "Yes, we have a visitor here. Do you know an older woman who has passed?"

The girl brought a ragged fingernail to her mouth and began furiously chewing.

Madison breathed deeply and spoke from inside herself. "Who are you here for?" It seemed as though the presence would not respond but then ever so faintly, the ghost moved her head slightly toward the door. It was a subtle gesture but one that effectively told Madison this visitor wasn't attached to the woman in the chair.

"I can't think of . . . I don't really know anybody—"

"That's okay." Madison cut her off. "Just remember it. Maybe it will come to you later."

"Oh, okay."

Madison looked back at the door. The corner was empty. She felt unbearably tired all of a sudden. This typically happened when spirits spent that much effort to connect with her. It was as if they tapped her energy to create a link. She felt the weariness settle about her shoulders. She passed her hand across her face and turned her attention back to the reading. A familiar tingle rose behind her eyes. The sensation was a sign she'd get when she realized a heightened sensory connection. She hadn't felt this way in a long time. It took nearly all her concentration to finish the reading.

THREE HOURS LATER, MADISON was drenched in sweat. She looked down at her black spandex pants clinging to her generous thighs and was thankful for her extra long, two-piece yoga top. Her new blue tank layered over a white racerback definitely brought out the sass look. Madison was quite sure that yoga was her newest love. She wiped down victoriously with a towel and congratulated herself on a job well done as she pulled her sweats on. She felt giddy with endorphins as she walked with Janine to the parking lot. "Hey, got a question for you," she said as she stepped carefully over the patches of red ice fastened to the asphalt.

"Yeah? Shoot." Janine smiled at her from inside her heavy parka hood. *Jesus,* thought Madison. *It's not that cold.*

"I was giving a reading today and this woman from the other side dropped in. I thought she was there for the client. When I asked her, she didn't really answer. But J, it was so cool because she made it so easy for me to see her."

"Wow," Janine pulled her jacket more tightly around her. "How did it feel?"

Madison knew that Janine, despite her wacky nature, had a very sensitive medium's gift. By "it," she meant the energy, the focus, the atoms of attention and intention that combined to make up a visitor's impression. "It kind of felt, I don't know, soft." She shook her head, trying to find a better way to describe the encounter. "She absolutely wanted to give me a message of some kind."

"Are you sure she wasn't a grandma, an aunt or somebody like that?"

"The client told me she didn't recall having an older woman who'd passed. And when I asked the spirit who she was here for, she tipped her head toward the door, like somebody out there, not in the office. But it wasn't . . ."

"Wasn't what?" Janine prodded.

"It was like she wasn't ready to show me who she wanted to connect with. It kind of felt like she was, I don't know, introducing herself."

"Ahhh," Janine looked up to the stars, partly hidden by rolling clouds. "Could be she's someone for you?"

"Yeah, but dontcha think I would have gotten that?" Madison shook her head. "Plus, I think I've talked to just about everyone I've ever known whose passed."

"C'mon now, you know better than that! There's always one more who wants to come in and leave a grain of wisdom. Think of all those who fill up that place! How many have we got in each life congregating around us? At least 200 souls every lifetime. You know that!" Janine waved her hands around her in a hula dance motion, as if summoning the invisible minions.

Madison watched her friend float through the frozen lot, feet skipping in the cold, swinging her arms gracefully.

"I bet if she's really got something to say, you'll see her again." Janine skimmed across the slick, frozen surface to her car.

"Yeah, probably. Well, I'll letcha know."

"Nice! And Madison," Janine pulled the car door open and eased herself in. "Be patient. Be available. You know what I mean? Wait for the pictures."

"Right."

Madison turned away and walked toward her Taurus at the other end of the lot. "Tally ho!" She waved and yelled as Janine drove past. Her friend responded with a peace sign and maneuvered her Mustang into the street.

CHAPTER
FOUR

IT FELT GOOD TO BE HOME. Despite the fact that the weather in Minnesota was terrible, Katherine had been ready to come home long before she did. The trip to Sedona had been a welcome distraction and actually motivated her a bit. God knew she needed some inspiration. Her life felt as if it was spinning out of control and jammed to a dead stop at the same time. The stress that had been with her for a year had abated a bit but she realized that it still clung to her. She was the glue that held the family together, but that glue was cracking under the realization that they could lose everything if circumstances continued.

Coming home had helped quell her nerves. Both boys were home for Christmas, Wes from the University of Minnesota and Wayne from the University of Southern California. Despite the fact that Grant had no job and even worse, still no prospects, the relief she felt at having her boys around took the edge off. After the holidays were over and the decorations were put away, she'd fall back into the pattern of quiet hysteria. But not now, if she could help it.

"What are you thinking about?" Grant's voice, from the other side of the car, interrupted her thoughts.

"Nothing. Just glad to be home."

"Well, it's nice to have you home." He smiled at her and she smiled back. Despite all the difficulties that trapped them, they still really did love each other.

Grant went on to bring her up-to-date on the last three weeks. The dogs had gone through the neighborhood on several walk-abouts (they rarely stuck around when she was gone). The weather had been ridiculously cold. Wayne and Wes had been home for a week and already seemed bored. No new job prospects . . .

At this point, Katherine checked out. It was as if Grant had pushed an emotionally charged button. It was an amazing testament to habit and patterns that, when he said certain key words, she felt panic slowly rise up again. She sat wordlessly as buildings decorated with Christmas lights sped past in streaks of red, green, purple and incandescent white.

"They said that the people in those accidents were so lucky." Grant's words danced about her head and tangled with the lights.

"What?" The colors outside darkened into black as they drove over the bridge spanning the Mississippi.

"Well, those people are awful Goddamned lucky," he said.

"Who?"

"Katherine, have you not heard a word I said?"

"I'm sorry, honey. Tell me again."

Even before Grant spoke, she knew he was annoyed with her. "Three different people were badly injured, the same day, almost the same time, on the bridge, last week."

"I'm sorry honey. I was worrying about Barb getting back okay, with her flight cancelled and all. Tell me again."

"It's just really terrible. I mean, two spinouts in one week, two days in a row." She could see the outline of him shaking his head in the dark.

They said that it's just a fluke that both accidents would happen in the same place on two days like that."

So did the same thing happen both times?"

"It's crazy," Grant recounted. "Both accidents happened between six and seven in the morning." She watched his fingers grip the steering wheel more tightly. "There were two people in the first car, one in the second. They were both going along just fine, as far as anyone can tell, then they started spinning." Grant rotated his hand to illustrate. "They were so lucky." He looked over at her. "So were we."

She of course knew exactly what he was talking about. They'd been on the bridge the day before Thanksgiving the previous year. It had been so ridiculously cold. They had been driving back from a concert at Mystic Lake after spending the night at the casino. She remembered getting up early. Was it about seven? She couldn't quite remember. But she did remember the spinout.

The memory of their accident rushed back to her. She was not only in a crash, but she was watching it at the same time. The traffic had been light on the bridge. She had started planning her day when suddenly the truck had become free of the ground, launched by the invisible, oily black ice. The wheels had no grip and they began a slow, elegant spin, three hundred and sixty degrees going sixty-five miles an hour. She felt it again as if for the first time. Her stomach spun in the vertigo moment.

She saw and heard herself talking to her friend Maude on the phone. They'd been planning the Thanksgiving menu that Maude would have at her house. Then, Katherine was face-to-face with the people in the Suburban behind her.

"Oh my God," she had said to Maude, so calmly. "I'm going to die. I've got to go." With the flick of her cell phone flap, she fell into the helpless fascination of the spin. Round and round they whirled. Grant had maneuvered the axis of the truck perfectly. They made three complete circles amidst all the cars around them. It had happened so quickly, no other drivers could have stopped or swerved to avoid them. Yet somehow the truck slithered harmlessly across the lanes and slammed to a stop, lodged underneath an over-pass just off the bridge. The moment had shocked both of them. They should have been dead but instead they sat next to each other blinking. Her head hurt for weeks afterward from the bone-popping jolt, but that was the only injury she or Grant had. She'd figured they'd gotten off easy.

Katherine was silent. It was almost as if they'd just jammed to a stop underneath that overpass for the first time. "They say that the bridge is the most treacherous cold weather spot among all the Twin Cities freeways." Grant said.

"What are they going to do about that?"

"I guess they're revamping that system they installed a while back. It reads when the temperature is getting into that danger zone and then it sprays the bridge with some solution . . ." Grant searched in his head. "Potassium acetate, maybe?"

Katherine shook her head. How did he know so much random information? "What does that do?"

"Keeps it from freezing into black ice. I guess it breaks down the combination of chemicals that form when the exhaust hits the moisture on the pavement."

"Wow," Katherine wondered aloud. "Does it affect the bridge in a bad way? All that erosion?"

"I don't know. You sure would hope not. You okay?" His voice sounded gentle.

"Yeah, of course." She reached over and squeezed his arm. She moved closer to him and kissed him lightly on the cheek. "I'm just tired. That's all."

CHAPTER FIVE

MADISON MANEUVERED HER CAR onto the quiet street. Closer to the boulevard, the houses were larger. They had grand Christmas light displays heralding not just the birth of the Christ child but their owners' unique footprints on the community landscape. The further up the hill the darker the street became. Lovely houses became littler structures. Big yards melted into wider driveways and smaller lawns. Lawns! She had always found it laughable that Arizonians even believed they had lawns. Lawns were nice expanses, large or small, of neatly manicured grass rimmed with tidy bushes. In Arizona, lawns were a compilation of crushed rock and strategically placed cactus plants. Some landscaping.

As she pulled underneath her carport, she flashed back to her mother's house in New Jersey. It was severe and efficient. It blended into the ranks of other brownstones obediently. It gave no hint of personality or fire or rebellion. It was the perfect place for her mother to live. It had nearly been the death of Madison. The memory popped into her mind and just as quickly as it had come, it fizzled.

She stepped out of the car and onto the spare front porch. In earlier days, the dusty gray house had probably been charming. Now it needed a fresh paint job and new roof. Madison wasn't thinking about the house's aesthetics at this moment. She was focused on getting inside to escape the evening chill. True to form, the obstinate key didn't fit neatly into the lock. But Madison was used to this drill. She was patient. She jiggled it gently while she surveyed the front yard. An ironwood tree stood on the north property line, surrounded by small desert tea and wolfberry bushes. Evening primrose laced between clumps of cactus plants. She took a happy breath and turned her attention back to the door. The lock finally obliged. She opened the door and walked into the living room.

The furniture was simple. Two Laz-y-boy recliners faced the window, looking out towards Sedona's finest new shopping mall sparkling in the distance. Opposite them a long white couch faced the fireplace. Madison snapped on the overhead fanlight and dropped her purse onto the recliner closest to the door. She walked down the narrow hall past the front study and glanced inside, reminding herself that she needed to get more candles. The room served as a home reading area where clients could come and have more in-depth sessions. A freestanding Chinese mural hid a massage table in one corner where they could have Reiki and healing work. Three folding chairs faced a table holding Madison's thick deck of cards, aromatic spray bottles and a tape recorder.

She continued down the hall, past the open dining room. Madison rarely used the room for entertaining. A sideboard designed for fine china held piles of videos and DVDs instead. Stacks of paper and research books covered the dining table.

She walked around the corner into the kitchen and flipped on the light. Coriander lifted his head and blinked his ashen-colored eyes in protest. The mammoth tabby yawned in greeting.

Madison bent down to greet the cat, "Hi buddy!"

He yawned and stretched his legs in front of him. The motion arched from his head and neck, down through his shoulders, slowly rolling through his legs and into his perfect, velvet feet, which opened neat claws in a final release.

"Are you happy that mama's home?" He slowly pulled himself up and ambled toward her, giving her the familiar head-to-ankle bump as his reply.

Madison scooped him up and gave his furry head a loud kiss. She plopped him back down and rummaged in the refrigerator for dinner for both of them.

Two hours later, with the kitchen tidied and the cat back asleep in his spot, Madison sat down at the dining room table. She found her reading glasses and searched through the top papers to discover where she had left off reading. The piles of pages before her sat neatly. She pulled a heavy manuscript to her and opened it.

Heightened Spiritual Evolution was her latest acquisition. She had been working for months on an article on the topic. It was a heavy subject but one that fascinated her. In keeping with her life's purpose of introducing the supernatural to the average person, Madison endeavored to write words non-believers and people who didn't know anything about the topic would understand. Exploring the theme had become her latest obsession. She couldn't get enough of it, so the books and articles piled up on the table as she labored to become an esoteric translator. Throughout her research Madison had found herself wondering if she was really writing the piece to prove her own psychic credibility. It was a thought that constantly lingered in the background.

After about twenty-five minutes, Madison decided she'd had enough for the night. She laid the book down, took off her glasses and turned off the light.

Within a half hour, she was sound asleep. The wind outside her window played with the chimes hanging in the piñon pine branches that brushed up against the house. But Madison didn't hear it. She heard a different sound altogether.

THE SOFT BREEZE SIFTED over the lake where Madison suddenly found herself. It licked the surface and curled small waves into patterns. It lifted the golden leaves from weary trees and dropped them into sunlit circles on the surface. Nearby, a boat slapped up against a dock with a gentle clapping sound.

She sniffed the wind and watched it caress two small sailboats cavorting for one last time before the dry-dock days of winter. The thought of those two little boats going dormant for seven months gave her a sense of melancholy.

As Madison surveyed the picturesque scene, she noticed a woman standing on the lake's shore. Her gray hair was coiffed neatly in short waves. She wore a pale, pastel dress. Instantly, Madison recognized her as the woman who had been in her office just hours before.

"Excuse me," she said. Her voice came out in just a soft whisper. "Excuse me?" Again, the words fluttered quietly. "Well now, this is crazy," she said to herself. "I gotta get this broad's attention." She prepared to walk to the woman but just then, a chorus of laughs and yells rolled over the lawn from the house behind her. She turned and noticed the house for the first time.

Madison felt like she was looking into an aquarium, observing the activities going on inside this home. Then somehow, smoothly, she was standing alone in a corner by a French door in the family room. The cooperative senses of warmth and smell overtook her as she slid into the consciousness of the people gathered there. Nearly sixty friends and family members had joined together in this comfortable house. Madison had never noticed before how the odor of alcohol on the breaths of dozens of people could permeate the air so overpoweringly. But seeing the people hovering in circles holding cocktails and munching on sandwiches, and then looking at all the empty gin, scotch, and beer bottles on the bar told her that. Everybody here could feel the affects of booze today.

A man in his early forties held court in the center of one such circle gathered in the family room. His words decreased in clarity as they increased in volume.

"Ya know guys," he saluted with his glass, "there was no one better. My mom was so incredible." He lifted his glass higher. "To Helen Rhames, the greatest mom ever."

Muffled "here-here's" floated amidst the group. Nodded heads all around seconded the man's tribute. He looked at each face and gently smacked his lips. "Yup," he said softly again. "No one better."

A jumble of questions danced in Madison's mind. Where was she? Who were these people? What year was it? Why was she here?

She heard a sigh behind her and turned to notice a tall, quiet younger man leaning against the kitchen door. Somehow, she realized she was seeing a younger son watching his older brother grapple with the inevitability of this moment—a son losing his mother. It seemed like a moment of great spiritual significance, the instant connection with generations of sons throughout time. They were intertwined in a silken thread of grief that wrapped around them like a spider's web. But Madison felt something different from the young man. Did he have a different relationship to this timeless passage, being the younger son?

Suddenly the woman by the lake quietly materialized in the room. Madison was overtaken by curiosity. It seemed clear that this ghost wanted her to share this moment. What was the significance?

"Johnnie. John, come over here. We were just talking about the time Mom stood in the creek in January for forty-five minutes trying to get us to pose for that family picture. Remember?" Sloppily, the older brother reiterated the tale he'd just told the patient listeners, embellishing with new details so it didn't sound exactly like the same story. Once again, this loyal band of friends commiserated with him in a gentle smiling circle. A few even offered additional chuckles, as if to lend credence to the story.

But it all sounded hollow to this John, Madison realized. He really didn't want to put on a polite face and become a part of this scene. He tried to sidle past the oak-lined bar and sneak into the other room, but his brother would have none of that.

"Johnnie. Come on over, bro. Let's see if you can remember all these guys' names."

Now trapped, John walked obediently over to the ring of his brother's college friends. "Okay, Sam, okay." He gently slapped his brother's shoulder. "Hey guys," he volunteered dutifully.

"Hey John," all welcomed.

"How are things?" One blonde, curly-haired man asked.

"All right, man."

She watched John's face as he seemed to leaf through the mental rolodex of statistics. "How's the wife and . . . kids?"

Ben crossed his fingers. "Not yet, but we've only got eight weeks to go. Hopefully it will be a New Year's baby. Maybe the first one of 1973."

"Man, Ben," Sam blurted out. "You with a kid! What's the world coming to?" The gathered offered laughs.

"John . . ." A woman's voice floated from the living room.

He backed away from the group (rather thankfully, Madison guessed), suggesting they get a refill on their drinks and another sandwich while he walked into the foyer. Madison looked back at the older brother. He stood alone with his scotch, abandoned by his buddies.

It seemed like Madison was in the middle of a movie. She had absolutely no idea why she was there but she couldn't pull herself out of the scene. She followed John into the living room. The space had a cozy ambience to it, filled with simple furniture. Photographs on the walls showcased a life past. The room could have been in any house in any part of the country. It boasted nothing extraordinary. Yet all of its elements clearly spoke to the young man's heart.

Then, gently, the realization seeped into her center. Somehow, Madison suddenly understood. He was missing his mother but he was conflicted as well. She detected again the difference between his grief and his brother's.

The woman appeared next to her and Madison flashed her a questioning look. It seeped into the woman's spirit. The ghost nodded imperceptibly. Madison absorbed the tangle of images and intuitions. She was bewildered by how she could feel so completely invested and integrated into these strangers' lives. And the question that had sprouted from that realization grew into a stronger voice aimed at the ghost. "Why doesn't he grieve for you?"

She wanted to cry. She felt a huge wave of emotion sweep over her on behalf of this family, this boy, mired in suffering. Madison felt she was being introduced to something that had roots deep inside this family's history. Clearly a painful family secret lingered here. She looked again at the ghost. The woman's face came clearer into view. Now Madison could better see the wrinkles, the lines, the life lived behind the eyes. The woman looked at her and held her with her gray gaze. Madison felt a current of the spirit's shame and guilt roll over her. That, she realized, was what the lines on her face reflected.

A photograph on the wall captured her attention. It showed this woman in younger years, dressed in long pants and a blouse. On either side of her stood two little boys. The bigger one smiled broadly, the little one looked serious.

Madison's eyes came back to the woman's stare. A feeling of sadness tightened in her chest as she watched the woman wipe a growing stream of tears away from her cheeks.

When Madison had encountered souls from the other side before, their messages had always come to her in her own voice, as if she was mulling thoughts over in her head. But the words that came through now were different. They came through in the woman's voice, delivered in a soft, throaty tone. "Help me," the ghost said simply.

At that moment, a crash in the kitchen distracted her. She looked toward the sound of glass shattering then quickly turned her head back toward the ghost. Helen Rhames was gone, leaving Madison invisibly alone with the mourners and their wake.

THE SOUND OF SOMETHING falling over in the backyard shook her awake. A shock shot through Madison's body, as if someone had jabbed her with a cattle prod. Her heart felt like it was going to explode, it was beating so fast. Her skin tingled. She lay back down and blinked her eyes. What the hell had just happened?

Slowly the images crept back in. She saw the lake, the house, the people, the boys, Sam and John. She saw their mother and her tears. That was it. Madison couldn't escape the fireworks along her backbone. Her psychic synopses flashed in brilliant colors in her brain. She wanted to know more. It was as if she'd been introduced to a book she couldn't put down. She even wondered if she coaxed herself back to sleep, could she continue the scenes? No chance of that, she realized. Madison wouldn't be dreaming anymore tonight.

THE MORNING SUN WOKE HER. She turned away from the light. What a night it had been. She lay wrapped in her blankets recalling the images that had transported her.

Madison was fascinated with the dream. Nothing like this had ever happened to her before. The physical sense of reality pricked her senses, and yet, although it had captivated her, she decided she didn't want any more like it. Sleep was a precious thing to her and Madison had gotten little of it. More importantly, this had been an experience completely out of her control.

She got out of bed, went into the kitchen and let Coriander out. Today was going to be a busy day. She had five clients back-to-back, then a psychic reading class at the Center that she led every Tuesday night. There was little time to digest the dream anymore. She hurried to get ready.

CHAPTER
SIX

KATHERINE COULDN'T REMEMBER when she felt this good. The holidays were spare but the days were filled with her boys and their friends back in this grand house she loved. She had successfully pushed away the nagging finger that poked her shoulder, whispering in her ear that reality would come back. She dedicated herself to muting that insistent voice.

In the midst of these lazy, easy days she realized again how much she loved her boys. They were so big now. Wes towered above her, a jubilant six-foot-six giant of intelligence and wit and laughter. Wayne stood not too much below that, six-foot-four-inches of aquiline beauty and a carefree attitude so infectious, it could actually wipe her worries away for hours at a time.

She knew Grant savored her happiness. He had not been able to provide stability, security or hope in the past year. So when he saw her truly happy with her boys, the tears glistened in his eyes. She loved him for that.

It hadn't been an easy time for them. The demise of his business had taken so much out of him. His company had suffered during a local economic downturn and following the end of his passion and investment of time and money, his father had died. Grant had been barely able to put one foot in front of the other.

Katherine remembered all the moments when she had held him and stroked him and told him things would be all right. But weeks had stretched into months and disconcerting anxiety had gotten a fertile hold of her spirit. Despite all that everyone said, that Grant was bright and capable, that he would get another job soon, Katherine saw another picture in her kitchen every morning. Days stretched into weeks and weeks into months. After a year, Katherine realized, he'd been so deep in mourning that he'd been paralyzed. How could she blame him? This man, who was so good and strong and earnest, had lost two of the strongest anchors in his life, his business and his father—all within months of each other. How could he be expected to plunge forward with excitement and optimism?

"Beauty Queen?" Grant's voice echoed down the stairs.

"Hello sweetheart?" She called back.

"Wayne and I are going to get parts for his El Camino. Need anything?"

Katherine looked quickly around the kitchen, taking inventory. "Hold on . . ." She ducked her head into the refrigerator. "We need milk, Grant. Okay?"

He trotted into the kitchen with a smile. He looked so much older these days. More gray in his hair, more careworn lines along his brow. But at this minute, with his eyes shining at her, happy to be with his boy, Grant looked young and . . . happy. "Will do."

"Okay!" She sang back at him. "Have fun!"

"We will, Mom!" Wayne galloped into the kitchen, bearing so much youthful joy that it bounced from him to her and around all the walls in the room. He grinned an easy smile and swooped up behind her to give her a big hug and a kiss on the top of her head. Katherine knew she was in heaven. No place could be better.

"Stay out of trouble, you two!" She couldn't help but giggle. At just this point in time, life was perfect.

Her phone vibrated on the granite counter, dancing its way across the pile of bills she'd managed to ignore for a few days. A text appeared. MESSAGE FROM WES, the screen read.

There were few things in Katherine's life that lifted her like a text message from her oldest son. He was steadfast and sweet in his contacts with his mother. One time a day, four times a day, whatever the frequency, he was impossibly tuned in to her.

"What ya doing, mother?"

If she had seen herself in a mirror, Katherine would have observed a woman with a smile the size of Texas. "Nothing, sonny boy. How r U?"

"Good. Only 6 more hours of work."

"Can I bring u anything?"

"Na, get a dinner break at 7. U ok?"

Katherine's heart melted. She felt so connected to this child. She remembered moments even when he was so small, where he would intuitively know what she was thinking. His sweet voice would echo the thoughts that trolled in her head.

"U know it!" She texted back. "Give me a kiss when you come home, k?"

"Of course. Gotta go."

Katherine turned to finish cleaning the kitchen. She became lost in the thoughts of Wes and Wayne, of her and Grant. Once again she squelched the dread that reminded her of the circumstances of reality that robbed her of control. She pushed away the feeling, trying instead to replace it with the enjoyment of living in the moment.

CHAPTER
SEVEN

THAT TUESDAY WAS another day in the weeks that stretched endlessly through the winter. Madison was caught on a treadmill of days with clients and nights with her research. Since then she hadn't felt or seen Helen and after so long, the memory of the wake had nearly faded.

One afternoon she had a few spare hours to clean her office. She moved all her books and tablets around her desk so she could dust the glass. Her pile of notes was growing and she wondered, not for the first time, when she should start throwing the records of old readings away. After all, she rarely looked at them again unless she had regular clients to keep track of. Her phone buzzed on the desk. "Hello?"

Miriam's nasal tone greeted her. "Your next client is here."

"What? Can't be! It's only . . ." She looked at the clock. "Four! Already!"

"Yes, it's four and your client is here." Clearly Miriam had less than little patience today.

"Okay, I'll be down in a sec." Madison hung up and shook her head. She stood and turned to look out the window.

Amber sunlight sparkled on the wisps of snow along the creek's banks. The trees hung over the water as if bowing to introduce themselves to the rocks beneath the surface. The winter light had a peculiar color, more like a fall sunset. She headed down the stairs.

Madison walked into the main part of the store and maneuvered past the display cases. She came around the corner and found herself face-to-face with Janine. "Hey sister! What are you doing here?"

"Howdy!" Janine gave her a big hug. Behind her stood Lee Anne Kneely, Madison's regular 4:00 p.m. Thursday appointment.

"Hey Lee Anne! How are you?" She half-turned to introduce the two. "This is my friend Janine. Janine, this is Lee Anne."

"Nice to meet you." Lee Anne put out her hand and Janine took it gingerly. Madison wondered what kind of energy she would pick up.

"What are you doing here?" Madison asked Janine again.

"Oh, gotta pick up some new crystals and I was checking on that book I told you about. You know, *The Sense of Being Stared At.* But I guess it's still not in." She looked down at Miriam and smiled.

Miriam smiled back and shook her head apologetically. "I'm sorry, honey. I'll check with them again, okay?"

Madison never ceased to be impressed with Janine's effect on people. Miriam was in constant bitch mode but whenever Janine came around, it was as if the sun had come up for the first time. Amazing . . . too bad she didn't have that gift.

"C'mon, Lee Ann. Let's get going." Madison put one hand on the woman's shoulder and guided her toward the door. With the other she waved to her friend. "Good to see you, doll!"

"You too!" See you at yoga Monday?"

"Wouldn't miss it." Madison spoke over her shoulder. "Maybe we'll talk sooner." The bells on the door jingled a merry farewell.

As Madison began, they discussed recent events that had happened to Lee Anne. She was curious. Did every event in someone's life have meaning?

"Well, you could drive yourself nutty trying to put meaning to everything," Madison explained. "There's no such thing as random. Everything operates within a framework but do you mean, are you supposed to get a message from everything that happens?" Madison shook her head. "If you're meant to get a message, you'll get it." She absently shifted through the papers on her desk as she spoke.

"Okay, that makes sense."

"Just remember. Be open to whatever is going on around you. Be present."

The words had barely left her mouth when she sensed that someone from the other side was in the room with them. Madison closed her eyes, tuning in. Lee Anne sat in silence. She was used to this routine.

Who's here? Madison waited for a picture. Nothing. *Who's here?* She asked again. A whiff of lavender perfume tickled her nose. "Do you smell that?" She opened her eyes and looked at Lee Anne.

"Smell what?"

"It's like, lavender, like some kind of perfume. You sure you don't smell it?"

Lee Anne shook her head.

"Do you know anybody who's passed who used to wear perfume like that?"

Lee Anne sat for a moment and looked up to the ceiling. "No, I can't think of anybody. Do you get anything else?"

Madison sat very still and turned her palms upward. She waited. The perfume lingered but nothing else came to her. "I don't know, honey. There definitely is somebody here with us. I just can't get a picture of who they are." She straightened up and spoke in a loud voice. "If you need to tell us something, won't you try a little more? Can you show me a picture?"

She got a sudden sensation of heat surrounding her. It felt humid, heavy. She started to sweat. "Man, is it hot in here."

Lee Anne giggled. "Hot flash?" She asked.

"Ha, feels kinda like that. But no, it feels like a summer day. Hot as hell, sticky. You know what I mean?"

"Well, that's how all hot flashes feel to me." Lee Anne grinned. "Maybe the person whose here is having a hot flash of their own. I like to call those moments my own personal summer!"

Madison laughed. Just as suddenly, the heat dissipated and with it, the feeling of the energy. No more visitors.

"Guess we're alone again."

"Wow that was weird. That's never happened before."

"Well, not to you, but for me it's a fairly regular occurrence. In fact, it's becoming more regular all the time."

"I don't know, Madison. It would really bother me to have all these dead people dropping in."

"Well, honey, that's why I am the medium and you're not!" They both laughed. Madison continued the reading with no more interruptions.

As Lee Anne left the room, Madison picked up the tablet on which she'd been recording notes. Clearly printed words caught Madison's eye: BE OPEN TO WHATEVER HAPPENS AROUND YOU. BE PRESENT.

Madison couldn't help but wonder if those words were meant as much for her as for her client.

CHAPTER EIGHT

T HE EARLY MARCH SUN was a welcome sight. After a long Minnesota winter, the fact that spring was just around the corner made people want to run outside in their shorts. The early rains had cleared nearly all winter's remnants. Katherine steered the car east on I-94, noticing how much black roadside snow had disappeared in just the last week. That sight encouraged her.

She tried to peek at the Mississippi River beneath her as she maneuvered over the I-35W Bridge. The waters below flowed under the crust of ice. She imagined the ferocious current. It made her shiver just to think of how cold that black water probably was.

Just off the bridge she turned onto Fourth Street and headed west to Sixth Avenue. She glanced at the bags in the back seat to make sure they hadn't dumped their contents. She'd cleaned for the past few days to get extra kitchen items for Wes's new apartment. She figured most of what he needed, she already had.

Once there, she helped him put the kitchen together. It was a tiny space but it was all he needed while going to the U. He wasn't really close to the campus (in fact, the business school was on the other side of the river), but it was closer than living at home and would do as a start.

Afterward they had lunch and hugged goodbye. Katherine was so happy that her son was back in Minneapolis after transferring back from the University of Iowa. When she was going through kid withdrawal, there was nothing more soothing than knowing that if she really needed a fix, Wes was only a half-hour away.

She drove back toward home and felt the familiar dread of coming back to the house, wishing that things would be better, and then knowing, with such finality, that nothing had changed—Grant still didn't have a job and their savings were slowly slipping away. She wanted to scream most days. She couldn't control or change what was happening to Grant, to her and to the family. It was excruciating to live through this.

Sedona was supposed to have fixed all that, but the early excitement and optimism she'd felt burnt out quickly when nothing had changed at home. She and Barb had called each other dozens of times, trying to re-create the hope they'd found in Arizona.

The psychic said Barb would find the career path that would finally make her happy and Katherine would survive her family stress with grace. She picked up her cell phone and dialed her friend.

Barb picked up asking, "What now?"

Katherine had to laugh. There was some comfort in knowing someone else understood how she felt.

"God, Barb. I just came from getting Wes set up in his apartment. Everything looks great, we have a really fun time, yummy lunch and then as I'm heading back over the bridge, reality sinks in." She felt tears welling up. "I'm so sick of this."

"I know. I was so bummed out yesterday, I didn't leave the house. I mean, what's the point, really? I know we're supposed to shift our focus but it doesn't help."

That sense of gloom pushed a button. "C'mon, we're supposed to see the possibilities, remember?" She said it as much to herself as she did to Barb.

"Yeah, but we come home and it's the same old thing."

"I know. How are we gonna get out of it?"

There was a moment of silence and then Barb's voice sounded a little bit louder. "You know what?"

Was that a tinge of hopefulness Katherine heard? "What?" She desperately wanted a magic answer to all her problems. She needed the Sedona effect.

"I've still got that Madison lady's card. She said we could call her. Let's do it."

Katherine's stomach twisted into knots considering the possibility. "You think?"

"Yeah, why not? Let's just ask if she'll do a conference-call reading or something."

"Can't imagine how much that would cost."

"No kidding. We'll be bankrupt by the time we figure all this out!" The electrical current between them lit a new enthusiasm. A tiny bit of Sedona's spirit flickered.

"Do you have her card?"

"Yeah, somewhere." Katherine heard Barb fumbling for it. The thought of Madison Morgan's measured stare transported her from the freeway to the tiny office above Oak Creek for an instant.

"Ha! Got it! Wow, this whole thing freaks me out."

"I know! But what if she can get us back on track?"

"I am honestly up for anything at this point. Shifting has no longer become an option."

"I'm with you. Call her now and let me know what she says."

"Will do!" Barb hung up with a quick click.

THE PHONE RING JANGLED Madison awake. *Damn,* she thought. *Why didn't I turn the ringer off?* "Hello," she yawned.

"Hello?" Another voice echoed timidly.

"Yeah. Who is this?"

"Uh, hi, Madison? This is Barb Frey. I don't know if you remember me but . . ."

Lord, Madison thought. One more crazy person calling was going to drive her over the edge. She tried to place the name. Barb. Barb Frey. Didn't make a dent. "Oh, ok. What can I do for you?" Amazing how professional one could be with no sleep and no sense of humor.

"Well, we, my friend and I, came to see you in December. You gave us your card and told us if we ever needed to call . . ."

"Yeah, yeah, of course." Madison stifled a yawn.

"Well, you got us all shifted and on track and now we're all messed up being back at home." Madison could hear the woman's sigh from 2,000 miles away as clearly if she was sitting across from her in her office.

"Um. Sounds like you need a re-tool. What are you thinking?"

"Could we do a conference call, together?"

"Not really a good idea. I need to do people separately."

"Yeah . . ." Barb's voice sounded distinctly disappointed.

"How about this, you and I talk and if you think your friend needs some time, we'll add it. You never know, maybe our conversation will take care of everything."

Barb sounded much happier. "Okay, yeah, that's great."

"Okay," Madison was moving it along now. Her nap was waiting. "I've got clients all this afternoon. How about tomorrow, noon my time?"

Now Barb's voice sounded on the verge of jubilant. "Great, that's great!"

"Okay then, talk to you tomorrow."

"Awesome. Thanks so much, Madison."

"No problem." Madison allowed a yawn to finally emerge and hung up the phone.

THE NEXT DAY MADISON worked her magic once again. She spent fifteen minutes with Barb and after reviewing her signs, reassured her. "Stay the path. You are a number one."

"Right," Barb answered. She sounded unconvinced.

"I'm telling ya. You are in a good place for the next fifty-two days. And, remember. You are a starter, not a finisher. Find someone else to do the finishing. Understand?"

"Yup. Got it."

"If your friend wants to set something up, tell her to give me a call."

"Okay, will do."

MADISON HUNG UP the phone and thought about all the people she spoke with. So many needed life advice, just a little push in a direction or confirmation that what they were doing was really the right choice. She got the clairvoyant visits much less frequently. They were exciting but taxing as well. She liked to imagine that the energies on the other side were far more in touch than anyone really knew. So many self-described psychics would create the strangest scenarios of communication from the other side.

Most of these people were scam artists, of course. All the legitimate psychics knew it but the profession was goofy. One never really knew for sure if a person really did have the gift. And of course, everyone was in it to make money.

Madison wondered how the ghosts felt about all of this. Trying to navigate the connections and messages between two states of consciousness was like reading a mystery novel. There were twists and turns that kept one constantly wondering which way things would end up next. Madison figured maybe the energies had created this landscape as a psychic joke.

She shared her theory with Janine later that afternoon as they hiked up the airport mesa trail. Janine had laughed so hard, she'd almost fallen over.

"God, I can see it now. They're all hanging around coming up with various loops they can throw at us to keep us on our toes. You know what?"

"What?" Madison puffed alongside her.

"We should start a support group for exhausted mediums!"

"Like me, now?" Madison loved these hikes but boy did she hate them.

"Ah, come on! We're nearly there." Janine patted her shoulder and strode forward enthusiastically.

"Let's just see how fast you're walking when you're my age!"

They made it to the top of the mesa and took in the glorious views of the rugged red cliffs standing sentry over the town.

"Wow, this really is worth it." Madison panted.

"You always say that."

"Well, it's always true. You'd think that if someone wanted to get in contact with us from the other side, they'd choose right here to do it."

"Maybe they will." Janine turned to her. "Seen your friend lately?"

"Naw. I'm starting to think I'm making this up as I go along."

"C'mon, that's what people would say about us, not us saying it about ourselves!"

"Yeah, but you know J, she really is a different character. I usually get snapshots but when this Helen laid out moments in her life, or I guess the end of it, in like a huge video feed, it really freaked me out."

"So you've seen her a couple of times?"

"Once at the office. Once in that dream." Madison paused. "But that day I saw you at the center, remember when I introduced you to that client?"

Janine nodded.

"I was doing Lee Anne's reading and got a strong sense that maybe Helen was in the room again. I smelled some perfume-type smell. I think," she tapped her lip with her finger, remembering. "It was lavender."

"Ah! Let's see, the color has the magical property of intuition! Doesn't the oil have the property of purification?"

"Yeah, think so. I'd have to look it up again."

"It'd be cool if you get a scent of it again. All part of the twists and turns. Right?"

"Yeah, well I don't want to go through these . . ." Madison pointed down the windy trail, "in the dark, so let's get movin'."

The two took one last look at the sunset-kissed rocks and headed back down the trail.

KATHERINE HUNG ON EVERY word as Barb recounted her phone conversation with Madison. She'd been reinvigorated by the thoughts that this woman so far away had the ability, the insight, and the power to push them back onto the right track. She couldn't wait to call her herself. She meant to. She didn't.

Days slid together like links in a chain that tightened around her neck. She was having a harder and harder time staying up, staying positive. No job prospects for Grant, the kids back in school, her friends going on with their lives while she stagnated and slipped deeper into alienation and anger, bitterness and despair. It was everything she could do in the mornings to go through the performance of sunny words and bright smiles. Inside was another story. She sensed that Grant realized it but those were words that were never spoken. They navigated the hours of depression and anxiety living in the same house but so far away from each other.

Katherine found herself more often going out alone, whether to walk around Lake Calhoun or go to a movie. She considered these solitary moments "dates" with herself and when she actually went on them, they eased her worry for windows of time. But she would return home, his car would be in the driveway and she'd come in the house and find him sitting in the kitchen with his laptop before him. It made her want to vomit.

She was swirling into a vortex of self-pity that was sure to swallow her up if she didn't do something.

ONE DAY SHE SAT in a Starbucks, sipping tea. She stared out the window, fascinated by the large fluffy flakes of a late-April snow dusting. As the ice crystals floated and delicately dropped to the ground, she wondered how hard it would be for the real estate company to get the FOR SALE sign into the ground outside her house.

She couldn't escape it, the dread of losing the house, her soul spot, and her security. It was an emotional quicksand that sucked at her and threatened to swallow her whole. But the worst part was not the thought of going under. It was the lingering in the muck that was driving her mad.

Katherine laid her head back against the high-backed chair

and closed her eyes, not caring what the other customers thought. A stream of memories ran inside her mind like a slide show—images of snow in the backyard, recollections of long summer days and parties by the pool, stacks of random moments with the boys when they were little, watching May thunderstorms from the porch, Halloween, birthday celebrations, wintertime sledding down the back hill . . .

The images suddenly coalesced into a memory of that winter day last December, when she and Barb wandered up and down those Sedona streets. That was the day when she had met Madison.

The woman's face materialized in front of her. Barb had talked to her weeks ago and felt so much better. But wasn't it all nonsense? Wasn't it theatrical and ridiculous?

She searched her wallet, wondering if she still had Madison's business card. She finally found it, crumpled but readable, the psychic's eyes gazed back at her as she traced the phone number with her finger.

CHAPTER NINE

MADISON GINGERLY LIFTED her laptop out of the back seat and carried it into the electronics store. Working a lot had its advantages, but the big disadvantage was the drain of taking on other people's fears, anxieties, hopes and questions. She needed a vacation. Funny, she was so ready for a break out of her ordinary pattern that she was actually considering going to visit her mother. *That would be something,* she thought. Go drop in on her mom in Jersey? She could just imagine what the family would say. "Poor Madison. Couldn't hack it in Sedona! Well we all knew it was just a matter of time."

She had to teach herself to turn off these ridiculous internal dialogs. She was driving herself crazy. "Hi." She plopped the computer on the counter and greeted the tech guy.

"Hi. What can I do for you?"

"My computer's got a virus and it's messing everything up."

"Ah, okay, we can take a look at it."

"Cool. Must be mercury in retrograde," she said more to herself than him.

"No kidding." He chuckled. "We'll have so much business in the next two weeks! Mercury goes crazy in her lunar paths and communication of every type gets messed up. You'd think computers would be immune to all that stuff but obviously the Universe's influence is bigger than we know. At least we'll make some cash from it!"

Madison giggled with him. Where else but in Sedona would a computer guy know about the details of a planet's orbit and its effects on life?

Within minutes she was back on the road heading to her office. No computer, no clients for the day. It felt so nice.

She got back to the office and settled in her chair. The windows had a humid build up of light, fluid drops clinging to the edge of the panes. It would be another clear day, one where the cliffs felt like they were peeking just behind one's shoulder rather than towering a mile away.

She again thought of going back home. How long had it been? Seven years, eight? Jersey was probably pretty different now. She wondered if anyone in her old neighborhood still lived there. She imagined the long row of modest houses, the smell of the marshes and river beyond her house. It would be warming up there today. Madison leaned forward and pulled the last few dates off of her desk calendar. May first. Man, was the year going fast! Already almost half over. She surveyed her office and thought of the life she had created for herself here. It wasn't bad. It was simple, hassle free (except for virus-laden computers), creative, and fun. She'd made great friends. She loved the gentle sense of kinship she felt with the people who had migrated here, just like her. So what if she wasn't always sure it was for real? There could be worse ways to make a living.

Suddenly, she got a shiver.

The ghost, Helen, stood behind the chair facing Madison. Her energy wavered as if she were an image on an old television screen. Her image was tremulous but her message to Madison was not.

Helen held a clock, its hands slowly circumventing the face. They purposefully tick-tocked in even rhythm but Helen gently shook the mechanism and they sped up, spinning faster and faster. Soon the clock looked like it might spin out of the room as it ricocheted in the ghost's hands. Helen whispered, "Not much time."

The clock faded into a picture of a family album. It was thick with photos and the pages were yellowed from time. Madison watched Helen open the book and turn to a specific page. "Here."

Before she even needed to lean forward to look, the book was in front of her, its page as big as her missing computer's screen.

A collection of old snapshots sat in orderly fashion. The edges of the celluloid had become sticky and mustard colored. They showed two little boys in various stages of childhood.

They stood with a young Helen, holding melting ice cream cones, one boy grinning, the other looking perplexed.

They laughed, running shirtless through a rooster's spray of a sprinkler showering a lawn somewhere.

They perched on a large car in some long ago driveway, dressed in somber church clothes, hair flattened obediently to their heads.

A picture with a crease lancing it diagonally showed a huge oak tree on the edge of a cornfield. It rose from an underfoot landscape of mulberry bushes. The branches started low to the ground and stretched out to create a canopy of climbing and building possibilities. A handmade ladder leaned against the rough trunk. Next to that, a thick, corded rope hung underneath a grand, ramshackle tree house.

And then there was another photo. Madison squinted to get a better look. This one showed the younger boy—John, she guessed— standing with a small companion. The two boys stood in the middle of an alley snaking behind a row of homes. Madison could almost hear their young voices bouncing off the walls of the houses on either side.

Then suddenly, she did.

"Think he's there?" The little one's voice trembled in an excited whisper.

"Don't know. Can't see him." The bigger boy peered behind them, and then turned around to get a better look. "Do you see anything moving down there?" Both boys stood on tiptoes, ready to bolt. The street was silent.

"Maybe he's in the house."

The larger boy seemed less sure. "Yeah, maybe . . . well, let's walk real quiet and if he's there, maybe he won't hear us."

"He woulda heard us when we walked by, dontcha think, John?" The smaller boy sounded hopeful, yet doubtful.

"I dunno, Tim. I mean, he's so quiet sometimes, like he's ready to watch us before he hunts us down."

They stepped cautiously into a band of sunshine and tiptoed across the gravel road toward a modest gray house. Halfway across, John began to relax a little. Only a few more steps and they'd be on the sidewalk.

but they all figured this was because he took easy stuff—candy bars, gum, a rubber ball like Tim's, and last month, a pack of Lucky cigarettes. When the guys had gotten together to try and smoke them, none had brought any matches and Marty had to go back and steal those, too.

The crumbling cement gave way to hard-packed dirt as the boys made their way out of town. John remembered hearing his parents talk about the city council's current debate on whether to use funds to extend the sidewalk as far as the cemetery or to plant new Jasmine bushes along the main street storefronts.

"If the flower guild has anything to do with it," his mother had said, "we'll have those lovely Jasmines in by the Fourth of July. After all, how often do people go over to the cemetery anyway?" This had been before his grandfather had died. John wondered if she had changed her mind.

They took a sharp right and climbed up the steep incline to where the tree fort was built. John could already hear Clay and Marty arguing. Tim grasped the fraying, knotted rope and swung himself up to the lowest branch of the oak tree, just missing a clump of mulberry thorns.

Tim pushed the rope back to John and climbed into the tree house. John followed quickly. He looked up to find Clay and Marty bickering over their never-ending marble game. Rickie was lazily swinging in the worn, yellow hammock, watching the crows peck at a scarecrow in the field below them. It was a good day to be in a tree house. The late afternoon sun filtered through the branches and the floorboards creaked rhythmically as the wind gently rocked the oak. John took a deep breath and plopped down next to Clay.

"Ferget it, Marty. You're the biggest cheater I ever met."

"C'mon Clay. Yer just jealous that I finally got back the cat's eye," Marty crowed. Clay responded with a disgusted shrug and slumped back against the worn trunk.

John had never met two brothers who were more different. Marty was short and thin. What he lacked in strength and size, he made up for in cleverness. Clay was compact and sturdy. Even though he wasn't much taller, he seemed so much bigger than all of them. John looked enviously at Clay's tan arms and legs. His own were so scrawny in comparison. Being the tallest by three inches didn't help when you weighed the least by ten pounds.

John caught Marty eyeing his new royal blue shoelaces. His aunt Gloria had brought them when she came for the funeral. That had been the best part of the day.

"Where'd you get those neat laces?" Marty leaned forward for a closer look. "Newberry's?"

"Na, my aunt brought 'em when she came for the funeral." John drew his feet underneath him, shifting to sitting Indian style.

"How was it?" Rickie asked from the hammock. He swung a long brown leg back and forth to increase his swing.

"I don't know, okay I guess. Everyone was bawling, 'cept for me and Sam and my dad. I didn't know there were so many people in town that knew him."

Everyone from Mayor Coleman to Tom from the barbershop had come by to say how sorry they were. Sorry for what? The fact that this old man had died or that his grandkids had never known him and now never would? John was tired of thinking about it.

"Jeez, that's kinda creepy. Did you see his face? What does a dead guy look like?" Rickie sat up expectantly, causing the hammock to squeak in protest.

John looked up from his sneakers to see four pairs of eyes waiting eagerly for gruesome details—nothing like a little horror to wake the guys up. "He was in the coffin and he just looked like he was sleeping." John had wondered about his skin. It looked so much like wax he had wanted to touch it. Then he had recoiled at the thought. Imagine touching a dead person! The memory made him shiver.

"Wow! Well, did he look like he could come alive? Did he have blood and stuff all over him?" Clay whispered.

"Gawd, stupid!" Marty barked at his brother in disgust. "Don't you know anything? They don't let dead people have blood and stuff on 'em when people come to see 'em." He shook his head as his brother flashed a middle finger at him. "Whaddya think? Ya think he's all of a sudden gonna jump out of the coffin?" With a loud roar, Marty leaped toward Tim, rolling his eyes back in his head, tilting his neck at a hanged man's angle. He thrust his grimy hands out, clawing for the backpedaling Tim who squished himself into the corner next to the old ice cooler, squealed uncontrollably, then looked immediately embarrassed.

"C'mon, Marty. Don't be such an asshole." Tim tried to sound brave, his smooth cheeks were red and his lower lip trembled.

"Well, what else did he look like? Kenny Walmar said they put makeup on dead people to make 'em look better." Rickie leaned forward, both legs outstretched, his canvas sneakers flat against the floor to hold the hammock still.

John felt odd discussing this man. "I don't know." He shook his head crossly. "I mean I didn't just stand there and stare at him. He just looked dead. You know, that's all, dead. His hair was combed neat. He had his church clothes on. His shoes were even shiny."

The boys paused appreciatively as they digested the image of a dead man wearing shiny shoes.

"How come you didn't know him? Clay asked.

John threw Clay a sullen glance and shrugged his shoulders. "Guess he was too busy."

"Too busy!" snorted Tim. "My grandpa's never too busy. He likes to take me and Greg fishin' and he always brings us sugar donuts."

"You mean the kind from Thatcher's bakery?" The attention shifted away from John's dead grandfather to the merits of Thatcher's delicacies and John sat back, silently asking himself the same question. Why hadn't his grandfather ever come to see him? He'd never even given him birthday presents. Once, on Sam's birthday, John had picked up the mail off the floor as soon as it had slid through the mail slot in the front door. Mixed in the pile, he'd seen a letter addressed to Sam. The writing had been written in a bold blue ink with a shaky hand. In it had been a birthday card with a one-dollar bill that Sam exultantly opened as soon as John showed him the envelope. He was almost sure Sam had gotten a letter just like that on more than one birthday, but when he asked Sam about it at dinner that night, they were silenced by a menacing look from their mother, who deftly changed the subject.

John sighed deeply and wriggled his toes, watching leafy shadows roll across his feet. The guys had gone onto the subject of reinforcing the tree fort ladder. He stretched his back against the worn, knobby trunk. He wasn't in much of a mood to participate. He looked over Clay's shoulder and watched the tall corn stalks wave in the distance.

THE SCENE FADED and once again, Madison found herself sitting in her office. The ghost sighed a whispery breath and Madison felt a soft pain in her own chest. Helen's presence receded a bit, reminding Madison how taxing it was for a spirit to maintain this high energy level.

She wondered if Helen would go soon, but the ghost emanated a determined energy. She pointed with a silvery finger to another photograph of the family seated at a modest table set for dinner. In the photo's bottom right corner a scribbled caption read, "Cecil's 37th, June 9, 1948." Helen's finger forcefully tapped the photo. "Bad day."

Madison closed her eyes, vicariously feeling this woman's deep sadness. The sound of china clinking caused her to look up. She found herself standing in a corner of the dining room watching as a young Helen bustled around the table, neatening the tablecloth and rearranging the serving platters. She checked the clock on the wall and shouted up the stairs, "Sam, John, I need you boys down here."

Within seconds, the two youngsters tumbled into the room. Sam jumped in front of his mother with a brilliant smile. Helen reached down to smooth his dark tousled hair. John followed his brother, a study in stark opposites. Where Sam was husky with dark features, John had a soft thin face, light blue eyes and nearly white blond hair.

The brothers continued their heated discussion. "So what did ya get him?" John asked.

The best present ever," Sam answered. "You'll have to wait and see."

"C'mon, Sam. I'll tell you mine if you tell me yours."

"No way. You gotta wait 'til he comes home."

Their mother broke into the discussion. "Okay boys, that's enough. Nobody's going to get a chance to give Dad anything if we don't get dinner going first."

As Helen and Sam walked into the kitchen to make out a list, Madison watched John sit on one of the dining room chairs. His thoughts echoed in her head.

John drummed his fingers on the table. He was anxious for his father to come home. He and Sam had discussed for days what they should get him for his birthday. Ultimately, they had come up with one good idea. They'd at first tried to decide on a gift together but they couldn't agree. So they each got him their own gift.

From that point the competition had been on. John was determined. He'd give his father a special gift—one that molded them together, one that told with a hint of promise the good times they could have together, just the two of them. John had searched weeks for such a gift.

With hours of advice and insight from the gang, John contemplated all the possibilities. Tim suggested a baseball mitt. Rickie thought a painted rock to use as a paper holder might do the trick, but the others dismissed the idea as too simple. Marty offered to steal something from Newberry's or the new Sears going in downtown, but John just shook his head.

He was touched when Clay offered the cat's eye marble that he had won back from his brother. But John politely declined. "Nah, Clay. That's real nice but that's your marble. I want to give him something special from me . . . you know what I mean? Clay had nodded back and smiled gently. All the boys understood John's pain at not having the kind of fathers they did. They had discussed it on several occasions when John wasn't around.

Finally, John had decided on his father's special gift—a sleek Bassone Rebel reel, complete with line and flies. John had arranged with Ralph Goodman at the Sport Hut to sell him the package on a down payment and promised to pay the balance back on a weekly payment plan.

He just knew his father would be proud of his responsible and creative thinking. Even better, he would definitely beat Sam in the gift-giving department! He could imagine what his dad would say when he saw the gleaming rod and spinner. "You paid for this all yourself? Son, I'm really proud of you. I know I haven't been a very good father but now I'm going to change. Let's get up bright and early

Saturday morning and try this beauty out. What do you say, John, how does a day of fishing with just you and your old dad sound?"

"John!" Helen's voice scattered the image from John's mind.

"Yeah, Mom." John stared up at the ceiling, watching the afternoon sunlight dance in dusty streams.

"Are you ready to help me? Are you boys done with your homework?" Helen looked over her shoulder at Sam obediently following her with the list in hand.

"Yeah, all done," John said.

"Sam?"

"Yup." Sam rolled his eyes at John.

"Have you got the list? I just thought of one more thing." Helen turned to Sam and pulled a pencil out of her apron pocket. It fell onto the thick rug and she leaned down to pick it up with a shaky hand.

"You okay, mama?" John walked toward her and put his hand on hers. "What do ya need us to get?"

Helen stared at him for an instant, "Ah, oh, ah . . ." She looked from the pencil in her hand to his worried blue eyes.

"I'm sorry, honey." She manufactured a smile for his sake and patted his hand in return. "It's . . . I'm okay." She glanced at Sam and gave him a smile as well. "I want you two to quick run to the bakery for eight buttered rolls, to the butcher at Lund's for the whitefish I've ordered and, um, I guess that's all." She paused, and then continued. "Let's see. . . . maybe some butter, too."

By now, Sam and John both looked relieved to hear she had resumed somewhat of her normal mother-in-charge cadence.

"Sure, Mama. No problem," Sam declared.

"That's it, go quick. I've got so much to do still. Here's the money, now go!" She shoved the boys toward the front door and turned back to the kitchen.

Madison watched Helen survey the kitchen. She walked purposely over to the cupboard above the refrigerator and reached for a bottle of wine from the top shelf. "How the hell," she muttered under her breath, "am I to get through this?" She opened the bottle and shakily poured herself a glass. Behind her, through the front window, John watched. He then turned quickly to catch up with Sam.

Within minutes, it seemed to Madison (although she knew it must have been far longer than that), everyone sat cleaned up and quiet at the dinner table. Cecil sat down heavily in his chair and began to serve the plates.

He furrowed his heavy brow as he concentrated on dishing out the fish. Madison could see that despite a slight paunch of on-coming middle age, he'd been a handsome younger man.

"Honey, this looks great," Cecil nodded to Helen. She smiled radiantly back.

"Well," he said upon finishing the blessing, "how was school today?" He looked at the boys and Sam immediately launched into a verbal report of the day's activities. His father chewed with a smile on his face. He asked Sam questions and laughed at his jokes.

John settled back in his chair and shook his knees impatiently under the table. He couldn't wait until after dinner when they would gather in the living room and he could present his father's gift.

"What's wrong, son. Not hungry?"

"No, I mean, yes." John picked up his fork and attacked the scalloped potatoes, carefully steering clear of the whitefish.

Cecil lifted a glass of wine to his lips. John watched him gulp the entire portion and refill the glass. He wished his father would slow down. Across the table, Helen mirrored Cecil in her lusty attack on the wine bottle. Before John even got a start on the fish, he could tell his parents were tipsy.

Helen began gurgling. "I'll tell you, I had such a time trying to find some good quality fish today. I'm really getting disgusted with the meat department at Lund's. You'd think we were Indians or something, with the quality of meat they sell."

Cecil grunted in answer and piled more potatoes on his plate.

"I don't know," Helen whispered conspiratorially and leaned toward the rest of them, resting her elbows on the table. "Could be that Jack Lund has other things on this mind these days." She clumsily sliced through the fish and sent a pearl onion skidding across the table. "Whoops," she giggled and swept the offending onion onto the floor.

"Helen, can't you control yourself? Stop throwing your food."

Helen gulped and carefully brushed away the crumbs by her plate.

Cecil's countenance changed as he watched his wife fumble with her napkin. "Is there ever going to be a time when you don't drink so Goddamned much?"

Sam and John sat ramrod straight at their father's outburst.

Cecil shifted in his chair and shot a disgusted look at his wife. "I'm really getting sick of you and your drinking."

Helen face went white with shock. She recoiled at his anger, leaned back in her chair for a second and then, unconsciously, poured herself another glass of wine. "I'm sssorry, honey." Her stuttering fed itself, "I dddidn't mean to."

The boys looked at one another sharing a glance of fear. Cecil sat unmoved by her apology. For no apparent reason, he launched into a tirade. This small, seemingly unimportant incident was evidently a breaking point.

"I'm sick of it, Helen," he hissed. His face grew redder in his inebriated anger. "I'm sick of all this," he swept his arm around the table. "And," he snarled, "I'm sick of you."

Helen dissolved into tears. "Honey, I'mmmm sssorry." She sobbed in deepening breaths. "I'm sorry. What can I do?"

Cecil stared at his wife. Sam and John were glued to their chairs in horror while their mother shivered miserably.

"What can you do?" Cecil asked. He leaned toward Helen with an ugly sneer. Years of what seemed to be repressed anger boiled to the surface. "You can take your bastard son and get the hell out of here. That's what you can do."

Madison gasped. The room's emotional electricity seemed to suck out all the oxygen. She couldn't take her eyes off the little boy at the table as she read his thoughts.

John stared open-mouthed at his father, then his mother, and then his brother, who returned his incredulous look. He didn't know if Sam knew what the word meant. But he was pretty sure he did. Wasn't it a swear word you used when you really wanted to put someone down? Didn't it also describe someone without a father?

John stared at the man across the table. Which of them had his father been talking about? He'd only said "bastard son," not "sons."

Helen gasped and bolted from her chair. "Cecil!" She screeched at him then launched forward. In mid-motion she pulled herself back and barked at the children. "Get upstairs you two!"

But her command went unheeded as her husband hoisted his heavy frame out of his chair and sent it crashing backwards. "I'm tired of this!" He roared. "I'm fuckin' tired of workin' to support a family that doesn't even give a damn whether I come home at night." His words slurred more as his tempo increased. "Take them both, Helen. Take my son," he nodded in Sam's direction. "Take your son." He cast a look at John of pure disgust.

"Take the fuckin' house. Take everything. I'm done . . . I'm goin' out for a drink." He turned like a lumbering bear and grabbed for his coat from the front closet. He jerked open the front door, sending it crashing into the side of the house, and stomped into the darkness.

Madison stood in the corner riveted by the scene. The violence, the rage of it made her feel like she was going to throw up. She could tell the boys and their mother felt the same way. She saw John sway. His face flushed. His eyes filled with tears.

Helen sputtered again at the two boys. "Ggget upstairs."

Sam scurried out of the room. John didn't move. Helen looked guiltily at her son. His blue eyes looked back, holding shock and despair. The charges of emotion whirled around the room. They hovered between Helen and the boy.

Madison felt like an intruder. It was almost as if she was watching a car crash but she couldn't turn away. She saw a look of realization settle across John's face.

"John, sweetheart . . ." Helen moved toward him with arms outstretched.

"Is it true?" His trembling voice stopped his mother.

"Honey, your daddy didn't mean it. He just had a little too much to drink and a hard day, that's all."

"Is it true, Mother?" No more Mama. Never again. His words sliced through the air.

Helen stared at him, almost as if she was weighing her options. Lie? Deflect? What could be done? She slowly nodded wordlessly, slid back into her chair and laid her head on her arms. Her shoulders shook with sobs.

Without a word, John moved slowly from his seat and walked out of the room. He trudged up the stairs, not bothering to look back at his mother who, with her head cradled on her arms, was wailing her heart out onto the white chintz tablecloth.

John steadfastly walked step by step up the wide staircase. Madison could see him pass Sam in the hall and go into their room. A moment later he came out again, carrying the shiny pole in one hand, the prized collection of lures in the other. Under the arm that carried the pole he had a colorful package.

He stepped heavily down each step and stopped at the top of the landing, where Sam stood. Carefully, John unwrapped the reel and stared at it. He put it down gently and opened the landing's large window, which looked out over the alley. He drew the glass up with a crack and with his other hand, grabbed the reel.

With one large movement, he threw it out the window. It clattered on the ground below. Then, he picked up the rod. He rotated it in his hands, leaving smudges on the smooth hard surface from the oils on his fingers. Madison, Helen and Sam watched John hold the Rebel up to the window. With a smooth motion, he snapped the pole hard across his thigh and cracked it in half. He held the two pieces, still connected by the thin fishing line, in his hands and launched them into the alley.

The shattered pole followed with the pile of flies. They glittered in the light of the street lamp and tinkled as they hit the pavement below.

Madison could feel that John's leg stung where he had broken the pole, but the tears, which came unchecked, had nothing to do with that pain.

He stepped closer to the window and whispered into the air, "Fuck you, Dad. Fuck you." He turned and plodded up the stairs, went into his room and closed the door.

Madison felt like she'd been kicked in the stomach. She looked from Sam to Helen. Sam sat down with a heavy thump on the stairs. He put his chin on his knees and stared at his feet. Helen continued sobbing, mired in her private place of despair.

Madison had never wanted to get out of any place as much as she wanted to leave here.

And in an instant, she was out of that room. She was back in her office, alone, staring at the wall where the images had played out so cinematically.

She was really shaken, trying to digest the reality of that moment so far back in time. Not only that, she wondered, but what did all of this—Helen, her sons, the revelation of this terrible secret—have to do with her?

Her head hurt and her body felt like she'd just endured days of the flu. She ached and quivered and realized she'd better do something to remove this negative energy. She picked up the phone and dialed Janine's number.

"J," she spoke carefully.

"Hey, girl, what's up?" Madison heard Janine draw in a sharp breath. "Madison, what's wrong?"

"I've got to see you. I just had a hellacious experience with this woman, Helen. Janine, this is starting to scare me."

"What happened? Are you all right?"

"Something so crazy is happening here. I'm being pulled into her life. She's drawing me in and I'm witnessing such sad, terrible things . . ." Madison's voice quivered as she tried to take a breath.

"Okay, okay, honey. Don't worry, we'll figure it out." Madison could tell Janine was trying to sound soothing and reassuring.

"We've got to, Janine. This woman is definitely trying to tell me something and she's sucking me into her life."

"It's okay, Madison." Janine repeated. "We'll figure it out."

They made plans to meet that evening at the base of the airport mesa trail. Madison called down to Miriam and cancelled her two afternoon sessions. She then searched through her drawers and retrieved a large bundle of sage. The densely wrapped leaves felt soft to her fingertips. She lit the bundle and waved it around the room. The pungent smoke made a wavy line in the air; the withering sage leaves dropped traces of ash on the floor. She lifted the silvery stick high to all corners of the ceiling. She held its reddened, burning edges low along the floorboards. She tried to guide the wisps throughout all the quadrants of the room. And, in typical Madison form, she found herself counting numbers, singular, combinations, formulas. Some of them floated before her mind's eye in an easy, drifting way. Some had a hard, marching feel to them. The numbers drifted, danced, stomped and filed into a haphazard line that finally felt right.

Madison circled the room and let the numbers still her anxiety. Numbers were her friends. They were steady and logical and always gave her a sense of order. Even when she'd been small, if some psychic experience had rattled her, the reciting or writing of numbers had calmed her, just as they began to do now.

When Madison felt more back to her own self, she waved the sage stick a few more times until she was satisfied the quieting embers had wiped away any remaining negative energy. She pressed it against the ceramic dish on her desk, extinguished the last burning flakes and set it back up on the bookshelf.

Madison quickly grabbed her coat and purse. She felt an almost hysterical need to get out of the office. She couldn't be in that space anymore today.

MADISON'S MEETING WITH JANINE brought back the discomfort in her center.

"Be patient," Janine advised after Madison had recounted the experience. "Be open."

"How much more open does a medium have to get? I mean really, Janine. I get that I've got this gift and all but isn't somebody taking it too far?"

"You lit sage, didn't you?"

"Yes," Madison answered wearily. She looked at her friend who she knew had easily as much or more of the gift than she. *Damn*, she thought. *This is getting serious . . .*

CHAPTER
TEN

THERE WAS NOTHING BETTER than the smell of dirt in spring. It predictably happened when the last crusts of ice had sunk into the grass and the small blades of new growth peeked out after months of frozen hibernation. Katherine sat on the front step of the house and breathed deeply. She watched a robin hopping about looking for a wandering worm. It almost made her feel normal, seeing these comforting signs of rebirth.

Just as quickly, the cloud of reality broke over her. She shook her head and tried to clear it. The despondency lingered around her like smoke in the air. *Stop whining!* She commanded herself. Katherine figured she needed to have a much more demanding tone of voice. Herself wasn't obeying a bit.

"Kath," Grant called from inside the house, "Wes is on the phone."

Ah, a moment of true sunshine. She hopped up and went in the kitchen. She sang into the phone, "Hi, honey!"

"Hi, Mom. Watcha doin'?"

"Oh, just sitting outside on the front step. I swear it's gotta be almost fifty degrees today."

"About time," her son's voice sounded quiet. She immediately sensed his worry. "How's your week been?" He asked.

The litmus test again. She knew he had an incredible radar reading on her tone of voice. "Oh, it was good." She said carefully, cheerfully. "Got the boys' season all wrapped up." She worked to fall into a normal, confident patter. Could he read through it?

"When does the season start?" He asked. So far so good, she thought.

"The thirtieth. Actually, the season starts on March twenty-third but the kids won't be back from spring break 'til the twenty-ninth." It sounded complicated, she knew, but Wes understood all the ins and outs of high school boys tennis coaching. After all, she had coached him as a senior, when she took over her first year.

"Well, how do they look?"

Katherine smiled and walked back out to the front step. She pressed the cell phone up to her ear and closed her eyes. If she imagined just right, he would actually be sitting next to her, instead of in his apartment thirty miles away.

She proceeded to give Wes a run-down of returning players, her finalized match schedule, entertaining stories of annoying parents. They laughed together in an easy, comforting camaraderie.

"What are you doing today, honey?" She asked, thinking of all the possibilities that her twenty-year-old, very independent boy could be entertaining.

"Umm, I don't know," she could hear him extend his long frame in a stretch. "I gotta work on my internship proposal for next fall. And," he added emphatically, "I decided I'm gonna valet again at Wayzata."

"Great! You and your brother both. How fun will that be!" She loved the fact her boys worked at the country club where she taught tennis in the summer. Katherine never tired of hearing how polite and charming her boys were. *Remember that!* She told herself. *A bright spot!*

"Yeah, it'll be good." He paused. "I can't wait for summer."

"You and me both."

"Mom," his voice softened. "Are you okay?"

Just the question, delivered in the concerned tone instantly brought the sting of tears. She was determined not to let him hear her desperation.

She had made the mistake before of sharing with Wes her frustration and anger at Grant and the circumstances. It was a selfish thing to do. Her son had less control over the situation than she did. She knew the grinding depression of living with it daily but it wasn't fair to suck him into it, too.

"Yeah, honey," she willed her voice to sound optimistic and cheery. "I'm good. It will be nice to get to work again."

"Yeah, well, keep your chin up, Mom." He didn't sound at all convinced.

"I will sweetie. You too. Love you." She waited for his predictable response.

"Love you, too."

Katherine pushed the end button on the phone and leaned back against the pillar. The moment felt so surreal. Here she was sitting in her favorite place in the world on a day when promise sprouted all around her. But she could only think about what she could lose. The sight of the birch tree in the driveway island, ready to sprout its new buds, depressed her. The lawn's new greenery sickened her. She hated her incredible ability to transport herself into the worst possibilities of the future and thrash about in them. It was really almost more than she could bear. Automatically, Katherine thought of all the things she had to be thankful for. There were more than she could count but she couldn't count hardly any of them today.

Then she remembered something and walked back into the house. She found her wallet and picked through it until she found the folded business card. With a deep breath, she tiptoed back to the front porch. She squinted at the numbers and punched them into her phone. She was a bit surprised at the boldness of her choice, but that was offset by the despondency she found herself drowning in. She needed a slap in the face and she could think of no other person at this instant better qualified to give it than Madison Morgan.

The message answer brought instantly to Katherine's mind an image of Madison, staring into her eyes, holding her hands over the table. She was transported back to that airy little office with the Sedona sun streaming into the window. "Sorry I missed you. I am anxious to speak with you and will return your call as soon as possible!" Madison's voice sounded strong and inspiring.

"Hi, Madison. This is Katherine Simon. You gave me a reading back in December. I live in Minnesota and I was wondering if there would be a time I could arrange to have a phone reading or something with you." What else should she say? "My number is six one two . . ." Katherine tried to speak clearly and slowly. "Thanks for returning my call," she finished, somewhat lamely, she thought. She put the phone down and wondered when she'd get a call back.

The phone rang as if on command. She pushed Send hurriedly and looked at the screen. No Madison, just a certain son in California. "Hi, Wayne!"

"Hi, Kath. What are you doing?" She loved the fact that Wayne played with her, calling her by her first name.

"Just sitting out on the porch, enjoying the blistering fifty-degree temperature!" She let herself enjoy the rare moment of a phone call from him. "What are you doing?"

"Getting ready to go to the beach."

"That is absolutely an unacceptable way to talk to your mother! In fact, I think I'll have to ground you. When are you going to be home, again?"

Wayne laughed, a sound unfettered by frustration. He led such an enviable, uncomplicated life. "Two months. You hold onto that threat and we can talk about it when I get off the plane!"

Wayne's voice, the warming sunshine, the conversation with Wes, all morphed into a moment of peace. Life was good, after all. She got the update from her younger son on classes, fraternity life, and funny stories. Then he asked her for the updates. She was careful to leave out the depressing reality details, instead focusing on coaching and teaching in the summer. "That's right!" She remembered. "You are going to work at the club with your brother."

"Yeah, should be fun. Unless," his voice dropped down an octave, "I get a job bartending in Ireland."

"Are you serious?" The jubilant bubble began to deflate.

"Well, I'd love to do it if I could but it probably won't work out. I'm working Natalie B.'s dad for it. He owns a pub in Limerick."

"Wow that sounds really cool." Could he hear the sadness in her voice? She hoped not.

"Yeah, just think! How sick would a summer in Ireland be?"

"God! That is so great!" She said. "Do you think you'll get it?" She took a deep breath. "It would be so perfect for you, honey."

A slow teardrop slid down Katherine's cheek.

"Oh, hey, Mom?"

"Yeah, sweetie?"

"I've got this assignment in theatre. I'm supposed to find a relative I don't know much about and perform an imagined dialog scene with them. I was thinking that Grandpa, you know, your dad, might be good for that."

"Wow, well, what do you need?"

"I've just got to know a few basics about him." Katherine heard voices summoning Wayne away from their conversation. He responded to them shouting over the phone. "Hey guys, fifteen minutes, okay?"

A carol of protests rolled in the background. "I promise," he yelled. He returned to the call. "Sorry about that. They're all on surf mode."

"And good for you that you are at least partially on home-work mode!"

Wayne laughed back. "Right! But not for long! So," she heard the rustle of his papers, "this scene is one that you are supposed to ask a question of this person who was related to you but never part of your life."

"Hmm, interesting. What are you expected to ask?"

"If you could tell me one life-changing moment in your life, what would it be?"

"Wow, that brings up a lot of possibilities."

"Yeah," Wayne continued. "So I was thinking about your dad because you never really talked about him. How come?"

"Well, we didn't have the closest of relationships. "He was pretty demanding and strict and not the warm, fuzziest of guys."

"What was he like?"

Katherine tipped her head back and imagined her father's face. His blue eyes would be looking back at her, hooded under white eyebrows. His mouth would be set in a firm, thin line. "He was incredibly intelligent. He was a smart businessman—"

"Hey mom, the guys are stompin' all over the place. They want to take off to Malibu now. Can I call you later about it?" His voice was already far away from their connection.

"Okay, honey, no problem. Call me when you want. Have fun!"

"'Kay! Love you!"

"Love you, too!" Katherine looked at the birch branches creating a spindly canopy above the driveway. She closed her eyes and thought about both boys in college. How in the world were she and Grant going to pay for this? The branches weaved in the air above her. *God,* she thought. *How did we get on this path? Nothing's going to be the same.* Fear slid into her belly. If things didn't change, Katherine suspected the house would have to go. It was only a matter of time. What then?

CHAPTER ELEVEN

IT HAD BEEN ONLY forty-eight hours since Madison's experience in Helen's world. She'd tried to think of other things, book a few more clients to distract herself, but the encounter still hung about her like sage smoke. By the time she was finished with her last reading of the day, Madison couldn't get out of her office fast enough.

She sprinted down the stairs and out into the spring sunshine. Her phone vibrated with a call but she didn't even stop to look at it. Just as she was about to get into her car, she thought better of it and went back inside the Center. If she were right, her friend William would be finishing his Reiki training session.

She burst past the jewelry case and headed for the book room. A gathering of students had just broken up and William was standing in a corner speaking to a young woman with tears on her face.

The tall psychic's presence and his voice were quiet and calm. Madison honestly thought he was the most beautiful man in the world and if he were anything besides being an incredibly intuitive sooth-seer, he'd be a certified movie star. His long wavy hair framed a face of incredibly strong features. His eyes glinted under straight brows. They were the most delightful and magnetizing translucent gray-blue. When he looked at her, it was as if he saw nothing else in the world and he drew her into his energy gently. His eyes actually made her weak in the knees. His angular jawline ran from beneath his prominent cheekbones to his firm, square chin.

William embraced the woman he'd been speaking with and she moved away with a misty smile. He turned and looked at Madison as if he'd known she'd been waiting to talk to him. Of course he'd known . . .

"Hello, my sweet," his smooth British accent soothing.

"Hi, honey. Got a minute?"

"Of course, love." He looked around the store at the circles of people huddled everywhere. "Let's go up to my office."

Madison nodded and followed him through the small rooms and out the door to his office above. He turned and smiled at her as he held the door open. "C'mon girl, let's talk."

Madison tromped up the steep steps. Even walking upstairs made her feel better. Madison knew William would help her. He would ease her mind. He guided her into his office and she suddenly became aware of William's faint cologne. He smelled delicious. *This will never do,* Madison told herself. She determined to keep her thoughts in the friendship mode. Her attraction to him would only disrupt her focus. Besides, she knew he only considered her a friend.

"So," William's voice sounded peaceful. He offered her a seat on the couch. She settled in amongst the multi-colored cushions covered with sun designs, some hand-embroidered, some needle-pointed, some slick and satiny. Each sun had its own theme: One rose up behind Snoopy Rock in the desert, one smiled down on field workers who waved gaily back. One pillow had a pair of suns playing hide and go seek behind stern grey clouds.

"Ahh," Madison couldn't help but let out a deep sigh.

"Well, your energy feels better now than when I saw you downstairs! Tea, my girl?" William walked to the small sideboard next to his desk. He flipped the teapot switch on and picked through his box of teas. "I've got green, white, mint, acai . . ."

"Green would be great, thanks." Madison watched him find two ceramic mugs and plop the tea bags in them. He rolled his large office chair from behind the desk.

It was less than a second before the words began rolling out of Madison like a package full of pennies sliced open and tinkling onto the floor. She explained how the ghost had come to visit her the first time. She recalled the excursion to Helen's wake, the ghost's visits to Madison's office and then the encounter two days before. As she recounted the scenes in that tree house and in the dining room, Madison felt goose bumps all over again.

William nodded as she spoke. He got up and stirred the hot water into the cups. He brought Madison hers and set it down on the distressed mahogany coffee table. By this time, Madison had completed her story and she sat back amongst the pillows. "God, that was exhausting."

"There is clearly a focused energy at work here." William tapped his fingers on the teacup. "But she speaks very little, eh?"

Madison took a sip of her tea and shook her head. "It's strange that she actually transports me to these places in time. That's never happened to me before. I feel like I'm living in a flippin' carnival and the bearded lady wants to be my new best friend. Has anything like this ever happened to you?"

"Yes, but it was years ago. A man who had passed was trying to get me to give a message to his son."

"Well, I've had that, too, but the way in which she's doing it is crazy. There is so much going on, I can't figure out why she's got me there."

"When it happened to me with this ghost," William remembered, "he gave me a series of life experiences to share. They all added up to the reason for his message."

"Hmmm, what was it?"

"He had made a number of bad choices in his life because he held a deep belief that he didn't deserve good things. His father had abused him. He showed me that." William's eyes took on a distant look. "It was fascinating how he chose the various moments to bring me in on. But I'm sure he was right. Of course he was right." He looked at Madison again. "He found a way to show me why he needed to get that message to his son."

"Did you give him the message?"

"Yes, but I don't know if he took it to heart." William shook his head. "His father told him to stop riding motorcycles. It was strange because this kid, his son, lived in Durango not too far from me. I'd see him every now and then at the little grocery store or the gas station. You know, Durango's a really small town."

Madison nodded.

"So, whenever I'd see him, right after or right before, I'd get this visitation from the man who had passed. It took me awhile to figure out who he was for." William laughed. "I have to say during those two or three months, I gave a lot of people some very strange looks! I'd stare at them and wonder if they were the person this guy was trying to get to."

"I've got the same problem. This lady is stalking me and I don't know why." The image of the cosmic stalker set them both laughing. Madison felt the pent up tension releasing. "So what do I do, William?" She leaned forward toward him earnestly. "My friend Janine keeps telling me to just stay open to it. But if I keep having sessions like the one I just had when I was awake, I'm never gonna go to sleep again. After all, she started this business in my dreams!"

William took Madison's hands in his. "Listen, Mads," He spoke quietly now. "This woman needs to get something out to someone. My guess is that what you are getting now is back-story to *who* she was and *why* she was. Understand?"

Madison nodded again.

"Allow her to create this pathway to you. The stronger her connection with you, the clearer her intention will become. Try guiding her with questions. Think of them and write them down. Keep a list in your office and a list by your bed. In fact," he let go of her hands and jumped out of his chair. He went over to the desk and picked up a pad of paper. "You need to get some nutmeg, cloves and rosemary."

"For, love, psychic power and . . ." Madison couldn't remember what the rosemary was for.

"Mental power." William wrote down the words and then dug into his tea box again. He brought out a small bag with a silken cord and a tiny tag. Madison squinted her eyes to read the writing. Sweet geranium and narcissus tea. She looked up at William questioningly.

"The properties of healing," he explained. "Make yourself some of this tonight and offer it as a positive path to you. Whatever the reason, Madison, this woman has chosen you specifically."

"No doubt about that!" She fingered the tea bag.

"Now you need to move her along to find out what she needs said and who she needs it said to. My guess is," he stood rocking on his heels ever so slightly. "She may be working through a lot of this for herself."

"Well, I don't want to hurt the ol' gal's feelings but I really didn't bargain for being a therapist to the spirits!"

William offered his hand. "Up you go. You never know. You may have to change your business card, Miss Madison Morgan!"

She stood up and gave his lean frame a giant hug. He smelled of a sweet woodsy combination of cypress and patchouli. She breathed it in deeply then stood on her tiptoes and kissed his cheek. He replied with a brush of his lips across the back of her hand and a squeeze of her fingers.

"I'm always available, my girl," William smiled.

"I know. Thanks, honey, love you!" She gave him a wink and walked out of the office, down the stairs and out the door. She didn't notice that he stood watching after her.

CHAPTER
TWELVE

A S SHE LOOKED OUTSIDE the window, she realized she wasn't even
seeing what was in front of her eyes. She felt like they were
dead, two useless holes in her head that let out tears and let nothing
else in. She was so tired of crying and being depressed.

She very nearly didn't pick up her phone. She'd left it on vibrate and wasn't sure where it was. It sounded like a bumblebee
caught under a cup. She reached it just before the last buzz. "Hello?"

"Hello, is this Katherine Simon?"

"Yes," Katherine hesitated and tried to peer down at the
number on her screen.

"Hi, this is Madison Morgan." Katherine's stomach tightened.

"Hi," Katherine tried to keep the tremors out of her voice.
"Hi, thanks for calling me back."

"No problem." There was that boisterous baritone sound she
remembered from Sedona. "What can I do for you?"

'Well, I came to see you last December. I had some life questions you tried to help me with."

"Ahhh . . ." Madison's voice didn't sound as if she registered
any memory of their session. "Well, I do have to admit. I talk to a
lot of people."

Katherine took a deep breath. No, it was clear that this psychic didn't remember her.

Despite that, Katherine wanted to pour everything out, just
let it all come out in a wave of emotional bile. She restrained herself.
"I was hoping we could talk for a half-an-hour or so?"

Madison hesitated. Katherine could hear her leafing through papers. "Okay, let's see." Her matter of fact tone eased a bit of Katherine's anxiety. "Well, is now a good time? If not I could do four my time. You're an hour ahead, right?" Madison charged on. "Or, I could do eleven in the morning my time tomorrow, for starters. What are you thinking?"

Katherine swiftly ran down her to-do list. All of them could wait. "Now, would be really great."

"Oh, okay," Madison took a breath. What's going on?"

Now, Katherine let it all gush out. Once the words started flowing, she couldn't stop. She talked about everything, coming home, feeling somewhat positive, but then falling back into her old patterns of anxiety and desperation. She shared her fears of losing the house, of Grant not getting a job for another year. She went on and on and realized that for at least five minutes, Madison hadn't said a thing.

"Wow," Katherine said finally.

"Yeah," Madison growled, "I've got your crap all over me. Tell me somethin' kid."

Katherine took a deep breath, "What?"

"And I don't want the unabridged Webster's Dictionary edition. Okay? My God, my ear feels like it's ready to blow up."

Katherine was a bit offended by this; after all, it was her money. Couldn't she spend it anyway she wanted? And if that meant spewing her life for thirty minutes . . .

"Are you listening to me?" Madison barked.

"Yes, yes, what?"

"What are you gettin' from holding onto all this garbage? 'Cause it sounds to me that you are still whining about all the stuff we talked about before and that was," Katherine could hear Madison counting, "four, five months ago?" Madison harrumphed. "I don't know but it seems like you enjoy being stuck!"

Katherine also counted in her head back to that December afternoon when she had first met Madison. Had anything changed? Not one thing. Absolutely nothing.

"Oh my God, I am such a freak, why would I just want to sit in this?"

"I'll tell you one thing, you are a world class tantrum thrower and you've been at it for a quite a while now. Aren't you tired of it?"

"Of course I'm tired!" She hadn't bargained on therapy for her hundred bucks. She wanted something more.

"Well lemme tell you something, everybody else around you, the Universe included, is tired too. So you gotta knock it off. Ya see," Madison's voice grew stronger now and Katherine hung on every word. "You gotta stop looking for disaster and destruction. If you keep looking hard enough, you'll find it, all right. You gotta start looking for happiness and fulfillment and joy. You are absolutely not in this predicament by mistake. It's so obvious that you have to learn how to be okay with whatever happens.

"Some people are naturally good at that. But some, like you, they've gotta work at it. It's a life skill and one that you don't have. Because, Katherine, you never really needed it until now."

"How do I do that?" Katherine wanted to scream the words but just whispered.

"How do you do that?" Madison answered softly. "You have to create the person you want to be. You shed the old self. Shed that other person; She's like a snake skin. No," Madison paused. "She's bigger than that. She's like this alien that's growing inside of you."

"You've just been sitting around holding this pity party, walling yourself off because it's too uncomfortable to try to be okay with what's going on."

Katherine offered a miserable moan of agreement. Madison could hear the deep depression that Katherine wallowed in and could never shake, even when things were going well. Her next words were soft and gentle, a light hand on Katherine's shoulder.

"You can do this. It isn't about what's going on for everybody else and you should just shut up because so many people have got it so much worse than you do. Let them be there. That's their path. This is your path. Your job is to grow up and learn a new life skill. You have to make that your goal because you'll see answers as you stop holding on to what you used to have. Listen, I see your fingers in my head and they're holding on to what you think makes up your life, like tentacles. Like you are a Goddamned octopus!"

Katherine sat back and stared out the window, watching the chickadees in the back yard play dogfights in the air. "So what am I supposed to do?"

"Well you gotta put one foot in front of the other. I don't know. I'm getting the feeling that I'm supposed to give you something more but I'm not sure what that is. I feel a huge connection to your kids. They are so big in your life. Take your worries for them first of all and replace them with positive energy, prayers, whatever. That's an exercise you can do starting right now. Are you writing this down?"

Katherine hastily grabbed a pile of post-it notes, chastising herself for not thinking about writing all this down before. Her head was reeling. She scribbled furiously.

"Got it?"

"Yes," she answered obediently.

"And next, replace the thoughts that are jumping around in your head. They look like birds fighting in the air." Katherine looked at the chickadees outside and squinted her eyes. Was this actually happening?

"You know, our time is up but I want to think on this some more." Madison shifted the phone from one ear to the other. "I'm gonna sit on this and maybe I'll call you tomorrow. Sometimes, I just get so wired up, I start throwing out all this stuff and I can't remember what I said and it's hard for the client to interpret it because it's coming out so fast."

Katherine tried to take in all the words.

"Hey, sweet cakes, you there?" Madison asked.

"Yup," she answered weakly. "I'm here."

"Okay, well don't get all freaked out on me. Today there is a resolution for you. It's a jumping off point." Madison's throaty voice reassured Katherine. "Not like you're actually going to jump, I mean!"

"You are going to be fine. Consider this like a new adventure in your life. When things seem really rough, you got to train yourself to step back and observe and just notice and say, 'Hmm, that's interesting. What am I supposed to learn from this?'

"At least it's better than going through life like you're standing against the bottom of a cliff, at the ocean's edge, and you're just getting pounded with waves and sand and sea weed and dead fish and there's nothing you can do about it.

"You know, no one promised that this whole journey was going to be easy. You don't get to traipse through life and just bumble along. And I got to tell you," her voice dropped into a conspiratorial tone, "sometimes I get really tired of people asking me to sort it all out for them. I mean, Christ! It's your journey, why should I do all the work to give you the crib notes?"

Katherine had to admit that Madison's words did make sense. She couldn't believe thirty minutes had gone by so fast. Madison spent a few more minutes giving her key words to write down and ponder. She promised to do her best and when they hung up, Katherine realized she didn't feel as down. She didn't feel completely optimistic, either, but one thing was for sure, she was going to have to think long and hard about everything Madison had said.

"Well what were you expecting?" She said aloud. "All the answers tied up in a box with a neat little bow?" She was pretty sure that whatever this Universe was made of, it wasn't designed to put things neatly in order so they were just right. Katherine gathered up her post-it notes. It was going to take some doing to translate these scratches into the next great chapter of her life.

CHAPTER THIRTEEN

GOD, IF IT WASN'T one needy client, it was another. Madison was worn out from the phone call. She was also bothered by the nagging feeling that something else had needed to be communicated, but she didn't know what it was. She looked at her watch and realized she had three more clients that afternoon. With any luck, she'd get down to the bank and gas station and have enough time to get a sandwich before her next reading arrived at her doorstep.

She was chagrined that she was feeling so negative. It would never do to bring that energy into the readings. She recited a verse she'd learned years before:

> Charting waters is easy work
> Changing places, laborer's perk
> Finding faith takes miles of road
> Dusty tracks mean far to go
> Invitation is not easily given to
> Ones who hover in the garden of living
> But time will tell and signs will show
> Whatever was meant for you to know.

Those words centered her. She couldn't remember how many times she'd said them in her frantic moments but they'd always relaxed her, just like the reciting of numbers. And luckily, today was no different.

Forty-five minutes later, Madison stood in line at the deli, considering how to change the molecular pattern she found herself in. The woman at the counter broke into her concentration, "Can I help you?"

"Um, yup," Madison looked up from her wallet. She scanned the sign above the woman's head. Her eyes ranged over the items listed on the blackboard sign written in white chalk. TURKEY SANDWICH SLIM. HELPER'S ROAST BEEF. SWISS AND HAM STACK. In the space of an instant, her brain took note of all the choices on the menu. She looked back down at the woman but saw something else instead.

Her face went white, and the words tumbled unchecked from her mouth, "Oh, craaaap!"

"What? I beg your pardon?" The woman was clearly surprised and confused, but that didn't register to Madison. What registered was the reflection in the display case behind the woman. Madison could clearly see Helen looking back at her from the shiny glass. She whirled around to look behind her and saw a light purple aura in the space beyond the man who fidgeted behind her in line.

Madison twirled forward again and peered at the image mirrored behind the woman who was now clearly not happy with Madison. There Helen stood, just behind Madison's reflection.

"I'm sorry," Madison mumbled backing away, almost tripping over the shocked man behind her. "I gotta get out, I mean. I gotta go."

She turned and shuttled past the man, who stood clearly bewildered. The quivering aura shimmered in the space between him and the soda machine. She stopped long enough to come up even with the presence, which only she could see.

"I gotta tell you," she growled under her breath, so low that no one in the deli could hear. "We have to stop meeting like this!" She tried to walk out as calmly as she could when she really wanted to run out as fast as if her hair was on fire.

Madison was rattled. Her mind must be rolled up in a tight ball and the folks in the astral plane were playing soccer with it. She felt hysterical and pissed off all at the same time.

"Breathe," she told herself as she marched toward her car, head down, eyes focused on the warm Sedona dust swirling on the asphalt.

"Breathe, count." She started methodically, "One, two, three, four, five . . ." she'd gotten up to thirty-six by the time she reached her car and realized she'd been reciting those numbers out loud.

She practically threw herself into the car and squeezed the steering wheel. Slowly she took three deep breaths. In six beats, out eight. Her heart rate slowed a few strokes and she leaned forward against the steering wheel. Then with a deep push, she breathed out everything left in her lungs, slid the key into the ignition, started the car and pulled onto Mesa Avenue.

She was relieved when every stop light in her path turned green just before she got to each intersection. She realized there wasn't a part of her body not shaking and it would be a real shame if she took a pedestrian out because her foot couldn't stay solid on the brake pedal.

Back at the office, Madison sat in her chair and stared out the window. The ghost's appearance played in her mind. She could see the dull gray eyes staring at her. She shivered and looked at the clock. The next client wasn't due for twenty minutes. She left the office and trotted down the stairs.

The crack of the door closing gave her a snap back to reality. A quick stroll would do her good. She walked up the quiet street and carefully picked her way past the construction signs on the sidewalk. Everywhere the street was torn up and re-routed, making the town look like a patient with surgical scars.

Madison circled back on the broken sidewalk to the center parking lot. The bright green Alien Museum stood out in contrast to her purple building. The windows sparkled with glitter and twinkling lights. On the front side of the building a huge painted alien, lizard-like with cavernous black eyes, surveyed the road. Madison opened the door and let herself in.

The neat room smelled slightly of tacos. Along the walls, display cases held guidebooks for alien hunting, videos, and pictures of alleged sightings in the area.

"Be with you in a sec!" A deep voice boomed from an adjoining room.

"Hey Jake." Madion called back. "It's Mads. Stopped in for a break to say 'hi.' You busy?"

Jake walked into the room with a taco in one hand and a cellphone to his ear in the other. He waved Madison over and gave her a quick hug. "Yup, Stan, thanks again for the head's up. You say there were two of them?"

Madison looked around the room at the poster-filled walls. Everywhere aliens in different forms peeked out behind Sedona's red cliffs and vortex whirlwinds. A replica of a space ship hovered above attached to the ceiling with cable wires.

"Sorry about that, Mads." Jake walked over and plopped the last bit of taco in his mouth. He was a bear of a man with hands that looked more like baseball mitts. His long, silver-streaked hair was pulled back neatly in a pony tail and his gray beard wiggled furiously as he chewed the last bite.

"Don't worry about it. Just needed to get out of the office for a sec. I've got a ten-minute break before I have to get back."

"Well, lucky me for getting the quick visit! Or is it my buddies you're coming to see?"

"I've got ghosts everywhere but I still haven't seen one of your alien pals. Sure you're not making this up?"

Jake frowned at her. "C'mon Mads, that's not nice. You know it's all true. In fact, I just got back from the International UFO Congress and it seems like appearances are stepping up. Some researchers think it has to do with a rogue planet called Nibiru, due to pass by us soon. They say the aliens are trying to create flight patterns around the earth so they can protect us from the Nibiru's affect on our gravitational fields."

"Wow. That little bit was just enough for me. And I thought I had an exciting life with all these spirit visits. Can't imagine how thrilling it would be to hang with some extra terrestrials, too!"

Jake gave her a kiss. "Don't worry, girl, I'll keep you updated on all the latest! We can hunker down somewhere near a vortex and live off of cactus flowers and aloe."

"That's exactly what I needed. You've taken me out of my funk and put me back into reality. I feel refreshed and ready to go again! I should always stop by when the ghosts start to come at me."

"You sure they are really not aliens?" Jake raised his eyebrows. "You know that in nine out of ten experiences, the beings are humanoid."

"Oh my God," Madison turned to walk out past the life-sized stuffed alien standing in the corner next to a video display of the Roswell Alien Incident. "Let's hope I'm only dealing with beings from one dimension. I don't have the stamina to cross over parallel Universes!"

"Okay," Jake hollered from behind her as she went out the door. "Just remember I'm here when you need me!"

"Will do, Jake!" Madison walked quickly back across the lot to her office. She was glad to have gotten out. The thoughts of aliens and humanoid visits erased Helen's deli stalking from the front of her mind. Mercifully, here she was just a garden variety Sedona psychic again. She hummed the tune from *Gilligan's Island* as she prepared for her next reading.

BUT ON THE CAR RIDE home, Helen's vision seemed everywhere. Madison thought she saw the ghost by a stop sign outside The Indian Den. She was sure she caught a glimpse of the woman's face reflected in the Hillside Mall. Everywhere, it seemed, the air glimmered with her presence. Madison's anxiety grew as she wound her way along Highway 179 to her little house on the hill.

Once home, Madison nearly catapulted herself into the house. The front door acquiesced to her forceful push and swung open obediently. Madison charged past the plants that leaned so gracefully in their vortex hot house. She ran into the dining room and began scanning the piles of documents, files, papers, and books. She shoveled through a foot-high pile of manila file folders in a far corner of the dining room table. Nearly to the bottom of the stack, she found the curly-eared folder with her flowing script which read HILBERT UNIVERSITY.

She put tongue to thumb and flipped through the various pages, class schedules, graded papers, general information brochures from 1984—1988. "Ah HA!" Her voice rattled through the house. She rummaged now through the tables' stacks to find the phone and with eager fingertips, tapped in the number.

One of the wind chimes in the backyard tinkled softly. Madison smiled. At least, she thought, just as one of these spirits out there was pounding the streets giving her grief, others were hopefully perched around like crows on a tree, ready to help in any ethereal way they could. She held her breath.

Four rings later she heard his familiar voice. It felt like it had been eons since she had talked to him.

"Hello?" The gravelly voice said.

"Hi, Ben, Ben Masselink?" Madison's stomach twisted in a nervous pretzel.

"Yup, that's me! Hello?" Madison could imagine his sweet elderly face scrunched up trying to recognize her voice.

"Ben, it's Madison Morgan here. Do you remember me?" She asked, timidly. After all, it wasn't like she was calling a neighbor she'd lived for days on end near or a butcher she'd bought meat from for years. This was a professor who she had known for a brief amount of time years ago. How many voices had he received calls from?

"Wow! Voice from the past! Madison, how are you, kid?" She could feel his warmth through the phone.

"Oh, I'm great." She wanted to sing. He remembered!

She rushed on. She wanted to fill her former professor in on her life in a breezy, detached way. "Just doing the Sedona thing. Remember we talked about that, I think it was the last time I saw you?"

"Yes, course I do. Well," he sounded pleased for her. "I'm so glad things are going well for you, kid." He added cheerfully, "What can I do for you?"

Suddenly, Madison felt sheepish and stupid. Maybe she was out of her mind and this was a bad idea. Too late now, he was poised on the other end of the line.

"Ben, this is going to sound crazy, but I've been having these strange experiences. I've been reading a lot of different clients but this one woman from the other side keeps popping into my life. At first, it was benign, a picture here, a sense of her presence there. Then she got into life-hold mode."

"Ah," his voice relayed his interest. "Go on."

"I've had some really intense moments with this broad. She has not only come around in my dreams, she comes to the office . . . I even ran into her at the deli today! Can you believe that?"

Madison could imagine Ben's tan leathery face underneath that white mane of wild hair. She had always thought he looked like a surfer who'd just cleaned up from a morning ride.

"Jeez! That's great!"

Great wasn't the word Madison was looking for. She plunged ahead. "Ben, I really need your advice, your guidance. I've talked to a couple of other friends here but they can't really help. They just say 'stay open, stay available', you know . . ."

"Good advice, kid."

"I know, but I think this woman is ramping it up. She's really trying to get me to know her better, understand her more. She's taken me back to significant moments in her life and—" Madison stopped mid-sentence.

"And what?"

"And she's taking me into moments of her son's life, too."

Ben was quiet for a moment. She wondered what experience he was filtering her information through. He'd been a clairvoyant for all of his seventy-plus years. He'd known from early on that he was different, as most people with the ability did. He had become the head of Hilbert University, the country's largest school for study of the metaphysical, and was recognized as a leading expert in all things otherworldly. "Madison, this feels like something really big. It's not unusual for one of them to attach themselves to us but to bring in another figure really dominantly, clearly, is really special," he paused. "Is that how you see it?"

Madison thought for a moment. She tried to sink deeper to find the intuitive voice. "I'm not sure. She's shown me more of herself than of him. I only saw him as a little boy."

"Do you know who this woman is?"

"I got a name." Madison searched her brain. Helen . . . Rhames? "Yeah, I think her name is Helen Rhames. I'm not sure of the spelling but that's the way it reads in my head."

"Have you done any research on her?"

"No, not really." Once again, Madison felt stupid. She should have done some checking before she bothered this man.

"Ahh," His voice broke in. "This is all part of the process. Sometimes it seems so obvious, sometimes not. Of course, it's all obvious later!"

"Kid, I think you've got a bit of work to do here. If she is nudging you, follow it. Find out more about her. Find out who she is attached to. Could be someone for you but you'd probably feel that, right?"

"Right."

"So, as I say, go to work, do some digging. In the meantime, your connection may get even stronger. Help her out a little bit, Madison. If she's choosing you, she surely has a good, important reason for that. Remember in the early clairvoyance sessions, we talk about sensitivity to pictures and the energy of momentum behind them?"

"Yes, like when someone gives you the picture of hands on a throat, you have to interpret, murder or weeping?"

"Exactly right. Use your listening to discern if her message is for someone else or relates to you. From the way you describe this whole scenario, there is a specific reason behind all of this. Does that make sense?"

"Kind of."

"Grab some paper. Write down what I just said. Get into Sherlock Holmes mode and call me in a few weeks to let me know what you come up with." Ben's voice resonated with her as if she was back sitting in his sunny classroom. It could have been twenty years ago. But it wasn't. It was today, 2007.

"Thanks, Ben. I really appreciate your willingness to help. I mean, it's been so long. But I needed someone I trust to help me find what is correct."

"We trained you well, my friend. Integrity is the highest honor and calling of what we do. I'll help you stay on that path however I can."

CHAPTER FOURTEEN

K ATHERINE ROLLED OVER and opened her eyes. Grant wasn't in bed. The covers hadn't been moved so she realized that he must have slept on the couch, again.

She got up and put her robe on. She used to wash her face and neaten her hair every morning, but now she had little energy for that. It was enough to stand on two shaky legs and prepare to pretend herself through the day.

Walking through the hall toward the stairs, she noticed both boys' doors closed. How could the few months since Christmas feel like so long ago? She couldn't wait till they would come home for summer vacation. Even though it was weeks away, Katherine made a mental note to clean and prepare their rooms. She peeked over the stair railing and saw Grant huddled on the coach, barely covered with a blanket. The television in the wall before him was tuned to ESPN and on the fifteenth rerun of Sportscenter. Her husband rustled sleepily.

Ten minutes later, she had the coffee brewing and Grant's favorite cinnamon bread in the toaster. The kitchen felt warm and inviting. Katherine stood at the window and surveyed the incredible view. The patches of snow on the ground punctuated the areas of frozen water, separating them from the islands of cattails that had been blown, then iced, into place. The expansive landscape swept out beneath and around her. Out the patio door from the kitchen nook roared a fifty-foot waterfall still bubbling and gurgling beneath the dome of ice that had formed over it. Beyond that sat the pool, above a rolling lawn which stretched down into the marsh. Just beyond the three-season porch, the tennis court glistened under frothy snow drifts. Over five hundred pine trees surrounded the court. Grant had planted them six years ago as three-inch seedlings. Now some of them were almost as tall as the fence around the court.

The soft mingling scents of coffee and cinnamon drifted through the kitchen and transformed it into a quaint Norman Rockwell scene. Katherine turned to get the butter for Grant's toast and just then, he stumbled in. "Oh, my back," he moaned.

"What, from sleeping on the couch, again?"

"Yeah, probably," Grant rubbed his hands through his hair. Katherine noticed how gray his short curls were becoming.

"Made you some toast and coffee."

"Thanks, honey," he smiled and came up behind her, locking his arms around her. "You always start my day right."

Katherine softened at those words. She needed to remember that Grant was having a hard time, too. It wasn't just she who stood in the kitchen of this perfect little house and surveyed what could be lost. She'd seen Grant staring out the window plenty of times, too.

Katherine squeezed his hands then turned to face him. She gave him a light kiss on his lips and smiled into his eyes. As their gazes locked, she again felt the deep connection of years spent together, children raised together, experiences enjoyed together—all being threatened and dimmed because of the incredible stress they had been living under.

Two years was a long time for a man of Grant's qualifications to be unemployed. It wasn't easy for a businessman who had run his own company to find a job in corporate America. Companies weren't looking for entrepreneurial types. They didn't fit in the culture. And Katherine and Grant had little money left, after living on their savings. There were absolutely no funds available to start a new business, but Grant couldn't emotionally or physically do it anyway. He was still paralyzed by the loss of his father just months after the demise of his company.

So he'd sat in the kitchen for the past twenty four months, half-heartedly trying to drum up contacts and interviews. He spent hours on his computer looking through websites that promoted networking and then tried to create relationships to get possible job interviews. It was really frustrating for this man who had been a CEO of a multi-million dollar company with five Midwest offices to be reduced to creating a fragile web of possibilities. It killed him a little more every day, Katherine realized.

She'd made endless mental resolutions to be more supportive of him, but instead she'd get out of the house as fast as she could in the morning and stay away as long as she could through the day. When she came home she wouldn't ask how the search was going unless he volunteered something first—she didn't want to hear the same depressing answers. Despite her intentions, Katherine realized it was a highly effective way to insert cracks into a marriage.

Katherine poured Grant his coffee and handed him his toast. He leaned forward and kissed her again, leaving with her a painfully nostalgic stab in her chest. She shouldn't live in the past, but why live in the present when all it presented was worries, fear, anger, frustration and despair? She turned to the sink and began to wash the breakfast dishes, already planning the itinerary for her day. Her thoughts of Grant were pushed to the furthest corner of her mind, despite the fact that he stood right in front of her, staring out the window.

CHAPTER
FIFTEEN

MADISON'S HANDS TREMBLED on the steering wheel. A sharp squeal of tires caused her to nearly jump off the seat. Instinctively, she slammed her breaks as the car backing out of the spot in front of her missed her bumper by maybe six inches. Her stomach felt like it had launched into her throat and streams of sweat began a torrent. The other driver's glare didn't help to calm her. "C'mon, buddy," she shouted. "I know I'm an idiot. Let's just mosey your ass out of this spot so I can get in."

Her agitation grew stronger as she waited for the man to pull out. Sweat soaked through nearly every inch of her blouse. She took a deep breath and tried unsuccessfully to calm her racing heart as she finally pulled forward into the empty spot. The safe landing did little to improve her mood. She'd been anxious all day knowing her dental appointment was on the horizon. Madison considered herself to be pretty strong but a visit to the dentist always reduced her to a fearful quivering mass. She hated the dentist but her abscessed tooth held more influence than her hysteria. Her damn tooth hurt, her head was spinning and she was as wet as an Indian in a sweathouse. *All this,* she thought miserably, *is a fucking perfect way to start a day*. Madison shakily picked up her purse and headed to the dreaded Suite 212, where terror and agony awaited her.

The small blessing was that she wouldn't have to wait more than ten minutes. Madison knew everybody's blood pressure went up when she came into the office.

"Fear is contagious," a horse trainer back home had once told her. Her mother had owned a few race horses and they were green broke as yearlings at their farm. She used to love to watch the new crop of youngsters fly across the pasture, tails raised high in the sky, hooves barely visible dashing in crisscross patterns through the grass. Then, like a quiet gaggle of geese, they would stop and form a calm herd, still and dignified. Just as suddenly, one weanling would bolt at a source of fear and take off at a dead run. The others, not knowing exactly why, would raise the whinnying alarm of worry and streak away, following their frightened compatriot. It was a fascinating display of the horses' deep, instinctual "fight or flight" syndrome. "Fear breeds fear," the trainer had said with a shake of his head and a spit of chocolate brown tobacco saliva on the dusty ground. Madison remembered excitedly going to find her mother to share this new revelation of nature and the possible psychic connections (understanding the way fear behaved, as if it were an actual being and seeing how people also acted on fight or flight impulse) but her mother had been too busy and had shooed her away, telling her to keep her eyes in her books and her interest in worthwhile things, and to stop thinking those ridiculous, silly thoughts. They were wasteful and counterproductive, and Gawd, when was she going to grow out of it?

Madison had anticipated correctly. Despite the three other patients in the waiting room, she was ushered in quickly to a chair and fitted with a mini paper apron, managing to send Madison's blood pressure higher through the roof.

Of course, as her luck would have it, Dr. Pogue was not able to attend to her directly. There was an emergency, which had just come in, explained Mary the hygienist. A small child had fallen and chipped her front tooth and needed to be dealt with immediately.

Madison nodded and calculated how many steps it would take to tear out of the office before someone grabbed her and strapped her back into the chair. But then she ran her tongue across the offending abscessed tooth and thought better of escaping. "Would it be possible," Madison asked Mary in her very sweetest of voices, "to have a little valium or gas or something to calm me down a tad? I mean, you know how I am with these things and to have to wait . . ." Madison felt the sweat slowly slide down her forehead.

"Of course, honey. Let me talk to Dr. Pogue."

"Thanks ever so much."

Mary re-entered with a small paper cone and a tiny cup of water. "Now, just want to make sure that you've got someone coming to pick you up. We can't give this to you and let you drive, you know."

Madison lied sweetly. "Oh yes, my friend William is coming."

"Okay, here you go then, bottom's up!"

Madison greedily inhaled the little pill and the sip of water and laid her head back. Mary went back to help with the emergency.

Madison peered at the *Where's Waldo?* poster on the ceiling above her. Funny, at this time, twenty minutes was a Perfect time. She could feel her body sink into the chair and her teeth begin to tingle gently. Waldo was no where to be found but she really didn't care. She squinted to find him but there were so many other irritating characters dressed similarly that she soon lost her focus. Slowly in her spinning head, Madison made up a series of lyrics for a very grand Waldo song:

Where oh Where has Waldo Wandered?
With Witnesses Watching
And Well-Wishers Waving
Waldo has Wound up Walking
Despite being Weary and Weak
He Wiles away his time with no Worries
Want to know Where's Waldo?
He Whispers to the Willing
Well, Wait a While
Work and Wonder but don't
Worry because it's always Worthwhile
When you find Winsome
Wonderful
Me!
Come Find Me

Madison was exceedingly proud of her new song. She would have sung it again to the creatures on the poster but the words had somehow jumbled into a mess full of random *W*'s. She felt like all the thoughts in her head were shimmying around like the notes on a slide guitar. Her eyes fluttered disobediently and within seconds Madison drifted off to sleep.

CHAPTER
SIXTEEN

A QUIET TAPPING BEHIND her caused Madison to open her eyes and look around quickly. She gasped at Helen standing near the door. The ghost motioned for Madison to get out of the chair and follow her.

This presented a bit of a problem as Madison had seemingly lost all control of her limbs. She shook her head trying to clear the cobwebs. Was she really seeing the ghost or was it just the Valium? No, she figured, it probably wasn't the drug. If the Valium was talking, she'd probably be staring at a huge Waldo standing at the door.

Madison squinted at the apparition. Helen looked more vibrant and clear than Madison had ever seen her. Her lilac dress was no longer a pale, tired shade. It gleamed as if lit up from inside. Helen's skin was a bit more pinkish, not the waxy, dead look Madison had grown used to. The air around her rippled and shimmered in widening circles emanating outward from Helen's heart.

"Wow, this stuff is good," she purred to the empty room. "I gotta get me some to take home."

Helen stood tapping, insistent like a schoolteacher who waited at the black board for the correct answer.

"Okay, okay," Madison murmured and fumbled to lift the arm of the chair so she could follow Helen. At this point she realized she was about two-and-a-half feet above the floor in the raised chair. She peered around for the control but saw the only way to move it was by a pedal on the floor. "Oh well, gang," Madison slurred. "Anchors away!"

Madison slid onto the floor with a loud thump. She stood up quickly and held her finger to her lips to quiet the room. She waited for someone to come in but she could still hear the dentist working as his assistant cooed over the injured girl. *Nice security,* she thought. *I coulda broken my damn—*

Then Helen did the most incredible thing. She stamped her celestial foot with a loud crack on the linoleum floor. Madison took a wobbly step toward her, surprised out of her mind. "Okay, okay, I *get* it, ghost!" She slithered toward Helen, reaching for anything she could hold onto for support. She clutched the chair, then moved forward and grabbed at the overhead drill, "Wow, spirit, somebody must have put extra caffeine in whatever you drink out there."

She got to the door and looked back one more time. No one was around so she opened the door as Helen disappeared ahead of her. When she opened the door, she was no longer outside the dental office or even in the hallway, for that matter. She stood behind a very young Helen as she faced the massive oak front door of some very rich person's house.

Tap, tap, tap. Madison felt Helen's nerves as she knocked quickly then fidgeted in front of the imposing oak doors of the mansion. The young woman quickly pulled the slip of paper with the address on it to check the numbers once again. This was it—1420 Ferndale Road. She knocked on the door again.

The door swung open and revealed a tall, austere man dressed in a perfect butler's suit. He lifted one eyebrow in a look of surprise as he surveyed her. "Yes?"

Helen's gray eyes stared at him in wordless response.

"Yes?" He said again. "May I help you?"

"Uh, yes, I'm sorry. Hello. My name is Helen Rhames. I'm here for the job interview?"

Madison watched the man consider Helen more carefully this time. She was surprised to realize that she could read his thoughts as if she were an omniscient narrator. His eyes scanned Helen as if examining a bunch of garden vegetables or a fresh chicken. *She's smallish,* he thought. *A bit plump. A forgettable, unas-*

suming face. *Nothing spectacular. Good,* he said to himself. *Spectacular would not do well around here.*

"Yes, of course. Please come in."

Helen stared up at the butler in total awe. She'd never seen a man in a uniform like that before. It was a beautiful black suit. It reminded her of something out of *Jane Eyre.*

The man moved back and opened the door wider for Helen to enter. She raised her eyes from the bricks of the impeccable front entry to see a spectacular winding staircase at the far end of the magnificent foyer. It was all she could do not to gasp out loud with awe.

She stepped in front of him then turned around to see where he would lead.

"Please have a seat in the parlor. I'll be with you in a moment." He steered her to a softly-lit room and motioned her to a pale blue love seat.

Madison stood in the corner, watching Helen's expression. She looked around the room slowly with wide eyes, struck by its quiet splendor. Everything was exquisite, from the shiny floors underneath the thick oriental rugs to the beautiful textured wallpaper lining the walls amidst the delicate wood molding. A spotless crystal light fixture hung overhead, not as grand as the chandelier in the front room but just as impressive. Madison was fascinated. Who lived here?

The butler re-entered. "You may follow me, miss."

They traveled down a back stairway to the lower portion of the house. Down the hall, Madison heard the sounds of lunch being prepared in the basement kitchen. The warm air carried delicious smells of baking bread and some roasted poultry. The butler showed Helen to a sparse room and offered her a seat.

No sooner had he left her than a short, portly woman entered briskly. She introduced herself as Mrs. Greer, the housekeeper. Helen's interview was short and to the point. The job available was as nurse to the patriarch of the family, Louis Park. At age seventy-five, he was in failing health and even worse, failing spirits. The family knew nothing much could be done for him. His ageless energy had conspired to leave him an invalid with an endless cough, barely able to sit. But having someone with him daily would distract them all from the inevitable end and give them more comfort knowing a professional with medical knowledge was at his bedside.

Mrs. Greer gave off a no-nonsense air of responsibility. She examined Helen critically and asked about her experience and education. She seemed a bit put off by the fact the Helen had just graduated with her nursing degree, but Helen jumped in and recounted her experience helping out at the old-folks' home during the three years of nursing school. She shared her understanding of the particular needs of elderly patients and saw this information mollify the housekeeper somewhat.

Madison tuned into the thoughts whirling in Helen's head as she tried her best to remember all the advice that had been given her. *Be enthusiastic but don't appear naïve. Be calm but energetic. Be optimistic and confident.* The snippets of tips whirled around in Madison's consciousness as Helen answered the questions Mrs. Greer lobbed at her. Finally, the older women nodded. She asked if Helen could start right away, as Mr. Park's current nurse was only staying until a replacement could be found.

Despite the gravity of the patient's health, Helen was clearly excited to take the job. The surroundings were amazing and she would have meals provided each day as well. She would be expected to work from 8:00 a.m. untill 6:00 p.m. six days a week. Sundays would be most often free unless Mr. Park needed her because of an emergency.

The interview completed, Helen nearly danced down the mansion's back porch stairs. She trotted out of the stately black rod iron gates and around the two blocks to where she had parked her car.

Madison tried to absorb the barrage of details scattered around her. She wanted to slow down and categorize each new piece of information but the story was unfolding around her so quickly, she was challenged to just keep her clairvoyance in step. She shadowed Helen as she skipped toward the car. Helen's excitement seeped out of her in a breeze of joy. Madison could feel it swirl around her as clearly as if it had been a mist of rose water sprayed from a perfume bottle.

Helen slid onto the old Ford's smooth leather seat. She sat for a moment and fingered the shiny wood steering wheel. Madison could hear Helen's exuberant thoughts. She would have a wonderful announcement for her husband and for her baby, Sam, too! Helen looked decidedly cheerful, sitting in the faded Ford. She started the car, which gurgled a small protest then growled to life.

The sound rattled in Madison's brain and reminded her of something. Was this young husband the same man who had screamed and stormed out of that house that Helen had shown her before? Could this possibly be Helen's attempt to show Madison how she'd found herself at that dining room table that summer night? She sensed for the first time that this whole crazy, ridiculous, unexplainable experience was no accident. This was all part of Helen's purpose. Madison's head began to ache. The level of concentration it took to tune into Helen's thoughts exhausted her but she was unable to pull away from the scenes. She was imbedded in them as if she'd actually been there in real time.

Farmer's National Bank stood at the top of a rise that held a dozen similar brownstone buildings. Helen pulled up to the curb in front and hopped out of the car, smoothing her dress as she walked toward the building's grand doors. She stopped inside for a moment and Madison paused as well. It took Madison an instant to adjust her eyes in the gloomy grandeur of the old building. She watched Helen expectantly scan the desks at the back of the bank.

Madison followed Helen's gaze to a young man working halfway to the back of the large room. His dark head draped low, studiously reviewing some paperwork.

Helen walked quickly toward him. "Cecil, honey! Got a minute?"

Cecil raised his eyes to his wife then glanced around. "Hi. What are you doing here? Did you go to the interview?"

"Oh God, honey it was fantastic! They hired me!" Helen quieted her voice as others looked up from their desks nearby.

"Well Helen, that's fine!" Cecil beamed at his wife.

A short, portly man bustled through the aisle toward them. "Well, Cecil, what's going on here? Why, Helen, nice to see you." The man's tone was friendly, yet reserved.

"Hello, Mr. Fiorelli." Helen offered him a beaming smile. "I just came in to give Cecil the good news."

"News?"

"Yes, sir. Seems my wife has gotten herself a job at the Park mansion as a nurse for the old man."

Mr. Fiorelli turned his admiring gaze to Helen. "Well, congratulations, young lady. This should be a wonderful opportunity."

"Thank you, sir." She bowed her head slightly then looked back to Cecil. "Well, sweetheart, I'll let you get back to work. See you at home in a few hours."

"Yup." Her husband leaned back in his chair. Madison felt him taking note that his boss was happy with the brevity of their meeting. "See you around six."

Helen practically soared out of the bank and back to the car. Madison suddenly felt a whole new appreciation for the energy it took one soul to enter in to the astral plane of another. She was beginning to lose her focus. Her body felt shaky and her mind felt overwhelmed by the emotions, senses, and nuances spinning around her head. *Keep up!* She commanded herself.

THE DRIVE BACK in the old car turned into a coursing band of colors as Helen ushered Madison past the details of the following days. Madison felt as if she was being pulled through water, feeling the currents of experience rushing around her. She could see in an instant that the next few weeks had flown by in a flurry of activity. Helen had quickly learned the culture and expectations of the Park family. Voices were to be low. All requests and comments were to be addressed to Mrs. Greer. She was expected to arrive promptly and be ready to start Louis Park's day with a ready tray of breakfast, a newspaper, his medicines and a fresh box of tissues. As Helen settled into the routine, Madison sensed she was able to focus on her charge, learning when he was comfortable, when he needed his posture adjusted, when he needed time alone to nap, and when he was ready for the sparse conversation in which he engaged her infrequently.

It was clear to Madison that Helen had been terribly intimidated by the old man that first day. He had an air of a king on his throne, propped up in a huge bed in his third floor suite. Madison had to admit, she didn't know what was more overwhelming, the grandeur of the room, the expansive view of the river glittering in the distance, or the quiet commanding manner of this discernibly important man. He was obviously suffering from poor health. His breathing was weak, his voice a bit hoarse and quiet. But beneath the square forehead and white bushy brows, his blue eyes were still piercing. Madison felt it keenly as he gave Helen the initial once-over. Mrs. Greer had accompanied Helen to the room carrying the requisite morning items. Helen obediently followed her into the warm, black walnut-paneled room.

"Good morning, sir." Madison watched as Mrs. Greer competently smoothed a spot for the old man's breakfast tray and placed it across his lap.

"Good morning to you, Mrs. Greer. Who have we here?"

"The new nurse, sir." She unfolded the napkin and slid it across his chest. The exquisite linen brushed along his impeccable gray silk pajamas with a soft rustle.

"Ah, ha," His voice rumbled in a low rasp. "And you are?"

"This is Mrs. Rhames, sir."

Helen clearly took her cue from Mrs. Greer's raised eyebrow. She moved toward the bed with an outstretched hand. The hand that took hers was mottled and veined. "Nice to meet you, sir."

Those blue eyes considered her. "And you, my dear. I look forward to our mutual imprisonment." He laughed ruefully.

Madison watched as Helen instinctively launched into her optimistic conversation. "Ah, I am sure Mr. Park, that we will soon be enjoying spring days on your veranda. A little fresh air will do you good and you won't be a prisoner in your own bed!"

Mrs. Greer frowned at her and touched her elbow. "Well sir, if you don't mind, I shall take Mrs. Rhames downstairs and acquaint her with the policies. She'll return in an hour if that is acceptable to you."

The old man focused on his paper and his juice. "Yes, that will be fine."

The two women walked out the door and Mrs. Greer shut it quietly. She turned to Helen with a tilt of her head. "I must caution you, Mrs. Rhames. Mr. Park has not been out of his bed for several weeks now. It is highly unlikely that he will ever be again. It is unfair to put that thought in his head. We don't want to disappoint him and have his health slip further."

"Well, yes, of course, Ma'am." Helen answered quietly. "It's just that often with patients of his age, the trouble taken to give them as much mobility as possible is a very good thing for their attitude."

Mrs. Greer sniffed indignantly. "That may be, young lady, but in this house things are done a certain way and we would never put Mr. Park's health at risk in any way. Do you understand?"

"Yes, of course."

"Very well, then. I'll take you downstairs and have Marta get you settled in."

Helen and Madison followed the round woman down the stairs. It was obvious the housekeeper considered herself captain of this ship. As they padded down the back staircase Madison glimpsed the butler instructing a gardener on the installation of a new bed of tulips.

Mrs. Greer also caught sight of the two men. She muttered to herself something about spacing those plants correctly and how she'd have to see to it herself.

"Let's get moving," she said over her shoulder to Helen. "You need to learn the system as quickly as possible." She turned and glared. "Don't think there are any shortcuts here, Mrs. Rhames. We all have important jobs to do and I'm here to see they are done correctly."

Helen nodded. "Yes, ma'am."

THE PICTURES THAT HELEN showed Madison sped up in time. She felt she was experiencing Helen's life rather more as if scanning it through a microfiche machine. The visions would spin and blur with speed, then stop and snap into clarity.

It was through this process, the hurling through time and space and the punctuations of crucial moments, that Madison learned of the life-changing meeting Helen had one early summer day.

THE MANSION WAS QUIET. The afternoon sun had even baked the bees into silent submission. Madison watched Helen organize the medicine cabinet in the upstairs bathroom. In the bedroom next door, the frail old man slept.

A pounding from the level below caused Helen to snap her head up. She was instantly in caregiver mode, clearly unhappy with the noise that could so easily wake her charge. Helen went to the door and out into the silent, gleaming hallway. Madison smelled a hint of vinegar, mixed with the odor of linseed emanating from the mahogany-paneled walls. Helen walked down the hallway toward the huge, winding staircase and peeked over the edge. From down below, someone boisterously galloped up the back stairs from the basement. Helen quickly tiptoed down the wide, magnificent steps. She got to the bottom of the stairs and rounded the corner to the back stairwell.

At once, she came face-to-face with him. Madison's vantage point allowed her to see both faces at the same time.

Helen stared at this young, beautiful stranger and then immediately barked at him. "Please sir, Mr. Park is asleep upstairs and we don't want to wake him."

"Sorry," the impossibly handsome man said sheepishly. "Didn't mean to start a fuss." He grinned charmingly at Helen, who responded with a frown.

"Well, let's just keep it down, shall we?"

"Right, lieutenant!" He saluted her and clicked his heels. He noted that his attempt at humor hadn't been accepted in the manner it had been offered, so he tried again. "Hey, I'm sorry, didn't mean to tease. Why don't we start over?" His ice blue eyes were framed under long brown lashes and a prominent brow. When he smiled, his cheekbones rose up and highlighted the square, angular planes of his face.

Madison thought he was one of the most beautiful men she'd ever seen. She looked carefully at Helen's face, wondering if Helen had the same reaction.

It seemed as if, in that instant, Helen did indeed actually see the young man's face for the first time. His eyes gleamed with a transparent lightness. They were a sheer opposite to Helen's solid, gray. Helen stepped back and shook her head, offering a little laugh of her own.

The young man thrust his hand out in greeting. "Jerome Park," he offered an easy and brilliant smile.

Madison was struck at that moment by the thought that this handsome fellow knew how to put that smile to good use.

"Helen Rhames." Helen's voice was timid.

"And how do you find yourself here, Miss Rhames?" He leaned his lanky frame against the smooth, brown banister.

"Mrs.," she quickly corrected. "I'm the nurse for Mr. Park." Madison watched realization flicker across Helen's face. "Your . . . grandfather?"

"Ha ha!" Even his voice was beautiful. "Yes, ma'am."

He added with a tilt of his head, "Well I'm sure my grandpop is happy to have *you* around!"

Helen smiled at this obvious compliment. Her cheeks reddened a bit. Yes, Madison could clearly see now, Helen *was* drawn to this young man. The chemical magnetism soared into her simultaneously and tingled.

Instantly she recognized the pivotal moment. This gorgeous boy would become central in the background of Helen's life. Madison remembered the images from the night in the dining room that Helen had shown her.

"Now," the young man's voice claimed Madison's attention. "I have a feeling that if you are on my tracks, then Mrs. Greer won't be far behind!"

Helen was clearly flustered. "Of course!" She grinned. "You'd better get out of here, now! Mrs. Greer is not easy to live with when things aren't just quite right!"

Madison noticed Jerome's attention to Helen's expression. He reached over and squeezed her arm. Madison could feel the electrical shock reverberating through Helen's body. He leaned forward, one of his silky blonde curls nearly brushing against Helen's forehead. "I'm off now," he whispered closely to her ear. "But I look forward to seeing you again." He turned and quickly hopped back down the stairs leaving Helen breathless.

Madison sensed the instant incredible connection between these two people. But was she imposing herself onto the situation? She purposefully pulled her attention back and waited in the staircase's generous corner.

Helen stood for what seemed an inordinate amount of time. She gazed down the staircase where Jerome had just bounded out of her sight. She reached out and gripped the smooth, mahogany banister. Madison couldn't really tell, surprisingly, what Helen felt. But then the young woman turned up the stairs and Madison looked further into Helen's eyes. A connection and spark flickered there. "Oh my God," Madison whispered in the darkness. "This is the beginning of your secret."

Helen slowly walked up the stairs. Madison was left perched in the corner, feeling the waves of time and fate brush about her in swirling currents.

Then, without warning, the psychic was lifted out of the staircase, away from the house and dropped back down into real time, stretched out in the dental chair.

"Ahh, here we are! Had a nice nap?"

Madison struggled to open her eyes. They felt glued shut. She rubbed at her lids to unglue them and blinked her eyes open. She stared at Mary's smiling face. "Trouble getting those eyes open? It's okay, nothing to worry about. Sometimes the Valium makes us tear up a little. Let me get you a wet towel."

Madison pressed her back against the chair. She felt completely disoriented. The sterile dentist's office clashed with the lush atmosphere of the mansion where she'd just stood. A wave of nausea rushed over her. All her muscles felt tight. This experience was like no other. She'd had no control over herself when the ghost had beckoned. She'd been caught up in a trance of fascination but she also knew that her presence in this other plane was a dangerous journey and she wondered what the outcome would be.

The hygienist brought a warm towel and laid it over Madison's eyes. The heat erased a bit of the throbbing in her head but it did nothing to quench the knot in her throat.

CHAPTER
SEVENTEEN

K ATHERINE WATCHED TWO of her young tennis players working on approach shots and volleys. The three weeks since the boys' season had ended had flown by and now summer tennis was in full swing. It felt good to be on the court again. Coaching was at least something that took her mind off of the rest of her life.

She was concentrating so hard on watching Carly's slice backhand that she didn't really hear it. Behind her, the girls, supposedly working on serves, were now standing in a tight circle. Now she could hear them snickering and whispering as they gleefully watched her number one player throwing an over-the-top temper tantrum.

Claudette spun around and slammed her racket onto the ground as the ball hit the tape of the net and dropped onto her side of the court. From two courts over Katherine watched the temperamental teen fume and storm along the baseline. Katherine shook her head and made her way onto the court.

"Claudette," Katherine began gently, keeping in mind that this girl didn't want to hear a word from her. "Did you have a plan for that ball? Did you have any idea what you were going to do with it when you hit it?"

Claudette shook a wordless *no*, eyes filling with frustrated tears.

"No wonder you get so pissed. You have no strategy. You just randomly, reactively hit the ball. You make mistakes and the frustration just gets worse and worse."

Welcome to the club, Katherine silently breathed onto the petulant teen. *You've got so many years ahead to torture yourself. But take heart, you are in good company.* Claudette eyed her with a "tell me something I don't know" look.

"Listen, let's make a game plan for you. Let's give you something specific to focus on. If you can concentrate on a simple action then you won't be as likely to be afraid of missing." Katherine watched for any sign of interest. "What do you think?"

Claudette just rolled her eyes, nodded and turned away. Katherine, too, turned away and watched the players on the next court. Why was it that these girls were so negative and defensive when she offered coaching advice?

She watched on the next court over as Abby flailed at a ball rather than put any effort into moving her feet. It was enough for Katherine to not roll her own eyes in disgust.

"Hey Kath," Barb's voice floated from the end court. "Want these guys to play ten point tie-breaks now? It's almost five o'clock. Or we could play Olympics." Barb's voice was hard to hear over the giggles and groans of thirty-six teenage girls.

"Yeah, sure. Ten points. Sounds good." Katherine yelled back. She stuck two fingers in her mouth and belted out a sharp whistle. Instantly, the players stopped. *They're at least somewhat well-trained,* she thought.

"Okay gals, ten point breakers. Just play with the person opposite you. You guys at the top," she glared over to Claudette and Abby, "Take turns and step out so all eight of you can play your individual points. But listen up, ladies." She cocked her head at Barb who had joined her. Katherine gave her partner their familiar hand signal for "let's torture them." Barb nodded enthusiastically.

"Okay ladies, a little conditioning is in order. Before the breakers . . . two ball cardio pick up. Now! Go!"

The courts were immediately a frantic cacophony of muttered groans, dropping rackets, sneakers squealing, as each girl sprinted to pick up two balls at a time, run them back to the baskets and head out for more.

Katherine smiled at Barb. "Don't you love payback?"

"More than anything," Barb agreed. They stood enjoying a respite of yelling as the girls scurried across the courts.

Barb sighed. "It's days like this that make Arizona sooo far away."

"No kidding."

"Hey, talked to that Madison chick again?"

"No," Katherine shook her head. "You?"

"Naw." Barb clapped her hands at a tenth grader who was clearly taking her time getting to the balls. "Although I do think she helped me shift again, kind of."

"Lucky you. How many times in the past year do you think we've used the word 'shift'?"

"Probably not as many times as we've used the other s-word!" Barb whispered. "How do the boys like being home for summer?"

"They're on perpetual fun mode. They play more than they work, which they probably shouldn't, since they're going to have to help pay for school a bit next year."

"Well it's nice they're having fun."

"Yup. Plus, I love having them home again. It makes me a happy momma bear!" Her mind went into automatic mode—*be thankful for your kids. You are a lucky woman. You have nothing to complain about . . .*

They were interrupted by the panting girls who gathered around them like expectant puppies. "Coach," Libby, the wild one yelped, "Can we—"

"Yes," Barb interrupted her. "You guys can get a quick drink and then on to the breakers." She clapped her hands authoritatively.

Katherine headed off toward the farthest court to examine the net strap, which had snapped out of its place.

"Hey!" Barb called after her.

"What-up?" She hollered back.

"Today is Tuesday!" The word sounded so wonderful.

"I'm in!" Katherine turned back to the offending net strap and tightened it into place.

AN HOUR LATER, the two sat on the patio of the Red Rooster. The local bar was packed. Six o'clock every Tuesday, the locals swarmed to this favorite watering hole for seventy-five cent tacos.

"Nothing like taco Tuesday!" Barb exulted as she squeezed a lime into her beer.

"God, really." Katherine sat back against the steel patio chair and took a sip of her chardonnay.

"Barb, do you think Madison is just somebody who says general stuff and rips you off?"

"Probably." Barb nodded. "To be honest, I don't even really remember what she told me. Something about being a ten of clubs and I was a starter and not a finisher and I'm emotionally indecisive."

"Well she got that right!"

"What'd she tell you?" Barb took another swig.

"Umm, I needed to get un-stuck, oh yeah, I need to learn a new life skill."

"What? Like Abby needs to learn to move her feet?"

"Exactly. Wow, that actually freaks me out, Barb. I mean who is more likely to learn their new life skill, me or Abby?"

"Let's hope it's you 'cause I don't hang out with Abby all day and I don't really think she wants to move her feet!"

"Seriously," Barb leaned forward toward her friend. "How come you think you get stuck like this, Kath? What is it in your past or your family that causes it?"

"I don't know. I guess my parents were kind of that way. They used to get mad and just shut down and we'd have to tiptoe around till they came out of it or we figured out a way to get them out of it."

"Out of it?" Barb looked puzzled.

"Their moods. They would go from light to dark like this." She snapped her finger. "Then we were all held hostage to their emotions. Of course, one would start, then the other would get mad and it felt like you were living in a cesspool of yuck. Usually their spells lasted for hours. My mom got over hers faster, but sometimes my dad's lasted days. It was such a drag."

"How come he was like that?"

"I guess he had a tough childhood. Never talked about it much. But whatever the reason, it sure wasn't cool that he took it out on us." Katherine shook her head glumly.

She could tell that Barb felt badly, so her friend chattered and tried to get her mind off of the subject. They sat and watched the patrons lining up outside the door as the queue for the tacos spilled out onto the sidewalk.

"Listen," Barb slapped the table. "If you are going to start this new life skill that you just remembered you are supposed to have, we'd better get some food in you. Sounds like you're going to need a lot of energy!" She pushed her chair back and marched toward the door.

Katherine rose and followed her. "Let's hope we can just figure out exactly what that life skill is!" Barb turned and gave her a thumbs-up and they joined the line.

ON THE DRIVE HOME, Katherine tried to remember what it was exactly that Madison had said. She remembered trying to organize and translate those post-it notes. She didn't even know where the little pile was now. She remembered Madison talking about what a tantrum thrower she was. That was certainly still true. She also recalled the exasperation in Madison's voice.

When she got home she went directly to her office and dug through her drawers looking for the stack of sticky notes. Lodged behind the stapler in the back of the drawer, she found them. Reading the disjointed words (she remembered now how frantically she had written), she felt the connection again to that woman. She'd really wanted Madison to tell her that on a certain date, according to her unique cards or karma or whatever, she'd magically be delivered from this hole she dog-paddled in. Grant would get a job, money wouldn't be tight anymore, they wouldn't have to sell the house, the boys would do great in school, she would finally be happy.

But that wasn't what Madison had said. She'd told Katherine that she needed to grow up and move on emotionally no matter what the circumstances were. Katherine felt her old, screaming-self want to answer, "but how do I do that?"

She remembered Madison's other words. "Enjoy those things you love, like your boys, and replace the thoughts in your head." And like a timpani drum in the background an insistent beat fluttered, Madison's call to change, to change, to change . . .

Changing, of course, meant action and she was far too addicted to sitting in the same place like a toddler who would sprawl on the floor yelping and writhing when she didn't get her way. Katherine sat for a minute and built upon that picture. There she was in Target, completely pissed off. She sat down in the middle of the front aisle. In her mind, Katherine watched herself slam down and begin paddling at the ground, all the while crying and shrieking. She pulled back from her own image and watched the other shoppers stare at her. She studied their faces and saw pity on some, disgust on others. A woman with two little boys dragged her children away from the scene mumbling under her breath, "Where is that child's mother?"

Those words reminded her. She'd been that woman one day. The boys had been so young and yes, maybe they actually had been at Target. They'd walked down an aisle to find a little boy beside himself in rage, spitting and screaming, throwing the finest tantrum to be found. Katherine had pulled the boys to her and whispered conspiratorially. "Where is that kid's mother? That is absolutely no way to act!"

The boys had taken that moment to heart because months later they had been in the grocery store when another child threw a similar fit.

Wes had stood next to her very imperiously and declared, "Where is that child's mother?" Katherine had thought it hilarious at the time and she had felt like a good parent, too. Her children never threw tantrums, ever.

Then she saw herself again, pounding and screaming in just the same way. She suddenly felt embarrassed and humiliated. What was she doing? She wasn't just throwing a temper tantrum in some store's aisle, she was going through life, every day, making her and everyone else miserable. "Well, little girl," Katherine said aloud to that pitiful image, "Answer the question. Where is your mother and why does she let you behave that way?"

The image of herself suddenly stopped mid-cry and lifted her head, eyes red-streaked and swollen. "I don't have a mother. I have no one to tell me to stop."

Katherine realized that truth. No one would make her change. She was a grown woman and if she wanted to get out of this hole she had dug, she'd have to pull herself out one hand at a time. The drum's metallic beat floated in her head again, to change, to change, to change . . .

CHAPTER
EIGHTEEN

THE VALIUM WAS NOWHERE near wearing off. The damn procedure had taken forty minutes, but seemed more like an hour, Madison groused to herself. When released from the chair, she took extra care to raise herself off of the plastic covering slowly. She noticed it was much easier to get out of the chair this time and then she realized she didn't have the two-and-a-half extra feet to negotiate, as well as the pressure of a crabby ghost beckoning.

She did her best to appear grateful and composed. She hoped they'd forget the "designated driver" rule because of the Valium. She even stayed a bit longer and did a round of palm readings for free—to the delight of the office staff. Madison walked slowly in a most upright manner out the door and then when it was closed securely, she allowed herself a staggering gait to her car. She was getting really sleepy now but she had work to do. So she rubbed her face briskly, retrieved her keys and jumped (more like slid) into her car. "Home sweet home, James," she said to some invisible chauffer whom she was always wishing she would find in her car. Even though he was never there, she thought it good practice to assume he would be . . . laws of attraction and all.

The ride home was blissfully uneventful. Luckily, for the potential accident victims in Sedona, they were all elsewhere and so maintained their safety without even knowing it. She drove carefully, squinting out of one eye, then the other to try to maintain consciousness. Finally she pulled into the driveway, got out of the car, walked past the pomegranate bush and up to the porch. Mercifully, the key did not require an extended jiggle dance this after-noon, so she was able to go inside quickly. The effects of the drug were finally beginning to wane and the memory of her last Helen sighting pumped her blood faster. Within seconds, Madison's brain was whirling. She grabbed her laptop and sat in one of the recliners in the living room. She went over the puzzle that was Helen's life, putting together all the pieces she had. Name: Helen Rhames, Place of Death: Somewhere in the Midwest. It was possible that this was just a pain in the ass, attention-seeking energy that she could en-dure and try to ignore. But Madison knew honestly that the visits from this determined ghost were not inconsequential. She recalled her conversation with William and how he had definitely been as-signed a message from that deceased father to his son.

This felt somewhat like that but even bigger, and the main cause of her growing anxiety was her fear that maybe she'd never understand what the ghost was trying to get across—that she'd fail this desperate soul who had chosen her for a reason.

Madison quieted herself and allowed her mind a few min-utes of meditation. When she re-emerged from her center of peace and relaxation, she was more focused and steady. It was time to solve these astral questions in simple order. One, who was the ghost? Two, what was she trying to say? And three, who was she trying to communicate with? She went through the dreams and vis-itations like watching reruns of movies. There was never an indica-tion of any city, any state where she could have been specifically from. She furrowed her brow and tapped it with her fingertips. Was-n't there some clue?

Nothing came to her mind so she tried searching obituaries around the country. If only she had a date to give her a time range to focus in. She was growing frustrated. No obit search engine pro-duced anything.

C'mon, she scolded herself. *You're a freakin' psychic. This is what you do!* At the same moment, she felt Coriander's soft tail brush lightly against her calf, followed by the customary head butt and rubbing of his silken fur against the side of her leg.

"Oh, honey bunches," she lifted up the heavy cat onto her lap. He settled into her and pressed against her chest. His purr was enthusiastic and soothing.

"Mr. Coriander," she looked at his face, his eyes closed in ecstasy as she gently scrubbed under his chin. "How are we going to find this pesky ghost?" He opened one eye briefly at her then closed it again. He had not one whit of interest, it was obvious, in finding anything but a way to keep her in scratch mode.

The house was quiet. The room was warm, the cat's weight felt solid on her legs. She leaned back in the recliner and pushed backwards so she was more stretched out. The stillness of the room, punctuated by Coriander's methodical purr, invited her off to sleep.

A DRAFT THROUGH THE ROOM sent Coriander scurrying to his bed in the kitchen. It woke Madison and she drowsily looked around to find the open window.

She gasped with a start. Helen hovered next to the fireplace. She was barely visible, mostly hidden in shadow, but she was there nonetheless. Madison sat up clumsily, trying to extricate herself from the recliner. Her heart started beating faster. "Jeez, lady!" she squawked, "You gotta stop sneaking up on me!" She put her hand against her chest to slow her heart rate. The figure offered no response.

Okay, Madison, she commanded herself. *Calm down.* She forced herself to take an account of how she felt. She realized she was a little bit terrified and absolutely enthralled with the image that wavered in a spindly shiver. The advent of twilight didn't make it any easier to see Helen, as the day's retreating light shadowed her still more. Madison was reminded of the phrase in a poem she'd read long ago. "*And dreamier the gloaming grows . . .*"

Slowly, the woman raised her hand to her heart. Madison waited and tried to intuit the movement. Had the woman died of a heart attack? Did she know someone who was going to have a heart problem? No, neither one of those thoughts felt right. The woman's tiny hand hovered over her chest. She closed what Madison could make out as a fist and gently tapped herself. Her frame heaved in a sigh almost bigger than the ghost herself. Madison felt a familiar tightening in her throat . . . tears, sadness, overwhelming grief.

Helen then raised her hand to her face and brushed her palm across her eyes as if waving a cloud away. She moved her hand back and forth in front of those invisible eyes. Then she pointed her finger to her head. Madison heard the words softly but distinctly, "Past is past. Now, honor . . . help."

As if the words were coming out of her mouth with her own volition, Madison spoke the phrase out loud. Her voice matched perfectly the tempo and tone of Helen's. "Past is past. Now, honor . . . help."

The drifting presence wavered like a flame absorbing a gust of air. Then with a gentle whisper of a word Madison couldn't understand, the ghost faded and disappeared.

CHAPTER NINETEEN

THE WARM WATER POURED over Katherine's body and tickled her skin. She turned up the temperature until the heat made her head throb. She rubbed her neck, her shoulders, and the upper part of her chest and under her armpits. Everything was perfect in this moment. The boys were home from school and she and Grant were in a better place. Dare she say that life was good?

Then she felt it slightly. The marble-sized soft mound underneath her skin rolled under her fingertips. Katherine pressed around her armpit again, sliding her fingers up and down in the hollow. She felt it more prominently now. She drew in her breath sharply.

What were all the things she'd ever heard about lumps? Pea-sized, hard, not lumpy—always in the breast. But this felt different. It was in her armpit, for one, and it was both malleable and anchored to the point where her pectoris met her latissmus muscle. She pressed again, harder now, trying to make it go away. The lump responded by sending a gentle pain above her ribs.

Katherine turned off the water and folded herself into a warm towel. Grant stood with his back to her, concentrating on his shaving. He glanced up from the mirror and into her eyes. The look on her face turned him around quickly. "What's wrong?"

Katherine's face was white. "I found something weird." She automatically pressed the three fingers of her right hand into the crease under her arm.

"What does it feel like?"

"Like a soft bump," she whispered and pressed harder to force the thing to go away.

"Well, don't worry, honey." He turned back to the mirror to finish scraping his cheeks with the blades. "I'm sure it's nothing."

"Yeah, of course. You're right." Katherine tried to answer brightly.

He looked back at her from the mirror. "C'mon, don't freak out. You'll call the doctor tomorrow and get an appointment."

"Yeah, you're right," she said again, hesitantly. There was no reason to get hysterical. But deep inside, Katherine felt a stab of worry.

ONE WEEK LATER, Katherine was in the mammogram clinic at the hospital. She'd stood obediently as the technician manipulated her breasts into the machine. By the way the skin had been pressed nearly flat, she was sure anything hiding would be discovered. She felt a little more confident, after she'd been to see Dr. Nielsen and he had given her a physical exam. No need to worry, he'd promised, but she hadn't had a mammogram in a year so it was worthwhile to get one, just to be safe.

Katherine leafed through a magazine waiting for the radiologist to tell her the results were fine.

The woman came out and instead of sending her on her way, sat down next to Katherine and gently put her hand on Katherine's arm. "Well," she started slowly. "We've found an area of interest in the left breast."

Katherine's heart skipped a beat. The doctor continued, "What we have are a group of cells called calcifications. They appear like a little cluster of stars in the midst of the dark picture."

"What does that mean?" She could barely speak the words.

"To be honest, we can't really tell from just the films. Calcifications can be nothing but sometimes they are the trail that cancer cells leave behind."

Had the woman just said cancer? Katherine shook her head to make sure she was hearing every word. "Do you mean I have cancer?"

The radiologist maintained a calm, even tone. "Like I said, we really can't be sure, but it definitely is something we should look more into. I've given Dr. Nielsen a ring and he's actually in his office across the street. I'll walk you over there and then you two can talk."

Katherine numbly followed the woman through the lobby to the building connected by an underground walkway. The woman continued to explain general information about mammogram results such as hers but she didn't hear any of it.

Once in Dr. Nielsen's office, the heavy weight of realization pressed down on her. No, they couldn't tell her if it was actually cancer or what kind it might be, but they agreed that spot needed to come out. Katherine was overcome by the connection of her random self-exam and the existence of these stealth cells in a different part of her body. "How do you explain that?" She asked the doctor.

"Honestly, Katherine, I can't. Maybe it's a swollen lymph node. You know, we might end up doing a lumpectomy and finding nothing. We might find something and if we do, I'd consider it a Godsend that you came in now. Waiting longer would not have been a good thing."

How lucky she was! How cursed she was! She listened as closely as she could to the doctor's plan of action. He spoke with a surgeon who agreed to find the soonest time for surgery. He gave Katherine names of oncologists to contact. Her head was whirling by the time she left his office.

She waited to get home until she told Grant. He was dumbfounded. The weight of the word "cancer" hung between them. They decided to wait and tell the boys. Why get them upset if it really was nothing?

Katherine called a few friends and as she recounted the story over and over it became more real, more permanent. "Calm down!" she commanded herself. "You don't officially have cancer yet!" Her inner voice sounded sharp as it echoed out loud in the room.

What about the life skills she'd been working on? What would that psychic in Sedona say now? She shook her head as she compared how miserable she'd been in December when she had originally seen Madison. There had been so much less to be upset about then.

A small voice promised Katherine that the next few months would be life-changing in so many ways, and somehow, her intuition chirped, good things would happen too. But Katherine ignored that hushed whisper inside her. She was too busy making plans for her surgery in forty-eight hours.

THREE DAYS LATER, Katherine had encouraged Grant and the boys to go to the grocery store to get steaks. It was a lovely, late May Saturday evening and the garden brimmed with blossoming life. She sat down in the chaise lounge on the porch to enjoy the quiet moment.

Her cell phone rang. What had they forgotten? "What is it now? Don't tell me you're on the way home and you forgot the steaks!"

"Mrs. Simon," a serious voice spoke quietly on the other end. "This is Sara Campbell." Katherine snapped to attention.

"Hi, Dr. Campbell."

"Well, we've got the results back and they are disappointing. Your microcalcifications were indicative of DCIS. Do you know what that is?"

"No," she answered softly.

The doctor continued. "DCIS, or ductal carcinoma incitu, is a fancy way of saying that you have cancer cells within some milk ducts in your left breast. Now," the doctor's voice droned on. "Even though this seems like bad news, it's actually quite encouraging. You see, as far as we can tell, those cells did not penetrate the rest of the breast tissue. That means that you are a very lucky woman. Your ducts contained the cancer and kept it from spreading."

The words "cancer" and "spreading" made Katherine want to retch right there in her chair. She willed herself to listen as objectively as she could.

"So," Dr. Campbell's voice continued. "We will get you quickly into an oncologist's office. Do you know of Dr. Barbara Bowers?"

"Yes," Katherine answered.

"She's quite good. I know you will enjoy her . . ."

Enjoy her? Katherine's inner voice screamed. *How the hell do you enjoy anyone involved with a cancer diagnosis? Is this woman mad?* Katherine responded calmly, quite separate from the woman inside her launching into a huge anxiety attack. "I've heard great things about her."

"Yes. Well, I've put in a call to her office and they will be ready to see you early next week." The doctor paused. "Mrs. Simon, I want to reassure you, this is not obviously the news you wanted to hear but in these circumstances, it's some of the best you could get."

Katherine was sitting on the lounge in a stream of disconsolate tears when Grant and the boys returned home. Each one of them absorbed the diagnosis differently. Grant was determined. Wes was silent and Wayne was visibly shaken.

And so the next several hours and days fell into an unreal pattern of doctor's appointments and phone discussions with the insurance carrier. The process took on a life of its own. She scheduled meetings with the radiation oncologist and technical personnel. She made sure that someone other than her and Grant would attend every meeting with any doctor. That person would be there to listen and take notes. That person was an extra pair of ears when hers were clogged with the mind-numbing fear that she was going to die.

Within ten days, Katherine Simon had assumed a new identity. No longer was she just a wife, mother, tennis coach. Now she added the title "cancer patient" to her list. Six weeks of radiation stretched out in front of her. The last day of her treatment, proposed to be August first, seemed a million years away.

CHAPTER
TWENTY

MADISON K. MORGAN, Extraordinaire, was on a mission. She was fueled by the increasingly insistent ghost. Using every possible route to information, she began piecing together who this mysterious Helen Rhames had actually been.

No birth dates. No date of death except, after going over the visions, she thought she remembered someone at the wake implying the year was 1972. She scolded herself (not for the last time) for not paying closer attention to the details that had danced around her as teasingly as the fairies and dragons hanging from the ceiling of the Enlightenment Center.

She began recounting all of Helen's visits in a special notebook. Her brain had been overwhelmed by the degree of the information that had stormed her. Hanging out with Helen felt more like being trapped in the midst of a meteor storm than observing a life lived before. With each visitation and glimpse into the seemingly carefully orchestrated collection of moments, Madison became more confused and intrigued.

The main question that tickled her was why Helen chose her. What did they share that connected them? There wasn't one person she had regular contact with who seemed to have any link to this woman. Discovering Helen's attachment to any client Madison had ever read created the possibility of having to go through hundreds of pages that sat carefully stacked in her office. Madison hoped Helen would get more creative and specific about what all this was about. Until then, Madison would become the supernatural detective of Sedona.

The unsettling part of this quest was that Helen had found unpredictable ways to contact her. Madison half-worried that one day she'd be walking down the street and this spirit would accost her on the sidewalk. She tried to create more quiet moments in her life that would give Helen opportunity to speak. The times of silence and meditation were actually wonderful gifts she hadn't shared with herself for years. While trying to become more available to Helen, Madison was finding she was becoming more accessible to herself.

MADISON MULLED ALL THIS over one day while in the car wash. She sat in the midst of the coursing rainbows of suds and savored the isolation inside the car. The oversized brushes thumped rhythmically against the windows. She leaned her head back against the headrest and wondered, what was happening now in Helen's life. She remembered the mansion and the old man and she smelled the oily scent of the shiny wood. It seemed so real to her. She felt as though here, in this cement box of water and wind, she might actually be able to get herself back there.

Now you know you're losing your mind, girl. Madison shook her head. She spoke out loud, "You can't go back without being invited!" As if to reinforce that, the streams on her windshield turned from color to clear. The boiling rinse poured around her, followed by the blasts of hot air from the giant tubes above and around her. How crazy was it that she actually could think of this place as a time portal? So crazy that she was persuaded to go through it all over again.

She pulled the car out of the driveway and drove it around to the entrance again. Larry, the operator, looked out from his perch inside the small shed next to the large glass door. "Hey Madison," he looked puzzled. "Forgot somethin'?"

"Well Larry, my friend, you can officially consider me nuts. I want another wash!"

He looked perplexed. "If we missed a spot, the next one's on us."

Madison suddenly felt very adventurous and excited. "Great," she lied, "I think it didn't get my wheels clean enough."

Larry walked around her car and surveyed the nearly spotless hubcaps. He came back around to her window and leaned in. "Madison, honey, you've got the cleanest wheels in town." He shook his head. "But if you feel you need another go-round, this one's on me."

Madison shook her finger at his friendly, wrinkled face. "Wouldn't hear of it, Larry." She grabbed a five-dollar bill from inside her purse and handed it to him.

He waved it off and walked to the control panel. "Ah, it's worth it just to see your gorgeous self again!"

"Thanks, honey," Madison quickly rolled up the windows and steered the car onto the mechanized tracks. She saw Larry wave at her through her rear window, then step back as the huge glass door blocked him from view.

"Oh my God," Madison whispered to herself. "You really are losing it." She touched the steering wheel lightly, feeling it twist and shudder as it was led along the conveyer.

"Ok, ghost!" Madison shouted above the sound of the slapping brushes. "Let's get back to work!" She waited and sat expectantly in the car. The soap turned to rinse, the rinse to wind but Madison stayed in real-time Sedona. She felt disappointed in an odd way. She was ready to move on with the process. Why wasn't Helen? She waited a moment longer as the Plexiglas door lifted in front of her. Madison drove onto the blacktop, car spotless and ghostless.

She was frustrated. How was it that the ghost could always pick and choose the particulars for visitation? The thought entered her mind but she pushed it away. It surfaced again. *You are making this up,* her inner voice said, repeating the words her mother had repeated to her in her childhood. *You are a fraud. You're no psychic, just a screwed up woman with nothing going on in her life.* The road blurred with tears. It probably was true. She was really just inventing this whole experience. She needed attention. She needed connection so badly that her mind had adeptly created this fantasy from a simple party trick.

She pulled over into the parking lot of the Sedona Red Rock newspaper and stared at the large crimson letters posted on the top of the building. Was she just a nut? Was she so disconnected with reality that she was willing to make up a crazy story so people would listen to her? Spontaneously she closed her eyes and tilted her head back. She wiggled her shoulders and scrunched her brow. Her body relaxed a tiny bit. She willed herself to slow her mind. Her breathing became deeper. Madison lowered herself into a state of meditation.

The whirling questions and thoughts bounced around each other in the darkness of her brain. A clock-like ticking sound tapped out a rhythmic cadence and she tried to attach words to the tempo. Questions marks paraded in an animated march. It felt good to be back in this dark space. She allowed the thoughts to stream throughout her consciousness. *Trust,* she told herself. *Trust . . .*

WILLIAM. His name came to the forefront of her mind like a glowing Broadway theatre banner. No other message surfaced. His name hung boldly, written in capitals, WILLIAM. Madison's breathing quickened and despite her best effort, she emerged from the quiet place with eyes open wide. She looked up beyond the roof of the building and saw a swirl of clouds and dust towering in the air, like a delicate tornado. The grayish-white puffs pulsated in the sky, tinged in dusty red. It was a vortex of incredible proportions. Madison had never seen anything like it and she blinked her eyes again, to be sure it really existed. There it was—a spinning cone of air above the silent red cliffs, whose tips she could barely see above the building. She got out of the car and stood on her tiptoes to see how far it reached and nearly smashed the hand of the man next to her who was similarly opening his door. Madison looked at him, startled. She was about to complain that he had parked backwards in the parking lot and didn't he know any better when she looked at her own car and realized it sat facing the wrong direction, stopped at a haphazard diagonal.

"What the hell," the man said. His bearded mouth hung open and he shielded his eyes as he looked up to the sky. "See that?"

He didn't seem to notice at all that Madison had nearly amputated his hand. His fingers still rested on the door frame.

Madison looked back up at the vortex. It rose higher and glittered in the midday sun. The red dust particles filled the space with a pink hue.

They stood there in the parking lot, faces tipped to the sky for what seemed to be ten minutes. The circulating clouds rotated above the Sedona landscape and lifted higher and higher until the shape disappeared into the sun.

They looked at each other. "Well, that was something," the man said.

"You can say that again." She looked back to the empty sky. "Have you ever seen one of those in the sky?"

"Nope." He shook his head. Seen a few vortexes down by Bell Rock and Boynton Canyon, but never nothin' like that."

"Me neither." She said. "Wonder what it means?"

"Dunno," The man answered in a loud deep voice as he turned away from her. "I don't buy into all this Sedona crap but if I did, I'd say somebody is trying to tell somebody else somethin'. Have a good one." He waved a hand and walked into the building.

Madison stood alone in the parking lot trying to process the last few minutes. This city sure as hell was a crazy place and this had been a textbook Sedona day. First she'd hung out in a carwash begging a ghost to visit, and then she'd seen the most amazing vortex she could imagine. She thought back to the brief interlude in her car and once again, his name came to her. She needed to call William.

CHAPTER TWENTY-ONE

THE PHONE CALL she made to Barb was one of the hardest.

"Hello?"

"Hey girl, what's up?"

"Nothin'. Same old thing. Got five lessons back-to-back today. I can't tell you how much I hate summer."

Katherine laughed. "Listen, aren't you always the one telling me you gotta make hay while the sun shines?"

"Well, once again, I'm trying to figure out why I stay in this business. If only I could figure all this out . . ."

"Don't tell me. You want to go back to Sedona."

"Well, I would if anyone there had anything to say that helped."

"Yeah, I could use some help right about now, too."

"What's the matter, Kath? You sound weird."

Katherine reluctantly told her friend the news. Barb was stunned. "What do you do now?" She asked.

"Gotta start treatment in a week or so."

"I can't believe it. Kath, I'm so sorry."

"Hey, it's not your fault. I'm just pissed I spent so much time taking care of my body. Here I am in the best shape ever and I'm a fucking cancer patient." The words sounded foreign.

"Listen," Barb said. "You are going to blow right through this."

"I know." Katherine felt overwhelmed. "I just am so scared, Barb. I mean what the fuck? I have cancer? Me?"

Barb didn't answer. Katherine could tell her friend just didn't know what to say. How could she? They'd never been in this place before. She didn't know what to say, either.

"Well, no use dwelling on it. Can't do anything till the ball gets rolling."

"Want me to cancel my lessons? We could go for a walk or something."

"No, that's okay. You can't afford it. Just think about how difficult you'll be to live with next winter when we go back to Sedona and you can't pay for the drinks."

They both giggled and Katherine hung up the phone. She turned to see Grant standing in the doorway, watching her worriedly. She walked over to him and collapsed into his arms.

CHAPTER TWENTY-TWO

M ADISON SAT IN HER car and found her cell phone. She quickly dialed William's number.

"Greetings, love." He answered cheerfully.

"Hi, honey. What are you up to?"

"Just finished making new copies of my palm reading charts. I've decided to hand them out when I'm done with the sessions. A sort of party gift, if you will."

"Great."

"What's up, Mads? You sound a bit out of sorts."

"Oh, William. I just had the craziest morning. I actually went into the car wash to try to create a moment with my damn ghost friend. Then I decided I'm actually nutty and I am making all this up and I see this incredible vortex in the sky—"

"Slow down, love, you've left me at the carwash."

"Did you see it, William?" Madison charged on. It was red and pink and huge. I pulled into the newspaper parking lot and it looked like it was just sitting on top of the building."

"Well, ah, no, love. Didn't see it. But I've been inside all day." He paused. "Are you sure you saw this, Mads?"

Madison peeked out her windshield to see if the actual mass of clouds had magically reappeared. She felt a bit of panic seep in.

Had she actually seen it? Or had she made this up, too? She remembered the man next to her.

"Not only did I see it, William. This guy in the parking lot next to me saw it, too."

"Ah, yes, then, well, right. Nothing better than confirmation. What do you make of it?"

"I got no idea. But I thought maybe you might."

"Me! Madison, you of all people have far more intuitive skill than I. You are a quintessential clairvoyant!"

"Yeah, but what does that really mean?"

"Don't tell me you're really questioning yourself?"

"Well, don't you ever?"

"Not anymore. After years of struggling with this and wondering if it was true, sometimes wishing it weren't, I read this fabulous book which helped me put a large part of it in order."

"Yeah?"

"It only deals with mediumship but the feeling of confirmation that I felt afterward helped me believe, no, *understand,* that I truly do have these gifts. I am different. So are you. That's probably why we click so well."

Madison felt a tingle at William's words. He felt they had a connection too! She wanted to linger there but her desire to find out about this book moved her past. "What's the name of this book, William? I really want to get it."

"*Learning the Angels' Song.*" He said. "I know they've got a few copies at the library. That's where I found it."

"Great! That's it! I'll go get the book. I'll read it. I'll have my epiphany and all will be right with the world."

"You sound positively giddy. Go forth, love and—" he stopped.

"And what?"

"I was going to say go forth and conquer, but I think I'll say go forth and discover."

"William, you are the absolute best."

"Don't go forgetting about me when this launches you into the next stratosphere of psychic stardom."

"William," Madison said, "I will never forget about you."

"Cheers, then, love." He said as he hung up.

"Cheers," she replied and drove her car out of the lot and towards the Sedona library. The librarian promised to call her when a copy arrived from the Flagstaff branch.

Madison hurried back to the Enlightenment Center feeling almost cheery. She'd welcome anything to give her a fresh perspective.

Hours later, Madison walked down the stairs from her office to retrieve her last client of the day. She was itching to get this session over with so she could walk the Airport Mesa trail before the sun dipped too low in the sky. This day had been a whirlwind tour of astral energies and she was completely exhausted. She wasn't sure how she made it through her readings. She'd had to force all thoughts of Helen from her mind, hoping the ghost would leave her in peace for a while.

She stepped down the slim staircase and felt the wood railing slide beneath her fingers. Along the wall to her right were posters of jazz concerts Sedona had hosted in the past. One particularly grabbed her attention. It showed a tall, thin red finger of cliff scraping a gray-blue sky. The crevasses and cracks on the rock looked like knuckles on a hand pointed up to heaven. The words "Red Jazz" hung above the rock. She loved this picture because it instantaneously removed her from this rickety building to the soaring crimson stones set about the desert city. That particular cliff was one of her favorites. She had often hiked around its base. The currents swirling about the edifice brought scores of eagles swooping and soaring through the juniper-laced air. Madison hesitated for a moment before the last step and breathed deeply. She expected to inhale memory-induced wisps of Juniper. She smelled something else instead.

She tried to place the sweet scent trailing through the dimly lit hallway. Strange, it wasn't an incense fragrance she was familiar with. The mediums in their tiny offices throughout the center always had some version of blossoms filling the air. Perhaps William had found a new fragrance.

Madison reached for the doorknob and pushed the creaky door open when she felt a light touch on the back of her neck.

She released the doorknob and turned around to see Helen's slight shimmer in the recesses of the corner under the stairs.

Madison approached Helen's form and breathed in her essence. The scent grew stronger and she immediately recognized lavender mingled with another sweet scent she couldn't identify. She couldn't see any of Helen's face but she felt a stirring intensity. Helen was pulling her back.

"No," Madison murmured. "I need a break."

PICTURES WHIRLED AROUND her head. Helen was flinging her through time, catching her up. Madison saw an image of Cecil working late, alone at his desk in the darkened, cavernous bank. She saw a slide show of Helen's days at the Mansion: caring for the old man, talking with Mrs. Greer, driving to work. Then the parade of moments slowed and Madison was able to see more clearly instances when Jerome would happen upon Helen. He'd find her in the kitchen, by the carriage house, in the hallway outside his grandfather's room.

The instances increased in tempo and, Madison could feel, in intimacy. She watched Helen's body language. She leaned a little closer, and would touch his arm. Madison could also sense Jerome's growing connection to Helen.

"Excuse me!" A voice at Madison's shoulder pulled her back to reality. She turned to see a small woman frowning at her. "Are you Madison Morgan?" The woman gave off an irritated energy.

Madison nodded at her then looked back in the corner. It was empty. She sighed. "What can I do for you?"

"I'm Joan Averly. I have an appointment." The woman's tone put Madison off immediately.

"Well, Ms. Averly, why don't we just hop up to my office?"

"The lady at the desk said you'd be down in a minute. You know," she sniffed. "I don't have all day."

"Well," Madison said over her shoulder as she led the woman up the stairs,."We here in Sedona don't work on regular time!"

It wasn't pleasant reading the woman's energy. Joan Averly was arrogant and self-righteous. "You know, I don't really believe in all this stuff. The girls back home would be appalled at this." She sniffed and looked out the window. Madison rolled her eyes. Her brain was fried and her patience was frayed. The woman was wading into dangerous territory.

"Okay," she began. "I need all this information." She listed the questions, "Name, phone number, address . . ."

1438 Lindawood Avenue, Winona, Minnesota."

Madison felt a prickle. "Winona, Minnesota?"

"Yes," Joan sat forward indignantly. "What does that mean?"

Madison didn't answer. She felt Helen standing directly behind Joan's head. *Winona, Winona.* The word rapped inside her head. Joan was saying something now but Madison wasn't listening. Whatever the reason for the Winona reference, Madison felt it was meant for her to find. In the next instant, Helen was gone and Madison looked again at the sputtering woman.

"Really, this is just ridiculous. Are you going to give me something good? I'm paying a lot for this."

Madison stared at the spot where Helen had just hovered. Joan raised her chin up and glared. "You know what I think," she said, leaning closer. "This is just a scam. You're a fraud."

The woman obviously used this nasty tone regularly. Madison could tell she was a piece of work. She probably made other people's lives miserable for sport. It took all Madison had to restrain herself from reaching across the desk to slap Joan Averly's face.

Madison was done. She didn't have the patience to put up with this toxic presence. "You know what, sweetheart, you're right. You figured it out. Congratulations. Why don't you go tell everyone back in Winona that some crazy dame in Sedona tried to take you? But it couldn't be done. You're way too smart!" Madison slapped her hands on the table and stood up. She grabbed the page that held the beginnings of Joan's numbers. "We," she began tearing the paper into strips. "Are done. Don't let the door hit you."

Joan stood up and glared again at Madison. "You think I'm an idiot?" she spat.

"No, honey, you're wrong about that. I take you to be exactly what you are—a woman whose ass is leaving my office."

Joan grabbed her purse and hurried toward the door. "I'm going to let them know how rude you are."

"Yeah, well. Good luck with that." Madison sat down and waved her out the door.

Outside her window the creek rolled joyously over the rocks. Madison leaned back in her chair and put her feet up on the desk. Snoopy Rock lingered in the distance. Her thoughts drifted back to Helen and the craziness of this persistent ethereal stalker. The determined ghost had become her own supernatural Snoopy, hanging around her yard just within earshot.

"Ah, Helen," Madison said into the air, "what have you got for me next?"

"Girl," she said aloud, this time to herself, "you're losing it." The realization that she'd rather spend time with an unexplainable presence from God knew where was more than shaking her up. Below her the creek splashed and echoed the word *Winona*. Madison shook her head and then put her feet back on the floor. What she needed was a break from this reality and that reality and whatever was actually reality.

"Madison," she declared as she leaned forward in her chair and focused on her computer screen. "We gotta escape this crap. Otherwise, we're in the loony bin, and I know they don't serve chai lattes there!" She pulled up the listings of local movie times, then shut off the computer and walked out of her office, hoping to leave the ghost and the overwhelming psychic vibrations behind.

CHAPTER
TWENTY-THREE

KATHERINE WAS AMAZED at the inner-workings of a hospital. Having only visited intermittently, for her labor and delivery and emergency room visits for the boys, she'd never hung around long enough to see the daily details. Now she was a regular. The first diagnostic appointments had blurred in her mind. She'd met with her new doctors, learned the protocol for her treatment and been introduced to the radiation oncology facility.

The longest appointment yet was what she called "the branding." For two hours she was moved around on a huge mobile table underneath an infrared light to pinpoint the exact coordinates of her tumor. Then she received a tattoo which would allow the radiation techs to find the spot consistently every day. When she returned home that afternoon she was drained. She took a long shower to wash away the smell and feel of the sterile rooms and equipment. As she rinsed her hair for the tenth time, Grant walked into the bathroom and leaned his head into the shower.

"You okay, honey?"

"Yeah," she lied.

"You've taken what could be history's longest shower."

"Don't worry, I'm almost done."

"I've got an idea," he said.

"What?" She stepped out of the shower and took the towel he offered her. She covered up her breast quickly.

"Let's go to Blue Point. We can have an appetizer, enjoy the view of the lake. It would be good for both of us."

"Do we really have the money?"

"No." He admitted. But that hasn't stopped us from spending it, so far. C'mon. You'll feel better." He reached and pulled her to him.

"I don't know. I guess we could. I'm just so shocked by all this, Grant. Two weeks ago, the word 'cancer' wasn't even part of my vocabulary. Now I can't get it out of my head. Look," she pulled the towel away and pointed at the *x* tattoo. "This is so surreal."

"Kath," Grant lifted her chin and looked into her eyes. "This is just rotten that we've got to deal with this, that you've got to worry about this on top of everything else. I promise I'm going to go through it with you step-by-step, just like you've stayed with me for the past year." Katherine cringed. She hadn't felt supportive at all. Now he was showing her his love in such a powerful way.

"I don't deserve you," she whispered.

"Wrong there." Grant gently kissed her. "We deserve each other. We're lucky that way. That's how we are going to get through all of this. Agreed, Kath?"

She looked at him silently, thinking how blessed she really was in the midst of this disaster.

"Can I get a witness?" he smiled.

"You've got one," she said.

"Good. Put on your fanciest duds. There's a tuna appetizer downtown with your name on it." He slapped her on the backside and walked out of the room.

Katherine took a deep breath and stared at herself in the mirror. Grant was right. They would get through it . . . together. *No more hysterics,* she thought. Now it was time to get into battle mode. She brushed her fingers across the tattoo and walked into the closet to get dressed.

CHAPTER
TWENTY-FOUR

TWO HOURS LATER Madison was fast asleep in the movie theater. She was one of a handful of people on this early Thursday afternoon. She had gotten her favorite large popcorn layered in butter and had settled comfortably in the dark. Within five minutes, barely after the credits, she slumped, softly snoring, her nose inches above the greasy popcorn bag.

A sharp *Crack!* shook her awake. She snuffled back to consciousness with a start, spilling puffs of corn all over her lap. She looked up at the screen and was mesmerized by a low green glow pulsating in front of her. Inside the glow she could see images moving, but they were gritty and unfocused. Madison put the popcorn down and rubbed her eyes. She looked up at the screen again.

Helen had just slammed the door of her car and was balancing her purse and a bag of groceries. At the same time she maneuvered a tiny boy in front of her, herding him like a sheepdog.

"Sam! Let's go, honey. Into the house. That's it. C'mon, be good for Mama." She pushed the skipping child toward the house. Once inside, she put the groceries down and quickly got the boy a cup of milk and a cookie. "Now you sit and eat your snack, Sammy. Mama's going to start dinner."

"Okay, Mama." Sam happily gnawed at his cookie.

Helen moved around the sunlit kitchen methodically. The room was small and tidy. She unloaded the groceries and turned on the Detroit Jewel oven. Her fingers lingered on the dials of the immaculate oven/range. It was obvious she adored the thing. She then pulled a chicken from a brown butcher paper package. She cut it in half and placed it in a pan with a collection of vegetables. Meanwhile, Sam began the dunking game. Droplets of milk drizzled the table as he dove his soggy cookie over and over again into the frothy white liquid.

"Sam!" Helen whirled around to see her son in oblivious joy. "Stop that! You're making a mess!"

Sam answered her with an infectious giggle and Helen immediately joined him.

The moment was a pure and sweet one. Mother and son sat together at the table, smiling at each other.

The front door slammed and Cecil lumbered into the kitchen. He dropped his coat over the chair and swooped down to kiss his son's head. "What's going on here?"

"Attack of the cookie again."

"Ah, those cookies. They can never get enough of that milk. Like I can never get enough of my Sammy!" Cecil leaned down and scooped the wriggling toddler up in his arms. Sam screamed with delight as his father whirled him around the kitchen table.

The screen darkened, and then Helen and Cecil were sitting up in bed together. Their conversation was muffled and soft. Random words would lift from the screen, "Mr. Park," "getting worse," "bank's new policy." Cecil shook his head at a quiet question from Helen. "Don't know," he answered. He turned and switched off the light and the theater was silent and black.

Next, a bright light filled the screen. The glorious Park mansion towered in the background as Helen walked the impeccable grounds. The huge old house stood grandly, surrounded by the gardens and lawns stretched out around like a brilliantly colored Christmas tree skirt.

Helen seemed not to notice the landscaped grandeur around her. She strode purposely through the extensive garden where roses and daylilies gleamed, along a gravel path and then to a smaller yard beyond the perfectly manicured topiaries ringing the house. Her pace slowed and she paused for a moment, looking back to the house. Then she moved forward again. She continued to a small garden shack, hidden behind a grove of crab apples that stood exhausted in the heat, their bright pink blooms littering the ground.

Helen opened the wooden door and slid into the darkness. A man's hands immediately grasped her shoulders from behind and she gasped.

"You're late."

"He was uncomfortable. It took me longer to get him settled."

"I hate it when I have to wait. It drives me crazy, you know that." The man turned Helen's face toward him. She looked up and smiled a glowing, eager look.

Despite the darkness, Madison could see Jerome smile back and pull Helen to him.

In the dark of the garden house, it was impossible to see but easy to know what was happening. Their groans intertwined and made a low, melodic music. Their breathing hissed slowly, separately, then more quickly and in unison as their invisible passion grew.

It seemed as if even the theater held its breath as the two voices and bodies became one.

The screen became bright again as Helen hustled out the door quickly. She stooped a bit as if to hide herself even more. The small Hawthorne trees lining the gravel path scratched and clawed at her arms but she didn't seem to notice. She hustled toward the garden, past the towering rose bushes and ducked into the kitchen entrance.

She was so intent upon sneaking back into the house she didn't notice the face watching her through the second story window.

CHAPTER
TWENTY-FIVE

THE SEARING MID-JULY afternoon sun gleamed in an ice-blue sky. Katherine turned over in bed to get away from the glare. She wished now that instead of see-through grass shades, she and Grant had chosen black-outs. The sun tickled her shoulder. She sighed and closed her eyes again. She needed a nap! Why didn't her mind agree with her body?

The last twenty or so days (was that how long it had been? She wasn't really sure) had piled on top of one another, like bricks forming a crooked wall. The moments were jumbled with crystalline realizations. Yes, she did have cancer. No, she wasn't going to die (at least not now). The hours of tests and waiting rooms and discussions with doctors and techs and nurses and insurance representatives added more weight onto that wall of her life, which was crumbling with increasing rapidity. And yet, it wasn't. Here she was, tired, no doubt, but still going on. She made it to tennis and occasional workouts. She and Grant managed a dinner out every so often, even though times were still tough because he had not yet found another job.

In the beginning of the journey down Cancer Boulevard, Katherine had lashed out with tears and fits at everyone. She realized that she should be a grown up. But she still had not integrated any of those mystical life-skills that the psychic from Sedona had told her to grow.

Along the way she had quelled her hysteria to a manageable roar that only she could hear. She determinedly put a smile on her face and held her tongue. She drove the twenty miles from her house, over the bridge to the east side of the Mississippi, every day to treatment and behaved like a well-trained monkey, obediently removing her blouse and bra in front of whoever happened to be in the radiation bay, positioning herself like a piece of meat on the morgue-like slab of a table and holding her breath so she wouldn't weep when everyone left the room and locked the six-inch-thick bank-vault door behind them.

Each day, even though the treatment lasted a mere three minutes, Katherine would stare up at the woodland scene pasted to the ceiling and ask herself again, *how did I get here?*

One day she had found the daily treatment schedule for all the breast cancer patients that day. She had scanned the list. Twenty-three names lined up in order like planes ready to take off. Each name had an age, a radiation oncology identification number and a notation of whether the left or right breast was to be radiated. She remembered idly noticing that of the twenty-two patients ahead of her (she had chosen the last available spot—6:20 p.m.), eighteen of them had left-breast treatment. She'd pondered that, thinking of the irony that the radiation toxins were pouring around so many women's hearts, literally and figuratively.

Katherine turned back toward the window and the unapologetic sunshine. She squinted at the clock and sighed. Four twenty. Time to get up, shower and put on her bright "I'm a good soldier" face.

"Kath?" Grant's voice floated up from downstairs.

"Yeah, honey?"

"I've got to run to the tractor dealer. I want to see what we can get for it. I might not be in time to get back for the hospital. You okay to go alone?"

Katherine stared at herself in the mirror. She noticed the deepening brown square across the left part of her chest—nothing like a permanent radiation tan.

"Kath?"

"Yeah, yeah, that's okay. No problem. Go ahead. See you when you get home."

"Okay, I'll pick up Chinese on the way. Sound good?"

"Delicious!" She smiled, Barbie doll-like, at her reflection.

An hour later, Katherine was gathering up her keys when Wayne bounded in the kitchen.

"Hi, beautiful mother!" He swooped down for a kiss, an irrepressible puppy.

"Hello, darling boy." This was good medicine!

"Where are you going?" He helped himself to a banana and plopped on a barstool.

"Off to the fun house."

"Oh, yeah," Katherine could tell that Wayne felt bad about asking. What had she been doing every day at this time for the past three weeks? He looked up from his banana. "Want some company?"

Katherine looked at him in surprise. "Don't you have to work tonight?"

"Nope, got Wes to do it. I'm going to see Cy do his comedy at eight tonight. We traded. I'm working for him tomorrow."

"Ah, the convenience of having a brother who works the same job as you!"

Wayne grinned his perfect Abercrombie-model smirk. "Well that's one good thing! So waddya say? Want me to come along?"

"I would love it. You've absolutely made my day!"

"Wow! And I didn't even have to clean up my room to do it." He leaned down and pecked her on the cheek. "Your chauffer is ready, Madam!"

THE RIDE TO THE HOSPITAL was as good as such a ride could get. The warm summer air blew in through the windows and sunroof. Although it was nearly six o'clock, the sun's rays still radiated off the pavement, dispersing its heat to every surface in sight. Even the stretch over the Mississippi didn't offer much relief. The construction traffic on the bridge acted like logs in a flowing river, stopping the cars to all but a trickle of movement. But Katherine didn't care. For the moment it was just the two of them out for a fun ride on a summer's early evening.

"So, exactly how do they do this, mom?" Wayne's voice cut into her reverie.

"Do what?"

"You know, the whole treatment thing."

"Oh, well, we go into the waiting room but we never have to wait for long because they have the schedule down to the minute. Sometimes I have to hang out a little longer because I'm the last one, but not that often. Then we go into the radiation bay where they have all the controls. This machine is huge. It's got a monster panel with monitors so you can see what's going on inside the closet."

"The closet?"

"Well, that's what I call it. It's a room about the size of our family room. There's a platform you lie on that they can move up and down and there's this gigantic cone that hovers around the table. They can maneuver it all around you so it can shoot you from any angle. It kind of reminds me of E.T."

Wayne nodded and Katherine thought she sensed a bit of uneasiness. If he were unsure now, he'd really want to change his mind when he had to watch his mom strip and get locked into the closet.

"It doesn't take any time at all, so if you don't want to come back with me, you can wait outside."

"Don't you want me to come with you?" He peered at her, concerned.

"Well, you might not feel comfortable. I mean it might be weird seeing me stuck on that table."

"Do you want me to come with you, Mom?"

"I would love it but don't feel like you have to, okay?"

"Okay." Wayne exited the bridge onto Fourth Avenue and steered the car through the traffic toward the hospital. "I promise I'll come with you and close my eyes!"

Katherine watched Wayne's face closely as she introduced him to Deedee, the radiation technician. Deedee was obviously taken with Wayne. She showed him around the bay and explained briefly how the technology worked. If Wayne was completely freaked out, he didn't show it. He was a perfect gentleman and seemed genuinely interested in everything. He grew quiet, though, when Katherine and Deedee led him into the closet. He looked at the huge radiation machine hanging like a pterodactyl from the ceiling.

"Wow, Mom, nice scenery!" Wayne pointed to the woodland wallpaper on the ceiling. No matter which part of the room a patient might find themselves, when they laid on their back, taking in the cancer-killing rays, they had the idyllic scene to take their minds off of it all.

"Yeah, beautiful, isn't it?" Katherine smiled at her son. "I told Deedee maybe about the tenth day in that I try to find some wildlife among the trees. But luckily I never have enough time to find any so I have to start over every next day!"

"Well, let's get your mom ready," Deedee ushered Wayne out of the closet. "Want to wait in the waiting room?"

"Well, if it's okay with you, Mom, I'd like to hang out with you."

Katherine and Deedee smiled at each other. "That's so sweet of you, honey, but you can't be in here with me. Nobody can. See how thick that door is? You guys have to go outside so you don't pick up any wandering radiation."

Wayne eyed the door, then turned back to look at his mother.

Deedee broke in, "But," she looked at Katherine for confirmation. "If your mom doesn't mind, you can watch me work the machine from the bay. Okay with you, Katherine?"

Katherine shrugged and smiled. "Sure, why not? Maybe this will be starting a promising medical career!"

Wayne shook his head. "Don't count on it!"

Deedee showed Wayne back to the bay and came in and helped Katherine onto the table. She carefully lined up the machine with the tattoo Katherine had received on the first day, signifying the exact spot of the tumor. Katherine laid on the table perfectly still, her left arm raised above her head and placed in a plastic mold to hold it motionless. She wondered what Wayne was thinking of this as he watched through the monitor.

Then she suddenly remembered when her mother had been treated for a brain tumor. She had made the obligatory trip to the hospital one day and bantered uncomfortably with all the far-too-nice hospital personnel. She had watched from behind a similarly thick door as her mother's forehead was illuminated by a neon red square where the tumor-burning rays entered her brain. Her mother had been dead three weeks later.

This memory, coupled with the clunk of the door closing, caused bile to rise in her throat. She took a quick breath and forced herself to display a calm face. The urge to jump off the table and claw her way out of that room caused her heart to gallop. She tried to reach for a deep breath but could only find a shallow pant.

Deedee's voice seeped into the room over the loudspeaker. "Everything okay, Katherine?"

Breathe, damn it! She screamed at herself. She managed a slight cough.

Deedee waited. They'd been in this place before. Katherine closed her eyes and squeezed back the tears ready to spill.

"Okay," Katherine managed in a small voice. "Ready when you are!"

"All right. Your son has asked if he can push the buttons but I told him it's not appropriate to radiate your mother!"

Katherine offered a chuckle at the gallows humor. Wayne was probably officially freaked out now.

"Here we go, Katherine. Take a nice deep breath. You know the drill. Ninety seconds . . ." The huge machine grumbled and growled then emitted a streaming high-pitched squeal as it lasered its energy into Katherine's breast tissue. The routine was repeated four times as the beast slung over Katherine on the table, pouring its cell-killing atoms into her quiet, trembling form.

CHAPTER TWENTY-SIX

THE MOVIE THEATER was silent, save the whirring of ceiling fans far above, as the screen shaded to gray. The next scene showed Helen in the great house's kitchen, reading a newspaper at the enormous island as the cook's assistants peeled potatoes for the evening meal.

"Mrs. Rhames," Mrs. Greer's sharp voice echoed through the kitchen.

Helen looked up. "Yes, Mrs. Greer?"

"You're wanted upstairs."

Helen looked at the clock. It read 3:00. She shook her head and looked at Betsy, peeling potatoes. "That's strange," she said. "He doesn't usually wake 'til four."

Betsy shook her head back wordlessly.

Helen gathered herself and trotted up the back stairs. Her footsteps made hardly any sound as they sank into the perfectly raked, thick blue carpet treads. She came to his room and knocked gently on the door.

Inside, the old man was propped in bed, looking paler than ever. Next to him stood Brian, the dour butler who had first let her in that day two years before. She took two steps closer to the bed. "Yes, sir?"

Again, Madison was fascinated with the reality of this experience. She could feel the humidity in the air. She could smell the unmistakable scent of illness. As Helen approached the bed, Madison noticed another person standing before the window, with his back to the bed.

Helen leaned forward to hear the old man. He didn't have much air in the lungs for speaking loudly anymore.

"Helen. I am sorry to find us in such circumstances," Louis whispered.

"I don't understand, sir."

Brian sniffed a loud, disgusted grunt.

"It seems that you have been consorting with . . ." He paused. "This is a difficult thing, my dear. I have become quite fond of you but these things are unacceptable."

Helen's face went white. Brian's disgusted look slid into a greasy smile.

"Mr. Park. I—"

"Helen, don't." Jerome turned toward her at the window. Helen gasped in sickened surprise. "I told them everything. I told them it was my fault."

"But how, what . . . ?"

"It seems our dear butler, Brian, picked up on our . . . contacts."

Helen groaned.

"It is truly disgusting to me on various levels, *Mrs.* Rhames," the butler accentuated the 'Mrs.' "Not the least of which is a professional standard which you as a nurse I would assume should hold. Evidently not."

"That's enough, Brian." Louis, despite looking exhausted and frail, showed a glimmer of his former self. He waved the butler off and sighed. "I'm sure you know it is incumbent upon me to release you."

"Grandfather, it's me. It's my fault. Let her stay. I'll go." Jerome looked miserable.

"Son, I will deal with you later." Louis dismissed his grandson with a look of disgust. "This woman is not only in my employ, she is married, Jerome. She is a mother." Louis shook his head. "I'm quite disappointed. You were a fine nurse. You took good care of me." Louis' face dissolved into a soft grimace.

"But what is done is done, Mrs. Rhames." He sat up a bit straighter against the pillow. "Mrs. Greer has your final check. We will not speak of this again." He shifted away from her. "Good luck in your future pursuits."

Helen stared at Jerome, still stunned. He looked at her with a strange, furious look and turned back to the window. She took a step toward him but then looked at the old man settled in the pillows with his eyes closed. "I'm sorry." She tearfully mumbled. "I'm sorry to both of you."

She hesitated for a moment, looking at Jerome's back, but he did nothing to acknowledge her. She walked resolutely toward the door and opened it. Without a look back, she stepped quietly down the stairs, collected her check from the disdainful housekeeper and left the grounds for the last time. The deep summer blossoms waved around her in the breeze. She walked out of the gates and down the street toward the dusty Ford parked in the distance.

THE LIGHTS FLICKERED to full strength. Madison snuffled as her brain came back to Sedona time. She looked around and felt embarrassed, as if she was the last one at the bar who had napped through the final song. Around her the small crowd of Thursday afternoon movie buffs were migrating.

"I thought all those car chases were just too much," an older woman complained.

"Well," a smug man's voice answered. "Those film guys always try to do too much. I mean," his voice permeated the theater. "What are they trying to say?"

Madison watched the older woman and her younger, opinionated companion walk down the steps in front of her.

"Excuse me," Madison stepped toward the couple quickly.

The older woman was intent upon finding the next step and didn't look up. Her partner turned, looking at Madison.

"What did you think of the last scenes?" Madison barreled on, sensing that movie-critique momentum was in her favor.

"Which scenes?" The younger man turned to face her, clearly interested.

"You know," Madison forced herself to sound like a casual movie-goer. "Like the last fifteen minutes or so, did you think they fit in with the story?"

The young man stopped and in the moment, pulled the older woman with him to a halt. "That last car scene, you mean? I thought it was over the top. I mean, c'mon, they want us to think both are going to die because neither one can have her. But everybody knows the lead character never dies."

Wow kid, Madison thought. *You gotta meet some of the characters I know!*

He turned back and looked for concurrence from his companion. She nodded her head in weary agreement. The woman didn't look at all interested in anything but going home. Madison asked again. "What did you think of the end?"

"What, you mean the fact that Gage's car barely made it to the line and Cordello won?" He tipped his head toward Madison as he steered his wilting companion into the theater hallway. Then he stopped as if he had been asked a question from CNN and his opinion on the film was the only one that mattered. "Trust me," he whispered, "It was set up from the beginning." Madison took a quick breath. The mention of car chases pretty much guaranteed that she was the only one who had witnessed the scenes in the red sandstone house.

"Those two guys will live to drive another day in the sequel." The young man declared benevolently at Madison. "Wow, sweetie, wasn't that great?" His partner nodded and moved slowly to the exit.

On another day, Madison would have merrily created a movie plot of her own around this odd couple. But she didn't have a moment to evaluate their story. The awareness that she had seen a movie that no one else had completely unnerved her.

Honey, she transmitted to Helen, hovering wherever she was (Madison could tell she was close by). *I appreciate your artistic elegance, but I really wish you would get to the point. What the hell do you want with me?* Madison's head bobbed up and down as she conversed beyond the Sedona world.

She paused for a second by a huge, freestanding movie poster, pretending to look for her keys. She wasn't really sure she wanted to get in her car. Helen seemed to be following her.

A young theater attendant walked up to her. "You okay, Ma'am?"

Madison looked at him, startled. She managed a breezy smile. "Yeah, thanks. Oh, there they are," she jangled her keys at him.

He nodded politely. "Okay, well have a nice day!"

"Will do!" Did she sound as hysterical as she was feeling, now? She walked quickly out of the theater into the brilliant sunshine. The rays made her blink.

Jesus, she thought. *I'm losing my marbles. I gotta get this ghost out of here.* She walked to her car and drove home with one thing on her mind. She needed to talk to Ben Masselink. Maybe he could figure this whole thing out.

AT HOME SHE SHUFFLED through the papers on the dining room table. Notes and random pieces of paper scattered underneath her roving hands. She found Ben's number and dialed.

"Howdy?" Madison wanted to weep with joy. Ben's voice was a welcome anchor on this ridiculous day.

"Hey Ben, it's Madison." Could he hear the tremor in her voice?

"Madison, my friend! How goes the ghost hunt?"

"Ben, this whole thing is driving me crazy. This spirit is like, stalking me now. She's showing me whole time periods of her life. She even changed the movie I was watching today at the theater. I go in to see car chases and I get remembrances of her crazy affair!"

"Wow, how did she communicate it to you?"

"I watched it on the screen as if it was the real movie. I am so anxious right now. I have never had anything like this happen. I don't know what she's trying to tell me, I don't know who it's for. But one thing's for sure, I'm starting to lose my grip on reality. I really need your help Ben," Madison's voice raised an octave.

"Now, kiddo, don't panic. There are times in our lives, whether because we are more sensitive or the astrology just fits, when the messages do become overwhelming. It's happened to me a few times, but I have to say, never like the way you're describing."

"What do I do, Ben?"

"First thing is, get out of that environment. Can you take a few days off? Leave Sedona for a while?"

Madison leaned forward and put her elbows onto the table, her head into her hands. "Well, I guess I could just reschedule my regulars."

"Right, my girl. That's what you have to do." Ben's voice was friendly but firm. "You have to remove yourself from all this energy. Take a break."

"Then what? What if she frickin' follows me?"

"Let me work on that part. Can you write me an outline of everything that's happened? How long has this been going on, again?"

Madison counted back to the first day she remembered seeing Helen, that chilly day last winter. "Seven months now, I think."

Ben whistled on the other end of the phone. "You're right Madison, this one is persistent. And even though it's unsettling, you have to trust that there's a really important reason that she's got this message, and more important, that she's using you as a bridge to someone."

"Honestly, Ben, I'd rather not have the honor at this point. Seems like it's becoming more of a curse."

"Imagine, Madison, if you feel that way, how does she feel? There must be so much emotion that's allowing this phenomenon to happen—with such regularity, too. You definitely have to document all this. You never know, maybe your next chapter is here at school teaching a class on over-enthusiastic astral plane visitors!"

"Okay. I'll write down what I have and what I remember. I started keeping notes but she gives me so much information in such huge doses, it blows my mind. I need help remembering all the details. I also tried to do some research on the internet to find out who she was but I never got a location, and it's hard to find out who someone is or was when you don't know where they're from—"

"Madison, one thing I know about you is that you never shrink from a challenge." Ben's words gave her a small shot of courage. "Just remember, it wasn't a mistake, her coming to you. It never is. They choose us."

"Right. Okay, thanks, Ben. I'm back on track . . . I think."

"Yes, you are!" She could see that toothy smile that had been such a great part of his presence when she had taken his classes so many years ago.

Madison hung up and closed her eyes. When exactly had the ghost first appeared? She scribbled a note to check dates in her records back at the office. Above her on the wall, her grandmother's antique gold clock reflected glints of the fading sunlight. The worn, delicate hands stretched exactly opposite each other—six o'clock.

"All right," she said out loud. "No time like the present!" She gathered her notebook and hustled into the kitchen to refill Coriander's dish. He slept soundly in his bed and offered only the slightest tick of a whisker as greeting. Madison looked down at the orange and white striped form curled up so happily.

"Wow, cat. I wish I could sleep like that!" Coriander offered no response.

"You want to sleep?" she asked herself. "Then find out what this crazy ghost wants and take care of it!"

She walked back into the dining room and took a quick glance over the messy contents. She peeked around the side of the chimney to survey her plants. All were green and happy. The house's energy pulsated in a strong, healing vibration.

WHEN SHE GOT INTO her office the next day, the stifling heat met her head on. Being at the top of the stairs always meant summer's swelter was a constant companion. She opened the window and reveled in the calm, predictable bubble of the creek below. Behind her desk sat the two-foot high pile of used tablets. Madison thumbed through them. In the middle of the stack she found the January tablet. She leafed through the pages, trying to remember the faces that went with the numbers and names.

She continued to trace back through January and into December. The notes of dozens of clients held hours of conversations and revelations. Her eyes scanned back in the tablet until it settled randomly on one day, December 15, 2006. Four clients on that date, one in the early morning, one in the evening and two sandwiched in between.

She studied the notes more closely. The first client in the middle of the day had been a woman named Barb. The paper showed her address as Minneapolis. *That's weird,* Madison mused. *Wasn't that wench I kicked out of the office from Minnesota?* The word "Winona" surfaced and lingered in the back of her mind.

Madison leaned back in her chair and tried to visualize the client while re-examining the numbers. Nothing new leapt out. The next reading was another woman, Katherine, also from Minnesota. Madison read the notations "green" and "head." So there had been something she'd seen about some injury. She continued scanning. Again, nothing out of the ordinary until she reached the very last line—*C. Madison's finger hovered above the page. *C was her personal code for clairvoyant visit. In parentheses following the C was an added phrase—(elderly woman upon client's exit). There it was, the first pebble in the Hansel and Gretel path back to square one. Helen had first showed herself on December 15, 2006. But Madison wanted to be clearer . . . why had the ghost chosen that day? She tried to clarify her memory of those clients but she'd read so many people since then all she saw was a jumble of faces in her head.

"Okay, sister," Madison said to the ghost. "Now the fun begins. If you're going to go to all this trouble to hang out with me, I'm going to figure out what the hell for." She looked up to the ceiling. No presence visualized but Madison felt the slightest tickle on her arms and the back of her neck.

She opened up her notebook again and created the headline "First Visit Details." She put whatever facts she thought were relevant from all the readings that day, most importantly, each client's birthday.

Madison rolled her head around to try and release the tension built in her neck and shoulders. It was then the thought surfaced. What was the hurry? Why did she feel this strange need to solve the ghost's mystery so soon? That question tightened her neck and pulled her shoulders to her ears.

Madison chewed her pencil and tried to recall the day of Helen's appearance in her dream. She remembered Christmas lights had still been up (although in Sedona, lots of kooks kept their lights up all year, just in case aliens happened to visit the desert and were looking for a friendly drop-in point). Maybe that at least narrowed it down to sometime between December 15 and maybe mid-January. She tried to place herself back in the moment but drew a blank.

The phone rang. Madison punched the call button and answered in a distracted tone, "Madison Morgan . . ."

"Hey, Madison, honey!" Janine's cheerful voice sung to her.

"Hey, cupcake, what's up?"

"Um, nothing much. I'm working on this guy's chart and I'm having trouble with his yearly spread. What are your feelings with the Ace of Diamonds, King of Hearts and Two of Diamonds?"

"Hmm," Madison pondered the suits and numbers. "Does he have something major he's trying to decide?"

"Well, we've been working together on this new company he might want to create, but it's in a goofy industry."

"What's that?"

"Some internet thing."

"Goofy industry? Girl, you're dating yourself! Internet is the new, next grand frontier!"

"Yada, yada, yada . . . Honestly, I need a break. All these cards are starting to do tap dances on my brain!" She exhaled a deep, long breath into the phone. "You know what I need, Mads?"

"What's that, cherub?" Madison's eye roamed over her notes, only half-listening.

"I need a good yoga session!"

The words shot through Madison, slicing through and reverberating past her. Yoga! That day she'd spent an hour with Janine in an overwhelming yoga session. Following class they'd talked in the parking lot. The crystalline stars in the winter night sparkled in her memory. Afterwards, she'd driven home. She couldn't recall the particulars but Madison was certain that night was when Helen had first dream-dialed her. But that was so many months ago. Madison tried to remember any details that could anchor her.

"J," Madison was focused. "Remember that day back in December or January I think, and we were talking after that hellacious Bikram Yoga class?"

"Hmm, we've been to a lot of classes, girlfriend, how should I remember this one?"

"I talked to you, I think it was the first time, about Helen. Remember? It was so cold when we came out of the studio. The streets were all torn up." Madison tried desperately to find a detail that Janine would recall. She sat expectantly as her friend silently reviewed and searched in her own brain for that winter evening.

"I think I remember . . . Yeah, you were wondering who she was, right? She hadn't really revealed herself in detail yet? Yeah, Mads, I remember. How come?" Janine asked, clearly intrigued.

"What was the date, Janine? I'm trying to make a linear plan to go over everything this ghost has shown me."

"Wow, I gotta go back and see if I can find my 2006 calendar." Janine paused. "This whole situation is really becoming like, intense. Do you have any idea why this is happening?"

"Not yet. But I sure as hell am going to find out." Madison's voice rose theatrically, "I am on a mission!"

"Well, heaven help the poor soul who stands in your way. It's funny. This gal sure has some strong energy and she's on a mission, too! You guys are a match made on the other side!"

Madison and Janine laughed in unison. "Oh stop, I gotta go! You're killing me, girl!" Madison wiped her streaming eyes and struggled to catch her breath. It felt so good to laugh. The churlish anxiety that had been building up flowed out and away, through the window, Madison felt, down to the creek past the bent piñons and pines. Madison took a solid cleansing breath. The air filled her lungs then expelled heat from her center. She breathed again. "Okay, call me when you find that calendar, will you, love?"

"You bet, and Mads?" Janine stopped mid-sentence.

"Yeah?"

"Remember, this is all for a reason, every bit of it. This la-la lady needs you specifically. It seems like she's got a lot of catching up to do and you're the one to help her. You know what we used to call this situation back home?"

"What?"

"Being ghosted."

What?" Madison shook her head.

"Ghosted." Janine repeated. "You've been lassoed with an entity who's attached herself to you." Janine giggled. "My friend, you are officially a ghosted bridge from one side to the other."

"Great," Madison repeated. "I'm ghosted. Now I guess I have no excuse. I've got to listen to her."

"I'm no expert, but I think you don't have an excuse because she's not going to give you any. It's really cool, Mads, if you think about it. This wayward soul from who knows where has chosen you to make a statement, give a message, change something. That's way freakin' cool."

All this heady, ghost-to-human communication stuff suddenly felt like too much. Madison suddenly wished for the life of a nondescript psychic doing her thing safely in an office in the middle of nowhere. More than anything, she wanted to be rid of Helen, if just for a day or two. "Good luck with the chart," she chirped. "Tell the guy there's a reason the King is the only card to carry the sword above his head. Tell him if he doesn't follow his heart, he may just cut off his own head."

"I got your message but I think I may have to temper it a bit. I am no Madison K. Morgan, Extraordinaire. I don't have the natural talent for such flare as you!"

"Yeah that's true, there can only be one in the Universe at a time! Love you, honey."

Madison hung up the phone and reluctantly took up her pen. The thought of Janine's client's chart made her take a second thought. There was an answer of some kind in the cards and numbers. Madison needed to find it.

This was going to be an arduous process, she knew. According to the cards, each year of a person's life was divided into seven fifty-two-day periods, beginning with their birthday. She would have to sift through all four clients' birthdays who had visited her that day in December to see if any of them had something monumental coming up in their chart.

Madison looked at the reading date again—December 15. Then she checked each client's birthdates from that day.

She calculated all the birthdays for the clients and was disappointed. None of the numbers seemed to call attention to any remarkable event. She felt a drop in her stomach. She'd really hoped that the perfection of the numerical formula would offer new clues. The pinpricks wrinkled her skin again and then the fleeting thought grew stronger . . . it seemed as though December 15 was a significant date, but if not for her clients, then for whom?

This was no random date, Madison realized. Everything in her psychic sensitivities screamed inside. Her antennae were now on full alert. Whatever Helen was trying to tell her, it had started on that day seven months ago. But what? What was the thing she needed to hear and who was the information for?

Madison stood up and looked out the window to Oak Creek bubbling serenely within its banks. She stared, mesmerized, and realized that her focus was going in and out like a Mexican jumping bean. Ben's words came back to her. *Get out of town. Clear your head.* She sat down and dialed Janine's number.

"Yup?" Janine's cheery voice echoed in her ear.

"Okay, this may sound crazy, but what are you doing in the next two days?"

"I don't think I'm doin' much, gotta finish this guy's chart. I see him again next week. I've got two clients tomorrow . . . um, the next day . . . let's see, wow, I've got nothing. Boy, I'd better get on the stick. I can't keep my horse in hay if I don't get more work!"

Madison imagined Janine's horse, Blue, looking forlornly from the barn with a "when am I going to eat" expression. Blue was Janine's baby. Madison knew he ate better than Coriander probably did. "Well, honey," she shot back. "I think we should clear our calendars and get out of Dodge! Waddya think?"

Madison didn't expect Janine to answer quickly. Her friend was lighthearted and easygoing but didn't like to stray from her schedule much. Janine's words surprised her.

"Cool! Let me call my neighbor to see if he can watch Blue for me. Where should we go?"

"Wow, sister, you've just taken a step to the crazy side. You up for the consequences?"

Janine's laugh tinkled through the phone.

"I think we should go to—"

"Algodones!" Both women shouted simultaneously.

"Janine, get your horse taken care of. I'm packin' up, filling up the gas tank and I'll be over in two hours." Madison suddenly felt giddy.

"Madison, I can't believe we're doing this!"

"You only live once, sister. Here we go! Mexico awaits! Now get to work!" Madison set the phone down and peered out the window. She could see a column of tourists snaking through the trails in the distance, sliding this way and that, a line of black ants on a sojourn to Snoopy Rock. The familiar sight had always impressed on her the enormity of the land and the smallness of the humans swarming it. The constant flow of souls searching and wandering the craggy redness of the town and her cliffs was time worn. People would trek here for generations, just as they had in the past. She and all the others were just grains of sand deposited in this soil. None of them were anything more or less than another link in the human chain.

But just now, Madison felt a renewed spark inside. Algodones would tell her something. Ben had said to get away. She was willing to separate from Sedona's energy to find out the unique thing that the Universe seemed determined to show her. Madison was back on the warpath.

She quickly swept up the papers from her desk and moved to switch off her computer. *It's crazy,* she thought. *That the internet dictates so many life decisions and guideposts for right and wrong directions.* The cobbled spider web of information had become a boon to the world.

She saw a new email flash onto her screen, the latest word from Gratefulness.com. Madison liked this website. Every day, a new quote would appear in her inbox, urging and reminding her to remember the keys to being grateful.

This particular quote caught her eye immediately: "When the bridge is gone, the narrowest plank becomes precious."

Madison leaned forward and stared at the screen. The words of the Hungarian proverb hung in cyberspace. She couldn't believe she was seeing the exact phrase that her grandmother Nagymama had translated in broken English so often to her when she was a little girl. Madison remembered her grandmother's kind, wrinkled face. Childhood moments of kisses and hugs and sweetly spoken words in Nagymama's strangely melodic accent surfaced from years before. She hadn't thought about her Nagy in over a decade, yet here it seemed that now her dearest departed grandmother was trying to point out a truth that Madison needed to embrace. She was indeed called to build a bridge, an avenue between the energies passed and energies living.

She tipped her chin to the ceiling, closed her eyes and asked herself a question she had never dared ask before, because the possibility had never been allowed. Could it be that through this history of childhood experiences, lifelong questions, and mystical psychic connections, that she actually was that precious narrowest plank?

CHAPTER TWENTY-SEVEN

MADISON GLANCED AT THE CLOCK and saw that it was nearly six. The sun still stood high in the sky. It had to be about ninety degrees, she figured. Her arms were full as she walked down the stairs. The light streamed in the small panes of the old wooden door. She could see dust particles floating in the air, streaming, small silvery flecks in perfect rows, as if attracted to the sunlight. Then the rows jangled and melded. There was no breeze to change their formations but they changed nonetheless. The specks rolled and danced and became a shape. Helen.

This time the ghost was harder to see. The sunlight speared through her form. If someone had walked through the door just then, they would have blown right through her. She hovered, nearly transparent. Madison felt the sudden need to sit down.

She set all the papers and her purse next to her and settled quietly. She forced herself to push Mexico out of her thoughts and let the ghost find a stream of consciousness to connect with.

Helen's presence was light, as if she hadn't enough energy to bring herself to full strength. Madison couldn't blame the poor thing. This spirit would probably take a nap a few centuries long after all this business was said and done. But for now, Helen lingered. She showed no pictures this time, so Madison closed her eyes and felt.

It was a strange thing, this medium's business. She had certificates of study in mediumship from the Walter Wilken International Academy of Mediumship and Hilbert University, she'd learned all the ins and outs of increasing sensitivity, creating a personal language that spirits could use to communicate, deepening her listening skills. All of these tools were invaluable, but the strongest, most foundational connection was in her core. She'd had it since she was a little girl. Her mother had always been so derisive of Madison's desire to explore it more. Madison remembered being called a cocktail party trick pony once when she'd tried to explain to her parents' friends what this was all about, offering short readings to prove her gift. Throughout her life, the strange connection to another place beyond reality felt flawlessly normal to Madison. So as she sat quietly on the stairs, allowing herself to slip into a meditative place, she realized she felt perfect here. This was right. With a strange whisper around her head, Helen began to speak.

They weren't spoken words. This time they weren't visceral pictures, either. They were feelings. Feelings so strong, it seemed Madison was generating them herself. First, she noticed a soft ache in her belly. It was a wound that Helen had carried around for so long that it lived inside of her, like a tumor. This awareness of discomfort settled within Madison's center. Was it an illness, a disease? Was it desperation or grief? Madison waited for discernment.

Next, her chest tightened and the back of her neck grew hot. Her cheeks flushed and her pulse increased in such a tiny increment that it seemed to flutter up and down rather than rise steadily. This was a feeling of dread. This was a realization that something very bad had happened and now the heaviness of that experience would settle upon a person and hold them captive.

It reminded Madison of when she had been a teenager and she and her brothers had secretly taken two motorcycles from her uncle's garage. They had rolled them down the quiet street in the middle of one long-ago New Jersey summer night. When the three of them had slipped out of earshot, her older brother had gotten on one bike, and she and her younger brother had clambered onto the other. None of them had ever driven a motorcycle before. As they turned on the machines and careened down the street, they'd made it only a block before smashing into each other. There they had lain in the moonlight, a shocked, shivering huddle of scrapes and confusion. The motorcycles had massive damage and could barely be pushed home. As Madison and her brothers realized the scale of what they had done, she'd felt the deepest punch inside her gut. Her brothers, too, had felt it. They had struggled wordlessly home with the broken bikes, to be found out the next day and appropriately disciplined. But the getting in trouble wasn't what they all remembered. The potential disaster of the moment had scared their wits away. Madison had never looked at a motorcycle the same way again.

She sighed softly, and intuitively tied this feeling with the scenes she'd witnessed in the movie theater. Perhaps, no, most probably, this was how Helen had felt when she'd been sent packing in shame from Louis Park's mansion. That would explain the first feeling, the realization that life would never be the same. Madison suddenly felt a huge empathy for Helen. Granted, the woman had clearly created her own problems by her dalliances with the grandson, what was his name, Jerome? But the lifelong ramifications of that seemed insufferable.

Then, Madison had a mental image of the little boy in the tree house. John had been Sam's little brother. That night in the kitchen the terrible scene between Helen and her husband had ended with the little boy hearing the word "bastard."

No doubt John was the illegitimate child of Jerome Park. Madison was rewarded with a sense of completion. Helen's nodding head appeared in her mind's eye. This was correct. Madison knew it.

But what did all this mean? She held a question mark in her mind and invited Helen's energy into it. A swell of unease crept into Madison's consciousness. She tingled with a sense of despair and resignation. She could tell they were imbedded into Helen's soul. But there was something more. A second wave of anxiety and sadness surrounded her. It wasn't all emanating from Helen's energy. This new feeling was attached to her son. John's face took shape in Madison's mind. She held herself still to read the temperature of this energy and sank into the exploration of what caused this unrest in Helen's son. She invited all the images Helen had shown before to re-introduce themselves. She saw the photos in the album of two little boys, no father around. She recalled the summer afternoon discussion in that perfect tree house hideaway about a dead grandfather who had never visited his grandchildren.

Then without warning, she stood in John and Sam's room. The two boys huddled at the closed door listening to their parents' raised voices.

"Please, Cecil, honey, please!"

"Dammit, can't you see, I just can't take it anymore." A slam of a suitcase punctuated his words. "How do you think it feels to walk around this town, knowing everybody is talkin' behind your back? They all know my business. I'm not going to do it anymore."

"Honey, tell me what to do and I'll do it. I'll do whatever you ask." Helen's voice cracked with tears.

"It's too late. You already did it. We, no, *you* can't change it. What's done is done." Cecil's voice sounded weary. "It can't be changed."

"I'm going in there," John whispered to Sam.

"Are you crazy? He's on a rampage. That's the worst thing you could ever do."

"No it's not, Sam . . . Being born was."

Sam silently stared at his little brother. Madison watched his face carefully. She sank deeper into the boys' thoughts. Sam surveyed John's grim set mouth. He looked deeply into his brother's light blue eyes and noticed how white-blonde John's hair was. He really didn't look like Sam (or their father, for that matter) at all. Sam felt awkward and selfish as he realized that he had never paid much attention to his father's criticisms of John. Sam had lived in his own world. He also realized something else, that his brother was growing up before his eyes and there was no way Sam could stop him from this painful step.

From her vantage point in the hallway, halfway between the boys' and their parents' rooms, Madison could see the staircase where a younger John had understood for the first time what he really was. She recalled how he had destroyed his father's birthday present. She could still remember the sound of the lures clinking onto the ground in the alley below. It reminded her of the chinks of ice in a heavy liquor glass, a sound that these boys had grown up with. It also reminded her of the tears that John had so mournfully shed in the midst of that disastrous night.

Madison noticed Sam wanted to say something, anything to stop John but his younger brother brushed past him brusquely. Madison followed invisibly behind him to his parents' room.

John walked in to find his father's clothes strewn about the bed. One suitcase was filled and he was angrily stuffing more into another. John stood beneath the doorframe and watched.

"Cecil," Helen grabbed her husband's arm to stop him from throwing more into the suitcase. He angrily pulled his arm away and turned to face her when he saw John.

"Ah, the source arrives," he snarled nastily. John could smell the whiskey on his breath.

"John, get back in your room, now!" screeched Helen. Madison focused on her for just a moment. Her brunette curls were now laced with gray. Her skin, which had been so flawless when she'd worked at the mansion all those years ago, was lined with deep wrinkles of worry and frowns. Her eyes seemed more deeply set, the gray-blue irises surrounded by bloodshot whites.

"No, Mom. I won't." John said calmly. "I'm tired of hearing you guys fight all the time."

"Oh you are, are you?" Cecil glared at the boy. "I'm tired too, John. I'm tired of being the laughing stock of this town. I'm not gonna stick around and keep this charade up."

"What charade is that, Dad? The fact that I'm not your son or the fact that you pretend you aren't a drunk?"

Madison stood in the hallway, both shocked and proud. "Go get him, kid. He's the real bastard in this house," she whispered.

Helen gasped. Cecil shoved her out of the way and lunged toward John. He was within an inch of John's face when suddenly Sam was there, inserting himself between his father and his brother. Sam was the biggest of the three. Years of sports had given him a strong frame, well-muscled and lean. He was more than a match for Cecil or John.

Cecil took a half step back hesitantly. He bobbled a bit and wiped a large fleck of spit from his mouth with his sleeve. "You know, Sammy, I respect you for this," he slurred lovingly to his older son. "I probably wouldn't have had the guts to stand up to my old man, especially for someone like this," he spit as he said the words into John's face. "As for you, I want you to hear me and never forget this. I despise you, kid. You were never mine. I guess I knew it from the very beginning. And now, I don't have to see your face ever again."

Cecil turned toward Helen huddled on the bed. "I'm outta here. I'll tell my brother to come get my stuff tomorrow. I can't," he said turning back to John with a scowl so black it made Madison's chest ache, "stand the stench in here."

He stumbled by John, jabbing him in the ribs as he passed. Sam reached out to stop him but John stayed him with a firm hand on his shoulder. "Let him go, Sam." He looked deeply into his brother's eyes. "I want you to know, I am so sorry that I fucked up your life. If it hadn't have been for me, everything would have been so different, so much better."

"John, you know you will always be my brother. I'm here for you no matter what anyone says." Sam put his hand on John's shoulder and Madison felt tears stinging at her eyes.

John looked down at his mother sobbing on the bed and gave a big sigh. "It's okay, Mom. It's okay," he nodded at Sam and the brothers cleared all the clothes and suitcases off the bed. They pulled back the covers and gently eased Helen under the sheets as she moaned and shook. Sam leaned over to give her a kiss and she obliged blindly by turning her cheek to him. John leaned forward too, and moved to kiss his mother. This time, she turned her face toward him. "Please forget all this," she said in a slurred whisper.

"Sure, Mom. Don't worry." He kissed her quickly on the lips and tasted the vestiges of four or five glasses of wine. He smoothed her hair and backed away.

Sam turned the light off and closed the door quietly.

Madison was still hovering above and behind the boys. She watched them move back toward their room wordlessly. She wanted to reach out and comfort these two bruised souls. She wanted to reach out and strangle Cecil. She wanted to reach out and slap Helen.

Then, in a split second, she found herself sitting on the darkened stairs. The emotional tidal wave seeped away. It left her with a question. These momentous events would absolutely have a negative affect on a child's psyche. But how much? How much would Helen's son have taken with him into adulthood? She remembered the wake in the small house on the lake. Sam, the elder son, had been much more distressed by his mother's death. John had looked strangely disconnected.

Once again, Madison was filled with a firm feeling of affirmation. Her unconscious mind was getting the right picture. Madison felt like she was the lens of a camera that was recording all the information in a safe place deep inside herself. Here was an amazing connection from Madison's individual energy to the universal force that Helen had tapped into. They had reached across the spiritual divide and folded into one.

THE DOOR SLAMMED below her and pulled Madison back into the current moment. She squinted as the light flowed into the narrow hallway and partway up the staircase to just below her feet. William's loud voice jarred her.

"Well, there you are! The group's been wondering what happened to you."

"Group?" Madison blinked at William, still psychically hanging, not quite both feet back into the present.

William instantly sensed this. "You okay, love?"

"Yeah, yes, of course." Madison shook her head. Her words were slow and stumbled, as if she'd just woken from a heavy nap. "Just had the most incredible incorporeal experience, William!"

"Oh, the ghost again? Still?"

"Yeah, but this time it was really over the top. I haven't had this much connection since I was back at school!"

"Fantastic, love. Look," William leaned closer to Madison still huddled on the stairs. "Are you up for coming to the meeting tonight? Or would it be too much?" He touched her arm gently and a tingle ran through her. *Knock it off,* she scolded herself. *There's no time for this silliness.*

Then she realized what William was referring to. Madison had forgotten the Thursday psychic training group. What had she been thinking? She was supposed to be downstairs leading this seminar and she'd set Janine into a gallop to bolt to Mexico!

"Damn."

William leaned toward her. "You okay?" He arched an eyebrow. "You look a bit, well, green."

"You wouldn't believe how green I feel, William." Madison took a shaky breath.

"Wow, bad images? Violent?"

"No," Madison shook her head. "Not violent, just intense. Here," she offered her hand to William. "Help me up."

"You are sure you can stand up?" William looked doubtful. "I don't want to present you, love, as a sack of potatoes on the doorstep!"

"No," she grasped his firm, clutching hand. "I'm really fine. I just really spaced out and made other plans." She looked at him. "What the hell was I doing, William?"

"Clearly losing your mind, sweetheart." William smiled at her. "I'd cover for you but I've got an in-home reading in twenty out on Distant Drums Road . . ." He offered her an apologetic shrug. "Want me to tell Miriam to cancel the gals?"

"Naw. I'll just call Janine right now." She stepped gingerly down the stairs. "Actually, I feel a lot better than I have in a few days."

"You sure? Like I said, you look—"

"Beautiful!" She broke in laughing. "Right? Beautiful, together, psychically prepared to save the day?"

"Right, that's it! You are the picture of cosmic control!"

She reached up and pulled his chin down so she could plant a kiss on his cheek. "You always know how to put me right, William."

"Good! A renewed psychic is a happy psychic, I always say."

Madison suddenly felt so much lighter, and so chatty. "I've got all this energy now, William. It's like she redirected me." She bubbled as he led her out the door and toward the main entrance of the center. "Actually, I'm not *re*directed I'm *pre*directed!" Madison laughed at her own cosmic joke. "Get it William? I'm pre-directed? Like I'm seeing what already . . ."

William guided Madison underneath his arm, holding the door open. "I get it, Mads, my girl. Now you get in here!"

"One sec." She dug through her purse and found her cell phone. Janine answered gaily.

"All right, already! I'm working on it! God, you're a slave driver, Madison!"

Madison's voice slid into her trademark growl, "I don't want to stress you out, let's give you another hour and a half. Will you be ready then?"

Janine's sigh of relief fluttered through the phone. "Madison, you're the greatest. I promise I'll be ready. Around ten, then?"

"Ten it will be, my little traveling bandit." She slid the cell phone cover shut and plopped it into her purse. "Now," she said to William brightly.

Madison slid gracefully into the room full of women awaiting her arrival. "Hello, chickadees! Momma's back!" She brushed through the hallway lined with posters and incense sticks, waving her hands cheerily as she steered the women into the book room. Just before she turned the corner, she looked back at her handsome friend. He gave her a wave and went out the door into the warm Sedona evening.

"Ladies," Madison exulted to her tiny pack of spiritual seekers. "We are going to have some fun tonight!"

CHAPTER TWENTY-EIGHT

KATHERINE STOOD ON the court watching Barb drill the girls on volleys. It made her cringe to watch the majority of these kids barely move their feet and aimlessly stab their rackets at the balls. When were they going to get it?

Barb finished the cart of balls and sent the teenagers on a cardio ball pick-up drill. The teens scrambled all over the court, picking up one ball at a time, dropping them into the cart, and then trotting for more.

Barb walked over. "Hey, you feeling okay? You look beat."

"Yeah, I'm fine."

"How's all the treatment going?"

"It's okay." Katherine leaned against the net post and watched the girls' quasi-sprinting. "I've only got ten days left."

"Wow, it sure has gone fast. Does it seem that way to you?"

"Kind of. It seems partly like it's been so long, but I can't believe almost six weeks has already gone by."

"Well, you're at the tail end now."

"Yeah, thank goodness. They tell me the fatigue will catch up when the treatments are done."

"Listen, if you need me to cover for you, just let me know."

Katherine smiled gratefully at her friend. "Thanks, girl, I will."

Katherine's cell phone rang. She looked at the caller. The screen said WAYNE. "Hi, sweetheart."

"Hey, Mom."

"What's up?"

"Wes and I were talking just now and we want to do something really fun on your last treatment day."

Katherine's face immediately grew a smile. "Oh, sweetie. That sounds wonderful!"

"Great," Wayne's voice sounded so positive. "So, that last date is . . ."

"August 1."

"Okay, August 1 it is! We'll both come with you to the hospital and then will go out for a bite to eat. Sound good?"

"Sounds fantastic!" Katherine suddenly felt a little charge of energy run through her. Thank God for her kids!

"I'll talk to Dad and let him know what we're planning."

"Thanks. Now I have something to look forward to!"

"We're gonna make it a great day for you, Mom. Oops, it's almost three. Gotta run. I'm supposed to be at the club in fifteen minutes. Who's going with you today?"

"Gina," answered Katherine. "That reminds me, I've got to get out of practice early so I can pick her up." Katherine looked at Barb questioningly and Barb nodded back.

"Okay, Mom." Wayne's breathing sounded a bit labored as he galloped up the stairs, no doubt looking for a clean work shirt. Katherine smiled, "Your shirt's hanging up in the laundry room."

"Wow, Mom, you rock. Thanks!" He hung up quickly.

Katherine turned toward Barb who was organizing a new drill for the girls.

"All right gals, we're moving on. Rotate one court to your left. Those on the far side will feed a short ball. You guys on this side hit an approach shot, and finish with a volley. Everybody get it?"

The girls nodded and shuffled to their new courts. Barb looked at her watch. "When do you need to go?"

"Forty-five minutes?"

"No problem. You take the top four courts, I'll take the bottom." Barb moved away, barking out instructions. Katherine walked in the opposite direction, thankful for the umpteenth time that she had these days on the court and this friend. "Let's go, ladies!" She yelled. "We don't have all day!" The girls trotted onto their courts underneath the blistering Minnesota summer sun. Even the heat wouldn't get to her today, Katherine thought. The idea of Wayne and Wes celebrating her last day made her feel almost giddy. Ten days wasn't very long to wait. Ten days and it would all be over.

NINETY MINUTES LATER, Katherine and Gina were sitting in traffic on the steamy 35W bridge. Construction workers surrounded them, having overtaken four of the eight lanes.

"Wow, Kath," Gina looked worriedly at the clock on the dashboard. "Hope we're not going to be late."

"I know," Katherine stretched and looked over the railing at the fast-rushing Mississippi below. "Seems like this traffic is getting worse and worse."

"They've been doing this just about since you started your treatment. How long does it take to resurface a bridge?

"Yeah, that's kind of funny, isn't it? Me and the bridge getting some serious work done to our anatomies all summer long!"

Well, I just hope all this work and equipment doesn't overload it," worried Gina. "You think it could?"

"Naw. These trusses and girders and whatever else they've got holding this thing up have gotta be in good shape, otherwise they'd close it, right?"

"Yeah," Gina sounded unconvinced. "Guess so."

Katherine laughed. "C'mon! Aren't you always telling me to focus on the positive? Well you might not believe it, but I finally think I'm learning to do just that. Can you believe it? Here I am sitting in boiling hot traffic on a crowded bridge, waiting to go get my cancer treatment and I actually feel good!" She felt strangely light today. The knowledge of only ten days left of this whole process was liberating.

"Well, Kath," Gina smiled back at her. "I sure am proud of you. You've come such a long way. Well done."

"Couldn't have done it without you," Katherine said quietly. Gina nodded wordlessly, tears forming in her eyes.

Finally, after ten minutes of waiting, the line of cars snaked off the bridge and onto University Avenue. Katherine and Gina quickly pulled into their reserved parking spot at the hospital.

"Absolute best thing about this whole situation."

"You gotta keep this parking pass," whispered Gina.

"I know!" Katherine got out of the car and shut the door. "Too bad it doesn't work everywhere!" She put her arm around her friend. "You have been such a good support through all of this, Gina-girl. I'll never be able to thank you enough."

Gina smiled back. They both were thinking of the many days in the past six weeks where they had walked in these doors to the radiation clinic together. From the very start, Gina had set the tone that Katherine had been holding onto. "Kath," she had said firmly on the first day. "You may be walking in a cancer patient but you will walk out an athlete." And so, for nearly every day of her treatment, Katherine and Gina had walked out of the hospital and driven to one of the beautiful lakes in Minneapolis where they would run around them, shedding the smell and sounds of the oncology unit.

"You have done such an incredible job, Kath." Gina stopped and gave Katherine a big hug. "You're almost to the finish line. I'm so proud of you."

"Yup, well, let's get this one out of the way!" Katherine grabbed Gina's hand and together they marched into the cool waiting room.

CHAPTER TWENTY-NINE

MADISON WAS IN a mad rush. She was a whirlwind of energy and excitement. She threw her purse and papers onto the dining room table and had to nearly hop over Coriander, who was meowing his most excellent yowl. She strode into the kitchen and opened his can of cat food. He rewarded her with a triumphant tail switch as she set it down for him. His delicate slurps and purrs sounded heavenly to Madison. She made herself a quick sandwich and headed back to the dining room, humming. With the notes she'd brought from the office, she'd at least have something to start with. Plus, she'd have her own private detective in Janine, who loved digging for information.

As she packed her overnight bag, Madison felt more and more optimistic that all the blanks would be filled in. She made a quick phone call to her neighbor, Shawn, and made sure he would take care of Coriander. Once that detail was taken care of, she phoned Janine.

"Well?"

"I'm ready, boss!" Janine squawked. "Come and get me!"

"On my way, my little Mexican jumping bean!" She walked into the kitchen to give the huge yellow cat one last goodbye kiss. He lay in his bed, belly up, with one eye halfway open, although it was clear he was sound asleep. Madison dropped to one knee and gave him a gentle rub under his chin. Coriander twisted his head around to look at her sleepily. He yawned and gave Madison a whiff of tuna breath.

"Thanks, buddy." Madison patted his soft, white tummy. "I'll take that with me as a gift from you! Maybe I'll pick you up some Mexican tuna!"

She stood up, picked up her bag and her briefcase filled to the brim with scraps and pencils and pads, and turned out the light.

She sped to Janine's house to pick up her friend.

"All ready?" Madison said to her friend as she loaded her things into the car.

"Yup! Can't wait!"

"Very well, then. Off we go to fabulous Algodones!" Madison revved the engine and began humming Mariachi music.

The car glided across the darkened desert. Inside, Madison was lost in her thoughts of Helen and all the bits and pieces that needed to be cobbled together. Janine sat beside her, slumped against the passenger door, snoring softly.

Madison went back to the questions that constantly knocked about her brain. *Who is Helen? Why do I need to know? What did Helen's son have to do with the whole mystery?*

The jangle of her cell phone ringing jolted Madison. She glanced at the clock on the dash. 11:45 p.m. Who would be calling at this time of night? She quickly pushed the send button to stop the ringing. Beside her, Janine stirred only slightly.

"Hello?"

"Hello, my dear Madison! Ben Masselink here!" Ben's eternally cheery voice echoed in her ear. "Didn't mean to wake you."

"Hey, Ben! No problem. I'm actually on the road right now. I took your advice. My friend and I are on our way to Mexico!"

"Wow, for the margaritas, I assume? Not running from the law, are we?"

Madison had to keep the volume down. She glanced at Janine, and then whispered into the phone. "Yes to the Margs, no to the law! I feel like this is going to be great. We get to escape from all the crazy Sedona energy and put all the pieces together."

"Well, my dear, that is why I called."

"Yeah? What's up?"

"I have to admit, I was so taken by our last phone call that I got to talking with one of my grad students about this. He's fascinated, as well. Would you mind us doing a little bit of research for you?"

"Would I mind?" Madison couldn't keep the volume low any longer. "That's fantastic, Ben!"

Ben giggled back. "Glad you said yes because I actually took the liberty of—"

"Whatever you did, I'm thrilled about. Give up the goods!"

"Well, we are in the beginning stages but I have a question."

"Shoot, partner."

"Do you know the actual spelling of this woman's name?"

Madison sat back and searched her memory. "Gosh, I don't know, Ben. I mean, I think its spelled H-e-l-e-n R-h-a-m-e-s. That's what I see in my head."

"Okay," Ben's voice was encouraging. "We've been using that spelling but didn't get anything. Why don't we try some variations and see what we find?"

"Fine by me," Madison answered. "Where are you looking?"

Ben's voice raised an octave in excitement. "We are trying a number of obit sites. The university has access to quite a few channels. We'll play with it and let you know."

"That's so fantastic, Ben. It would be awesome if we found out who this woman actually was. Then don't you think all this information will make sense?"

"Well, we can only hope so. We'll try some old-fashioned detective work on our end. You use all your fantastic gifts on your end. You never know, maybe the margaritas will be the answer to all this!"

"For the sake of this dear, departed woman and all the other ghosts contemplating using me as their astral travel agent, I will attack my duty with true professionalism!"

"Great, kiddo. Have a wonderful time and we'll be in touch!"

It came to her in a flash. Madison didn't know what brought it to the forefront of her brain, but there it was. "Ben? Ben? You still there?"

"What's that, Madison? Did I miss something?"

"No, I did. I just remembered something weird. A few weeks ago, I did a reading with this really awful woman. She was definitely running for bitch of the year." Ben listened silently and Madison felt instantly embarrassed. "Sorry, shouldn't have said all that, bitch or not."

"You're right," he said. "Negativity never clears the water or the air. Just focus on her value. What is it? Why did you think of her?"

"Because I was taking down her vitals and when she told me her address, it was in Winona, Minnesota. I got a shock right then and all of a sudden, I felt Helen behind this bit . . . this woman. Maybe she was giving me affirmation. Could it be for Winona?"

"Hmm, could be. I'll add it to our criteria and see what we get."

"Thanks, Ben. You're the best."

"Ah, one soul assists another. It's all we have to give to the ones we care about. Have fun and I'll ring you when we have something."

Madison set the phone down and glanced at Janine. She was now twisted into a ball, curled against the door. Madison glanced down to make sure the doors were all locked. "All I need, Janine, is for you to take a tumble." Madison whispered to her sleeping friend.

"What?" Janine mumbled sleepily.

"Nothing, honey bunch. Go back to sleep."

"Um, okay. 'Night."

"'Nighty-night, cupcake." Madison rolled her shoulders back and shrugged off the fatigue. This trip was going to be fantastic. Just what she needed. She wondered if Helen would follow her to Mexico. *Maybe I should keep my eyes open for hitch hiking ghosts,* she thought. She looked down at her cell phone and noticed the date, July 27. Man, summer was half over! Where had it gone?

Madison steered the car onto the I-8 West. The landscape looked barren and vast. Above her millions of stars twinkled and kept watch over the car barreling along the freeway. One hundred and twenty miles away, Los Algodones waited.

CHAPTER THIRTY

Hey, Mom."

Katherine stretched and opened her eyes. Wayne plopped onto the bed next to her. He grinned and leaned over to give her a kiss

"Hey, honey," she said sleepily. "What's up?"

"I don't know. Nothing much. I don't have to be at work 'til five. So I can't come with you today." Wayne cast her a worried look.

"No problem, sweetie. Gina is going to come with me again. Then we'll go run Lake of the Isles."

"You are amazing, Mom," Wayne looked admiringly at his mother. "You know, you could take a break."

"Why would I want to do that? We're almost at the finish line."

"Yeah," Wayne lay on his back and stared at the ceiling. "How's it going to be when you are done? Do you think you'll get back to life as normal?"

Katherine sat quietly for a moment. This was time she didn't want to waste, but was she prepared to do the moment honor?

"I don't know," she sighed, praying for the perfect words to follow. "I don't think 'normal' will ever be the same."

"That's true." Wayne said quietly.

"Something up, honey?" Katherine propped herself onto one elbow and eyed her youngest son.

"I don't know. It's just that life is so different now. I mean a couple of years ago, we were just moving along and everything happened the way it was supposed to, I guess the way we expected it to.

"Now, it's like everything is upside down. My bearings are all screwed up. I thought when I got to college, life would be so fantastic and it is, don't get me wrong, but . . ."

Katherine brushed Wayne's forehead with her fingertips. He scrunched his face at the familiar tickle. "It's just what?" She asked.

"It's just now I feel like everything is just one step away from disappearing. Dad and his job, you and your cancer, selling the house . . ."

Katherine immediately pushed the mommy-mode button. "You know, honey, life goes in stages. We've had some fantastic moments and we've had some tough ones. One thing is for sure: life will never stay the same. We really are lucky. We are all healthy . . ." Katherine heard the words coming out of her mouth and started to laugh.

"What, Mom?"

"Oh my God! Those words are so ridiculous! How crazy is it that I didn't take into account that I actually have cancer! Isn't that funny? I mean that is really hysterical!" Katherine sputtered the words in staccato.

"I'm telling you to relax and go with life because everything is okay. We are really lucky and we are all healthy and by the way, I'm forgetting one tiny fact! I have cancer! How ironic is that?" Katherine roared. "Really, it's . . . okay! Don't worry, we've got our health! Are you kidding me? I am the antithesis of health! I've got frickin' cancer! How bad can it be?"

Despite himself, Wayne started laughing. "Oh my God, Mom, that is so sick. That is so funny! I didn't even pick up on it. We're so used to saying that stuff so often. We don't even know what's coming out of our mouths."

Their laughter released the months of frustration, silence, worry, and anger. Katherine and Wayne were rolling on the bed in hysterics, trying to catch their breath, when Wes walked in.

"Hey, what's going on?"

"Oh, honey," Katherine could barely get the words out. "Don't you know everything is going to be fine?"

"What?" Wes shook his head and looked confusedly from his mother to his brother. "What are you talking about?"

"I mean, we really have nothing to worry about with all this stuff going on . . ."

"Yeah, because," Wayne wiped his eyes and searched for a breath. "We at least have our health!" He burst out laughing again.

Wes rolled his eyes. "Of course we've got our health. Of course everything is going to be all right."

"Except for the cancer," Wayne giggled.

"Yeah, that small wrinkle," Katherine added.

"C'mon, Mom. Everybody knows this cancer thing is done. You're almost finished with treatment. They got most of it out with the surgery. You're fine. This doesn't count. Although," Wes shook his head and smiled at his mother and brother. "It does sound kind of funny to say everything's hunky dory, but p.s., you've got to go to the hospital in a couple of hours to get radiated!"

In a moment, all three were laughing uncontrollably. Maybe the joke wasn't good enough for the casual observer but for these three souls, the moment was perfect. They were celebrating and rebelling and pitching their best fits against the circumstances that held them hostage for months.

"Bring it on, you fucking cancer!" Wayne yelled.

"Bring it on, world!" His ever-so-conservative brother barked in relief.

"Bring it on!" Katherine screamed at the top of her lungs. She wanted this moment to be forever planted into her brain. She let herself enjoy all of it. For just this tiny space in time now was perfect—nothing else stood in the way of her complete happiness— no past anxieties and no worry about what would be. Now, in this space, she was a mom with her babies.

Both boys rolled in a puppy fight, laughing so hard, tears ran down their faces. Right here, right now on this big bed, she and her two boys were just enjoying life. They were taking in the oddity and irony of reality. Today was a good day, for all of them, at the same time.

CHAPTER
THIRTY-ONE

MADISON ROLLED OVER in the tiny bed and pressed her eyelids shut. It was never a good thing to wake up too early in the morning, wherever one found one's self. And even though she realized in the far reaches of her consciousness that she was in a good place, the magic of Algodones was not enough to wake her in a sufficiently happy mood. It was far too early for that. Maybe she could still lull her mind into an hour or so of quiet.

She had almost talked herself into the loveliest, quietest, calmest place when the image broke into her brain like a plane crashing on her front lawn.

The visions assaulted her. Cars, dozens of them, catapulted all around her. Madison's neck tensed as she felt the sheer stress of twisting her head back and forth to catch the heart-rending scene of cars and people launching into the air, above, around, below her . . .

The psychic suddenly had no bearing of where she was. She felt as though she were a startled fish, trapped with no warning and struggling in the midst of a huge undersea net. She tried to get her bearings, up and down, side-to-side, but the only thing visible through her darting eyes were strobes of white, silver, blue . . . colors flashing past and through her brain so fast that she couldn't distinguish the hues.

Madison recoiled, yet was transfixed by a wave of streaming energies. Emotions of fear, hysteria, dread, terror flashed as if electrical flashes in a heavily humid summer storm. And everywhere she sensed the people and automobiles plunging around and above her. They rolled sideways next to her; they dropped underneath her, huge capsules of rubber, plastic, leather, glass and steel. They twisted and flexed and exposed their startled, panicked passengers. Madison could hear and feel the groan of collapsing metal and the thunderclap cracking of cement exploding. She had a sharp feeling of being dropped suddenly, as if she were in a free-falling elevator.

And then, the room and her head were quiet. Madison sat up abruptly and looked around. A simple chintz curtain swayed in the desert breeze. A single fly buzzed aimlessly about the window-pane. Outside her hotel window, vendors and tourists began to fill the street. The noises of a yet-to-be busy avenue were still muted in low voices and the gentle bumps of merchants setting up their stands in the hazy morning sun. But Madison couldn't connect to those sounds. She sat in horrified paralysis, overtaken by the magnitude of this catastrophic disaster. The echoes of the shocking vibrations still reverberated inside of her.

She tried to wipe away the visions by rubbing her hands across her eyes. She rolled her palms over and over along her face, massaging along her temples and across her jaws. She tickled her cheekbones with her fingertips to try to relieve the pressure that had built underneath her eye sockets, around her cheeks. The ministrations slowed her heart rate a tiny tick. Her fingers pressed deeply into the muscles stretched under her scalp. Madison drew in a deep breath of warm Mexican air. The images that had assaulted her brain settled quietly into the background, almost as if they hadn't overcome her in the first place. She stretched out on the narrow bed and closed her eyes.

When she blinked them open again, Helen stood shimmering before her, caught in the light streaming through the window like a lightening bug in a jar.

The ghost gestured to Madison. She stood wringing her hands. Her long, bony fingers writhed around each other in a figure eight motion, as if she was washing her hands under a stream of water. Madison couldn't see Helen's face but she could feel the spirit's energy. It leapt out of the space she inhabited and covered the room. This was a different type of visit than Helen had ever projected before. She was not opening Madison up to past experiences. She was somehow trying to communicate a real-time message.

This visit played differently to Madison. Helen was not reliving a past moment. She was not bringing Madison to a long ago place this time. She seemed to be pointing forward to the future. Madison felt a huge stab of warning in her chest. Something terrible was going to happen. Helen could somehow see that and she wanted Madison to see it, too. The violent images crowded at the back of Madison's brain like a swarm of people waiting to board a train. She felt overwhelmed and told herself to be careful. It wasn't unusual, she knew, at times of heightened consciousness to pick up numerous messages from many sources. It was like her antennae were super-charged and open to all signals.

Madison stared at Helen and tried to get a firmer reading. Something definitely was wrong. Madison asked quickly, *has this event already happened?* The ghost shook her head. Helen's hands rose to her face as if she was seeing something terrible. She brushed her fists against her chest and then held her open palms to Madison.

A knock at the door nearly jerked Madison out of the bed. Outside she could hear Janine's muffled voice singing some sort of wake-up song in Spanish. Madison looked back quickly to the window but all that was left in its space was a sprinkle of sunshine through the wafting curtain.

"Mads?" Janine's voice sounded so light. "Madison, honey. Time to start our day! *Buenos tardes!*"

Madison shuffled to the door quickly. She opened it and grabbed Janine's hand, roughly pulling her friend into the room. She quickly shut the door and stared into Janine's face.

"Oh, shit," said Janine.

"No shit," said Madison.

"What?" Janine sat down on the bed with a thump.

"I'm not kidding you, Janine. I just had the fucking scariest experience. Somethin' bad is going to happen." Madison leaned toward her friend and grabbed her shoulders.

"What . . . ?"

Madison couldn't control the words. How did one explain what she had just experienced? "It was crazy. I saw shapes and colors everywhere around me. They were flying all around my head. But they weren't just colors, Janine. They were cars."

Janine stared, confused.

"There were cars, just everywhere—flipping and flying and dropping. I don't know where the hell this is but it's like a huge disaster—maybe an earthquake or something. Then Helen comes in and—"

"Wait, wait!" Janine waved her hands frantically. "I can't keep up. You mean Helen was there or here or wherever, in a car? What was she doing?"

"No, she wasn't in a car. She came at me after I saw the cars." Madison shook her head. "Jesus," she groaned. "I sound like a flippin' nut job. I'm out of it. Ooohhh," she plopped on the bed next to Janine and set her face in her hands. "Ooohh," she wailed again. "I'm a complete nut and this ghost is driving me crazy and now I've got this to worry about!"

Janine put her arm protectively over her friend's shoulder. "Don't worry, honey. It's okay." She gently held on to Madison as her friend rocked back and forth.

"Ooh," Madison was overcome. "I thought I was gonna get some clarity! I don't know if all this is one big message or I've got dueling energies chasing me." Madison really looked on the verge of hysteria and Janine had to do her best not to freak out right along with her.

"It's okay, honey." Janine crooned. "We'll figure this out."

"J, what if something terrible is going to happen?"

"Well, Mads, you can only do what you can do. I mean, if they or she or whoever is going to lay this type of information on you, then they have to give you more than just a dream or whatever it was."

"It wasn't a dream. I was awake. It was like somebody came in, jammed virtual reality glasses onto my head and turned a switch on!" Madison continued rocking. "Why the hell is this happening to me?"

Janine was an intuitive soul but she had no answer for Madison. She grabbed Madison's hand, and forced her to throw some shorts on and find her sandals. All the while she nodded and cooed at Madison's babbled rant.

Janine managed to get Madison down the stairs and away from the hotel. They wandered along the street, picking their way through the rapidly expanding crowd of vendors. Madison was quiet now. She seemed shell-shocked as she walked amongst the tables and booths filled with colorful blankets, colorful pottery, sage sticks, bumper stickers, gemstones and quickly settling dust.

Janine grabbed her hand. "C'mon, honey. I think you need a drink."

Madison looked up at her friend, "What? It's only . . . well actually, what time is it?"

Janine glanced at her watch. "Well it may only be ten here, but it's noon somewhere." She took off down the street, leading Madison like a protective mother elephant latched onto her off-spring with a tight trunk. Madison followed obediently.

IT TOOK TWO DRINKS (actually three, if one threw in the beer chaser behind the Bloody Marys) to calm Madison down. Madison remarked on the irony of the situation that alcohol could actually clear one's head. The truth was, she felt much better sitting on the sun-dappled patio with a cool drink in her hand and a plate of nachos on the table.

"This is so crazy," Madison said at last after a long sip and a munch of crisp celery.

"I'm telling you one thing, Mads," Janine smacked her lips after licking a string of celery salt off of the glass. "We should be taking notes about all of this because one day, this is going to be an amazing book!"

Madison laughed and tipped her head back, happy to be free for the moment of ghosts and visions. "I'm serious, though. I can't keep going through this. Can you imagine how loony I'll be if I keep havin' to endure all this stuff?" Madison shook her head and asked Janine for what felt like the thousandth time. "Why me?"

"I don't know, honey. I guess, why *not* you?" She waggled her finger in Madison's face. "You must be the one person who they need to use. Although," Janine sat back and pondered the Christmas lights strewn haphazardly above them. "Maybe we should check in and see if anyone else at home has gotten a message anything like this. Could we call William?"

"Great idea!" Madison nearly leapt out of the chair and sent a particularly loaded nacho chip spinning on the plastic red tablecloth. "I'll call William. He is so psychic, you know." Madison's voice rumbled as the Bloody Mary and beer trickled into her system.

"And cute, too!" Janine raised her hand and in an instant, their waiter, Paulo, was at her side.

"Another, *Señorita* Janine?" He leaned close to the women and gave them an inviting smile. Paulo was well acquainted with his two favorite customers. He loved them because they always tipped well when they came, and almost better yet, brought intriguing stories of the world beyond.

The two women adored Paulo because he was undeniably handsome. He had light chocolate skin and deep brown eyes. His perfect white smile glistened beneath high cheekbones. His dark, shiny hair was wrapped neatly in a ponytail. Best of all, he was absolutely ripped. His other job was as a cowboy for the local fairs in the area. His body was tight and athletic, and every time Madison saw him, she enjoyed his presence in more ways than one.

"Oh, Paulo, how generous of you!" Janine smirked at Madison who wriggled her eyebrows back. "I'd, I mean *we'd* love another!"

Paulo nodded cheerfully and cleared off the empty glasses. "It is so nice to see my beautiful American friends. It has been too long!"

Madison grabbed Paulo's hand in mid-glass collection. "Oh *Señor* Paulo, we have missed you too!"

"You know, Paulo," Madison whispered conspiratorially, "I've been getting some crazy ghost visits lately."

"Ah, *Señorita* Madison, you always have such stories to tell! I love to hear about the ghosts. You must read my palm before you go."

"You bet, my sweet."

Janine interrupted with a light tap on the table. "Mads, let our boy go so he can refuel us."

"Yeah, of course. Thanks, Paulo."

"I think," said Janine, "we should call William."

"Yup, we should." Madison took a long sip of her drink and then dipped her hand into her purse to find her cell phone. She flipped open the lid and quickly scanned through her contact list. "Ah, here he is." Madison highlighted his name and pushed SEND.

"Put it on speaker," Janine whispered.

Madison pushed the button and they sat silently as the rings increased. "Hello, this is William. Thank you for calling. I'll be happy to ring you back if you kindly leave your name and number."

"Hey, honey, it's Madison." Her voice boomed across the table and Janine cackled. "I really need you to call me back. We've had a . . ." Madison paused.

"A development," Janine offered.

"A development," Madison repeated. "I need your expertise." Madison squinted at Janine. "Thanks, pumpkin!" She flipped the phone closed and tossed it back into her purse.

Janine leaned back in her chair again. "I just love his accent," she said dreamily.

"Janine! Did you just have me call him so you could hear his voice, or do you really think he might be able to help us?"

"A little of both."

Madison was surprised that Janine's answer generated a strange feeling. She couldn't quite pinpoint it.

Paulo appeared silently at the table with two new drinks. Madison and Janine toasted each other. "*Salut,*" said Madison.

"*Salut,*" replied Janine. "Here's to finding out what the hell is going on in the netherworld!"

Madison bellowed a hearty "Here, here!" Above them, the twinkling Christmas lights danced gently among the tree branches laced over the cool patio. Algodones was sharing her magic spell once again.

Within hours, the two had scoured the shops and stands for bargains. Madison was beginning to feel the affects of the waning alcohol. "Let's go back to the hotel," she said to Janine. "I need a nap."

Janine willingly complied. They walked along the busy street, absorbing the sounds of tourists and merchants, the scents of roasting meats, savory tortillas and spices.

Madison's phone rang. She retrieved it from her purse and peered at the screen. "William."

"Ummm," smiled Janine. She silently mouthed a word.

"I know, I know . . . speaker phone," Madison flipped open the phone. "Hello?"

"Hello, lovely Madison? William here!"

Janine sighed.

"William, honey! Thanks for getting back to me. How are things back home?"

"Sterling, love. A new group of tourists has just arrived by bus, hungry for the answers to all their lives' questions. It is a psychic's dream."

"Of course we'd leave now," Madison said more to Janine than William. "Perfect timing."

"Don't worry. There will be plenty of pickings when you return. By the way, where are you and what is this development?"

Madison maneuvered to a bench and plopped down. Janine sat beside her.

"I took off last night after I saw you. I'm in Mexico."

"Mexico!" he laughed. "Never a dull moment with you, love."

"You know that's true, but I have to talk to you, William. I had a really crazy dream today. I saw some terrible images, like a premonition of something bad happening. There were cars flying everywhere and I felt like I was in the midst of them. They were crashing all around me."

"How awful."

"I know. It was very intense, very scary. I was wondering, have you or anybody else had an episode like this in the last couple of days?"

"Hmm, no, it's been quiet in my head. I could ask around. Although," William's deep British accent poured through the phone. "I think somebody would be talking if they'd had such an encounter."

"Yeah, you're right. That's what I thought." Janine nudged her in the ribs. "I mean that's what *we* thought. Janine's here with me too."

"Ah, lovely," He answered breezily. "Well, send her my hello!"

"Hi William," Janine answered back. "You're on speaker."

"Ah well, hello, peaches and hello to Algodones!"

Janine grinned at Madison, who shook her head. "Janine," she whispered in an irritated tone. "Let's work on the psychic-harmony part of this later, okay, cupcake?" Another call beeped in. Madison peered at the screen. "Perfect!" she screeched. "It's Ben."

"Sorry, sweets, couldn't hear you, say again?" said William.

"William, gotta let you go. "We," Madison smirked at Janine, "have another call. We'll ring you back."

"No worries, love. Enjoy your day, ladies."

"God, I love his voice, and his eyes, and his face and his body," Janine closed her eyes.

"Back to work, woman." Madison tapped the Send button. "Ben!"

"At your service," his cheery voice greeted them over the speaker. Two tourists walking by looked over at the sound. Madison leveled her none-of-your business gaze and they hurried off. "Got some interesting news for you."

Madison's stomach took a leap. "Great. My friend Janine is here with me, ready to lend her psychic powers to the cause. Go!"

"Well, it wasn't easy but I've got a bulldog for a grad assistant. We checked all the spellings of Helen Rhames and sure enough, you had it right."

"Ms. Extraordinaire strikes again!" piped in Janine.

"She sure did. Must be the great instruction she had about, hmm, let's see, how many years ago? I think it was . . ."

"Zip it, Dr. Masselink," Madison warned. "Otherwise I'm settin' you up with a nasty Sedona spell!"

"Okay, okay! I know you've got the Universe on your side. You've clearly got something magnetic to stay hitched to this enterprising energy. I promise.

"Turns out, Mrs. Helen Rhames died in 1972. She was . . . hold on, let me read the obit for you." Ben rustled the papers on his desk. Madison held her breath. "Ah, Rhames, Helen Frieda, born September 22, 1907, died September 8, 1972. Lifelong resident of Minnesota City. Survived by son, Samuel, his wife, Caroline, son,

Jonathon, his wife, Doris, and five grandchildren. Funeral to be held at the Watkowski Funeral Home, Winona, Minnesota."

"Wow! Winona, Minnesota!" That crazy dame pointed me straight to the source!"

"Yes, that was the final clue we needed," Ben agreed. "Thank her for making our job easier when you next speak to her."

"Will do, my investigative guru, but wait. I don't get something else."

"Do they say anything about preceded in death by or survived by a spouse named Cecil Rhames?"

"Nope."

"Well, I guess that's a bit more investigation for me to follow up on."

"Don't worry, Ms. Extraordinaire, we'll stay hot on the trail as well! I'll send you a copy of this and we'll look for other versions. Sometimes some obits are more detailed."

"Ben, I just love you. Not only are you a fabulous friend, you are a true magician!" Madison shook her head at Janine, who stood with hers cocked sideways, looking back. "How did you find this obit? I looked everywhere."

"Ah, my friend. You probably looked in newspapers, right?"

"Of course. Isn't that where you find the latest info on stiffs?"

"Sometimes, sometimes not."

Janine piped in and whispered to Madison. "God, I love this guy! He's a regular Matlock!"

Madison rolled her eyes. "And so?"

"You really want me to give away my secret?"

"Yeah, Ben, especially because I'm standing here in the middle of," Madison's voiced raised to a lovely dramatic shout, "Algodones, Mexico where all my friends . . ." she whirled in a circle and swept her hands out wide, "are with me waiting to hear!" By now more people had turned their curious eyes to Madison and Janine holding court in the middle of the street. Madison looked them all over and offered a gallant bow. "My people!" she shouted. "Join us in our quest for the Truth! The wizard is about to speak!"

"Did you ever check the funeral homes?" Ben's voice echoed.

"What?"

"Did you ever check the funeral homes?"

"No, never thought of that."

"We've created a program to find names through lots of avenues. Some towns don't have papers. Some papers don't have obits. But you can look in other places—city records, hospitals . . . We found this Rhames name pop up in Minnesota City, and then found this Watkowski funeral home in Winona. Seems the two cities are just a stone's throw from each other. The mortuary was started in the early 1900s, changed hands a couple of times. Now, for your information, it's just gotten a new name as of April—Watkowski-Mulyck."

"You are a genius!" Madison tossed the phone up and danced a jig.

Janine lunged and caught it in mid-air. "Madison, you've completely lost your marbles!"

Madison grabbed the phone from Janine. "So, my leader, what do I do now?"

"Well, as I said, we'll keep looking for other records that might make the picture clearer. In the meantime, my dear, that's up to you and your ghost. Seems like she's given you lots of clues. We filled in one blank. She's probably standing behind a churro stand with her arms folded nodding her head. I can see it now. This wrinkled old ghost is either furious or overjoyed that you've gotten one step closer to her."

Madison rubbed her eyes. "Thanks, Ben. I owe you."

"You've said that before."

"Yeah, but this time I really mean it."

"Okay, twinkle toes, get back to the hunt. Like I said before, you'd better write all this down. It's going to make one heck of a movie."

Madison winked at Janine. "Okay, then. Who do you want to play yourself?"

"Obviously," Ben Masselink sniffed from 3,000 miles away. "Clint Eastwood."

"Done. We're off to toast the wizard!"

"Sing the margarita song for me."

"What's that?" Madison asked as she watched Janine make her way back toward the bar.

"Why, whatever you want it to be! Remember, you can celebrate your place in the Universe any way you please."

"Hey, Ben, I have one more thing."

"What's that?"

"Well, I had this really scary vision this morning. I think I was half-awake but I could have been completely dreaming. I saw this huge catastrophe of cars smashing and crashing all around me. It was like there was an earthquake or something. The cars appeared to me first like schools of fish but then I realized they were actually all colors, shapes and sizes. They were falling everywhere," Madison shivered. "It was so horrible."

"I've got to say, that sounds really disturbing. It's seems more apocalyptic than your other recent experiences. Was Helen involved?"

"She showed up at the end of it. Her energy felt so fearful. But I can't be sure if her visit is related. You know how sometimes you get lots of messages at the same time?"

"I do. It's not easy to sort them out." He said. "Be sensitive to this increased connectivity. If you have more than one entity, the visions will separate and clarify. It may take some time."

"I hope I've got some," Madison frowned. "What if this event is coming soon?"

"You can only do what you can do," answered Ben, echoing Janine's words from this morning. Madison nodded at her friend.

"Make sure," he cautioned, "that you don't attribute. You are a translator, first and foremost."

"Got it, doc. Thanks for the instruction. Looks like I may owe you a bit more for tuition."

Ben laughed. "On the house today. Get back to work!"

Madison snapped the phone shut and skipped her way up to Janine. They made their way back to their table on the patio, underneath the twinkling multi-colored lights.

CHAPTER
THIRTY-TWO

KATHERINE SNAPPED her bra straps back together and shrugged her shirt back on. Why did doctor's offices always have to be so damn cold? She took a deep breath and eyed her oncologist warily.

"You're on the right track, Mrs. Simon. We'll set you up with the aftercare program as soon as you've completed treatment," he said.

"Thank you," she said politely, offering her hand. He awkwardly shook it, nodded and backed out of the office.

Dr. Monyag, she knew, had little ability to make her feel comfortable. For the last four-and-a-half weeks, he had intermittently come into the radiation bay and made infinitesimal adjustments according to his never-ending computations. With the contraction and expansion of Katherine's breast tissue and skin throughout the radiation, the measurements of where the rays should focus always changed. He would stand over her as she lay stretched out, topless, on the table and dispassionately direct the techs to move her body sideways or forward or backwards.

She grew to despise him, which she knew was ridiculous. He was the one who had the keys to her healing, but as he hovered over her the day before she had completely lost it.

"Move it two degrees left," he said. He pushed his glasses up on his nose as he studied the columns of numbers on his chart. "Make sure the arm is fully extended. Don't let it bend forward." He never looked up.

Suddenly, she sat up and screamed at the man. "I am not an *'it'*!" Katherine stared at the doctor, ignoring the two shocked techs' looks of astonishment. "Look at me. I am a patient. I am a person!" Katherine couldn't stop the dam burst. Too many hours of fear and frustration boiled over. "I bet you don't even know my first name!"

The doctor was clearly taken aback. He looked down at the numbers on his chart, then back up to Katherine.

She leaned her bare chest forward and poked the embroidery on his white coat. "I see your first name is David. Don't you think you should know my first name since you have been handling my breast regularly?"

One of the techs gasped. The doctor backed out of the bay, muttering awkward apologies.

"I'm sorry. I've got to take a break. Can I have my robe?" Katherine thrust forward a shaky hand to retrieve the mold-green garment from a speechless resident. She hastily wrapped it around herself, hopped off the table and rushed into the restroom, where she promptly threw up.

Almost immediately, Deedee rushed into the bathroom. "Are you okay, Katherine?" Her voice was soft, gentle, concerned.

Katherine lingered over the toilet, feeling the bands of sweat stream down her back. "Yeah, I'm okay." Did her voice sound as weak to Deedee as it did to her?

"Can I get you something?"

"Oh, how about a new body, a new life, and for fuck's sure, a new attitude."

Deedee turned on the water and wetted a paper towel. She handed it to Katherine underneath the stall door. "Feel like you can c'mon out?"

Katherine took another shaky breath. "Okay." She took the paper towel, wiped her face and opened the door. Upon seeing Deedee's concerned look, she broke into tears again. "I don't know what's wrong with me!" She wailed. Deedee put a comforting arm around her. "Why am I acting like this?" Katherine shook her head angrily. "I'm almost done. What's wrong with me?"

Deedee's voice was like a sweet balm. "Katherine, this is not unusual. It takes a lot of energy to stay in this fight. You've been in a battle for weeks. You've been trying to keep a brave face for your kids, obviously, and for your husband. You're still working, outside nonetheless, on the courts every day and it's hard to do all this. I want you to know we recognize and stand with you in this."

"Oh, God, Deedee. I've been such a bitch. I'm so embarrassed. Although," she wiped the tears away. "I have to admit, Dr. Monyag is kind of a troll. I just couldn't take being an 'it' anymore."

Deedee laughed. "Well, it's true, he's not high on the list of those with people skills. But Katherine," she leaned forward and whispered. "He's the absolute best you could ask for."

"Great. The least I could get is the best doctor and one who looks like a movie star instead of nerd poster boy."

"Let's hope you don't get another reason to get a new doctor in the future." Deedee put her hand on Katherine's arm. "Ready to come out?"

"Yeah. I feel so stupid, though."

"Katherine, I promise. I've seen breakdowns that make yours look like a Maypole dance! Remember, there is no wrong reaction to this process. Your world is rocked. Everything is upside down. We understand!"

Katherine grabbed Deedee's hands. "I want you to know that it's people like you who save patients like me. When we feel like we are in the midst of a never-ending horror movie and everything is crashing around us, you guys—the techs, the nurses, the office staff—you are the people who keep us anchored to hope through this disaster." She squared her shoulders, suddenly feeling strong and in control again. "Thank you," she said somberly.

"It's what we love to do, Katherine, and patients like you are what keep us motivated. So, let's get today out of the way and move back on track!" Deedee smiled a strong, cheerful smile. Katherine was ready to go out again.

Katherine walked out of the restroom and across the waiting room floor. She noticed the evening sun streaming through the windows. Outside, the atmosphere was steamy. A thunderstorm hovered, angry and blue, on the western horizon. She surveyed the steel-gray clouds on the horizon outside the window. Then her gaze dropped to find the only person left in the waiting room. An older black woman sat quietly, working on a crochet piece of some kind. Deedee's assistant, Claire, walked over and bent down to speak with her. Katherine stopped and watched.

"Okay, Lorraine, almost time for the bus."

"Wow," the woman looked at Claire with a brilliant, open smile. "That seemed like no time at all!" She carefully put her yarn and needles in her oversized canvas bag.

"Need help walking over?" Claire asked, looking carefully at the woman's face.

"Oh, no, darlin'. I'm fine, just fine!"

"Are you sure? It's no problem. I would love a little break."

Lorraine nodded at Claire. Katherine felt touched by the woman's warmth. She actually wished she could be sitting in one of those worn, fake leather chairs next to her. She looked over to where Deedee talked with one of the techs and decided to sit for a moment. She edged over to the frail woman who gently packed her things.

"You know what, I would really enjoy a walk with you," Claire said. "Let me get my station covered and I'll be back in a jiffy."

Lorraine primly closed her purse and folded her hands over the canvas carefully. Katherine leaned back and stared out the window next to her. She closed her eyes and tried to forget the incident in the restroom. She tried to focus on the woman's calm energy.

As if in response to her unspoken request, Lorraine leaned toward her. "I hope you don't mind, honey, but you look a bit cross." Her voice flowed over Katherine like warm melted caramel. "Anything I can do to help?"

Katherine opened her eyes and looked at the pinched face with the skin stretched tightly over the cheekbones and the eyes sunken under drooping lids. Katherine felt as if it were the most beautiful face in the world. She sighed.

"It hasn't been the best of days," she said.

"Well, not every day can be a picnic or a party." The smile beamed from beneath the sallow skin.

"I know that's true but it seems like every day is a struggle here. Every minute, every second, I'm thrashing around trying to come to grips with . . ." she waved her hand at the tidy now-empty waiting room. "This."

The gray head beside her nodded. "Tell me how it is for you today, darlin'. My Grammy always used to say that a burden shared is half the weight."

Katherine couldn't stop the torrent that Lorraine's prompting unleashed. She poured out everything that had happened in the last ten months, culminating with the diagnosis, her treatment and her meltdown minutes before. All the while, the old woman patiently listened and stroked her hand.

"What is it about me?" Katherine felt the tears welling up again. "What did I do to deserve this?"

"Ah, that's God's special secret. Why He chooses to bless us in the ways He does. I don't believe we'll know that 'til we stand before Him in all His glory."

Katherine stared at her through red eyes. Had the woman heard a word she'd said? "Blessed?" she repeated.

"Of course. We are the lucky ones." She tapped Katherine's hand with a spidery veined finger. "We have found God's presence. We can see it every day in the wonderful people who care for us and in our own knowin' that life shouldn't be taken for granted, no matter what that life looks like. Most other poor folks go wanderin' around the world searching for a sign. Look at us!" She sat back and straightened her fragile frame. "We see God's favor, every day."

Katherine looked out the window and watched the blue-gray sky morph into a steely dark shadow, backlit by what was left of the sun's afternoon streaks. "Favor?" she asked. She turned to Lorraine, confused. There certainly was no favor in her life, just loss, anger, piss and moan paralysis.

Lorraine lowered her chin close to Katherine's ear and whispered. "You have favor. My people could always see those who carried it. It's a talent we have." She raised chin face proudly. "Now go out and live like it."

Before Katherine could respond, Claire came over and helped Lorraine out of her chair. As she turned to leave, the bent dark angel whispered, "you remember what I told you, now. The main thing about favor is it grows bigger the more you accept it. It's working even now. I believe you're to see more and more. Don't know why," she said. "But I learned long ago not to question my gift." With that, she launched into a lively discussion with Claire as they walked out the automatic doors into the late, humid air.

Katherine turned to Deedee, who had slipped silently by her side. "I've seen that lady so many times," she said.

"She's an incredible woman," Deedee said quietly.

"I'm the last one for treatment every day. Why is she still here?" Katherine stood and moved forward toward the closet.

"She's a couple of slots before you. Actually," Deedee checked her watch and guided Katherine forward. "She takes a bus from Blaine at about 3:30 and gets here at 5:00ish. Her time slot is 5:45."

"She takes a bus?"

"Yup. She gets here at 5:00 and then takes the 6:30 bus home. I guess she gets home around 8:00. It's really amazing," Deedee said. "Lorraine cleans houses from around 7:00 a.m. 'til 3:00. Before she came for treatment, she worked twelve-hour days."

"Isn't there someone who can drive her?" Katherine asked.

"She's a grandma of two little ones, twelve and eight. They live with her because their mom has issues . . . You know what," Deedee whispered to Katherine. "I've shared too much."

"Wow," said Katherine as she walked slowly back to the radiology bay. "I guess I really need to shut my mouth and get over myself."

Deedee smiled. "Katherine, don't expect yourself to live anyone else's experience except your own. Lorraine is an incredibly amazing person. So are you and remember, you're getting closer to the end every day."

Katherine felt tears well up, mingled with disgust at herself. As she walked through the waiting room she thought of the past year. So many silly, empty things had nearly sidelined her, had paralyzed her in so many ways. She felt a new spark inside her. Life wasn't easy . . . for anyone. The idea that she deserved a pass because she just didn't feel up to the challenge curdled in her mind. She had lived with this falsehood driving nearly every day of her life. *No more*, Katherine decided. *Like it or not, it's time to grow up.* She needed to redeem herself for her ridiculous behavior, and now was the moment to start. She lifted her chin and wiped her cheek. Inside the bay, the group had assembled again. The resident checked his notes as one tech helped Katherine remove her robe. Dr. Monyag was nowhere to be found.

"Okay, kids," she announced cheerily. "We're back and waving to the crowd. Sorry for the breakdown but let's put it behind us. Cool?" Katherine smiled bravely at the young resident and two techs. Deedee applauded behind her.

"Well, folks," Deedee's voice was light and airy. "We're all eager to carry on. We've got our marching orders, right?" She looked at one of the techs. He nodded his head. "Well then, let's get on with it. Katherine, ready?"

Katherine looked at all of them and then at the hulking machine and the lovely wooded scene plastered on the ceiling. Her resolve began to crumble. She wanted to run. Then she imagined Lorraine, beaming a cool, peaceful smile in the midst of yet another three-hour bus ride to treatment.

"You bet," she nodded to each person in the room. "Let's rock!"

Two blocks away, the older woman waved goodbye to Claire as she boarded a bus in the late afternoon heat. "Where've you been, Charles?" Her friendly greeting echoed inside and outside the metro bus.

"Sorry, Miz Lorraine! Ten minutes late. Won't do it again!" The aging bus driver cheerfully offered his hand to help her up the steps.

Lorraine settled into her seat as the bus pulled away from the curb. Claire tugged at her scrub shirt, listening to the fading voice of the woman. "Young man," the velvety voice sang, "can't think of better company than you!"

Inside the radiation bay, Katherine took her place on the table with her left arm stretched above her head. "One week left," she whispered, and turned the word over in her head . . . *favor*.

CHAPTER THIRTY-THREE

MADISON AND JANINE ambled among the booths. The city was full of tourists and visitors who had come from over the border in Yuma to get medical and dental treatment. Los Algodones was famous for its medical and pharmaceutical services where everything from prescription drugs to face-lifts were cheaper.

As they walked closer to the restaurant, Janine suddenly whirled and grabbed Madison by the shoulders. "I've got it!" she shrieked.

"Jesus, girl! You nearly stopped my ticker. I gotta sit down. What exactly is it that you've got?" Madison searched for an empty bench.

"I've got another way we can fill in the blanks!" Janine sputtered in excitement.

"Stop with the intrigue. Spill!"

"Okay, I'll give you a hint."

"Jesus," Madison moaned again.

"C'mon, Mads, lighten up."

"Okay, okay. What's the hint?"

"What do I carry with me wherever I go?"

"Your cell phone," Madison offered.

"Nope. Think less high tech."

"Great." Madison screwed up her face and considered the question again. What was Janine always carrying around with her?

"Your wallet?" she guessed.

"No, again. You are way off track, chickie. Need another hint?"

"Sure." Madison was wearying of this game. "Go for it."

"This is a thing that we both use but I'm more into it. We use it for work."

"Use it for work," Madison repeated, thinking of objects Janine carried with her everywhere. "Hmm, oh! I know! A pendulum!"

"Right on! Good job, Mads!"

"That's a great idea, J! We can ask all sorts of questions!"

"Think it will work better with margaritas and chips?"

"Well, there's only one way to find out. I'll race you to the bar."

BACK AT THEIR SPECIAL TABLE complete with fresh margaritas, sumptuous fresh salsa and loaded burritos, Janine pulled her pendulum kit out of her purse. She kept it carefully stored in a blue velvet bag. Madison thought it looked appropriately magical.

Paulo came by with a dish of guacamole and watched Janine set up the pendulum and a collection of question boards. "Do you mind me asking, *Señorita* Janine, what manner of thing is this?"

"It's a pendulum, Paulo." She showed him the brass cylindrical pointer connected to a thin string. "We hold it over this small board, see?"

"Ah, I see." Paulo read the different answer squares on one of her four boards. "'Positive Side,' 'Negative Side.' I don't understand this thing."

"Look," Janine held up the board. "There are a number of possible answers on the board, on both the positive and negative poles. You can get answers like, 'good outcome, some gain' or 'balanced outcome, no loss, no gain' on the positive side and 'poor outcome, some loss' or 'negative outcome, significant loss'."

"Oh, yes, this is clear." Paulo nodded his head. "I see one can also get 'try again later' or 'poor question.' It can even tell you it doesn't know!" He leaned over and tapped Janine on the shoulder. "This is supposed to know everything, *sí*?"

"Yes, theoretically, but we don't get it right every time."

"How does this thing find these answers?"

Madison sipped on her margarita, watching the chemistry between the two.

"You hold this up over the center part of the board with your right hand about two inches in the air. You hold it very still and pretty soon it will begin to vibrate and then to swing back and forth. It will find the correct answer and continually swing to that answer." Janine looked at Paulo's now doubtful face. "It really does work, Paulo. Let's try it on you."

Paulo took a step back. "I don't know, *Señorita* Janine. This is, how does one say, too fear?"

"Oh, you mean spooky?" Madison popped in. "Nothing to be scared of, Paulo, let's do an easy one. We'll ask a question you already know the answer to."

"Ah! Like a test, no?"

"Yep." Madison smiled up at him. "Let's set this up, J. This should be fun."

Janine quickly laid out the board with the dates and birth times of every astrological sign. She placed it in the middle of the table and rubbed the pendulum gently between her fingers. "Ready?"

"*Sí*, yes." Paulo looked quite unsure and Madison had to giggle. "Don't worry, friend. This is not a bad thing." Paulo looked at her and nodded.

Janine held the string attached to the brass pointer above the table. She placed both feet firmly on the floor, took a deep breath, and quieted her arm to total stillness. "Okay, Paulo," she said. "We will see if our little friend here can discover your birthday. You obviously know that, right?"

Paulo nodded his head.

"Do you know the time you were born?"

"No, Señorita, but I can call my *mamá*. She is at home now."

"Great, even better. Well, here we go." Janine held her hand still and they all waited. Slowly, the pointer began vibrating slightly, then more obviously. It whirled in an ever-broadening circle, going around and around in the air. Paulo leaned over the board. Both Janine and Madison had their eyes fixed only on the board's center.

The pendulum continued its circular route. Then the speed slowed a bit. The movement changed to an oblong motion, cutting the board in half. It then narrowed to a straight line from one side of the board to the other. And then, ever so slightly, the pointer's movement was reduced to moving back and forth from just the center to a specific month. It held its course and gently swung to and fro. The direction shifted vaguely. The date the pendulum pointed to was April 20. However, the swinging brass fixture didn't specify between seven and eight in the morning. It seemed as if it couldn't make up its cosmic mind. Janine gave it another minute to clarify the information, and then she lifted the pendulum away. "Did you get that?" she asked Paulo.

"Yes," he said, incredulous.

"Let's validate the information." Janine turned to Madison. "Got a piece of paper?"

Madison rifled through her purse and found an old index card.

"Write down what you saw for month, sign, and time of birth."

Madison nodded and began writing.

"Now, Paulo, you and I will do the same." Do you have some paper and a pen?"

"*Sí.*" He pulled out his waiter's notebook and a pen. Janine found a pencil and a piece of paper in her purse as well. "So, write the month, the day if you saw it, the astrological sign and the time." They all wrote in silence. "Okay, let's see what we've got. Mads, you go first."

Madison pushed her paper to the middle of the table. It said, APRIL, TAURUS, AND SPLIT BETWEEN 7 AND 8 A.M. Janine went next. Hers said exactly the same thing. Finally, Paulo showed his paper with a shaky hand. It too, said *ABRIL, TAURO,* AND *ENTRE Y SIETE Y OCHO*—April, Taurus, and between seven and eight. "Wow," said Paulo, his face a shade paler than before.

"Cool, huh?" Janine high-fived Madison.

"Not so fast," warned Madison. "The between seven and eight thing bugs me."

"Let's have Paulo call *Mamá*. That cool with you, Paulo?"

"*Sí*, but *Mamá* has six other babies plus me. Maybe she forget the time?"

"No way!" Madison assured him.

Paulo left the table to find the bar phone. The two women took a couple of sips of margaritas and began munching on their burritos. "You'd better watch you don't get cheese on that thing," said Madison. "We still have a lot of work for it to do."

"Let's put together a list of questions that you want answered," Janine suggested.

"Good idea." Madison looked for a larger piece of paper. Unable to find one, she went to the front of the restaurant and asked the hostess for a pad.

"*Sí, Señorita*. Right away." The girl disappeared for a moment and returned with a wrinkled tablet.

As Madison returned to the table, she was nearly bowled over by Paulo. "*Señorita* Madison! It is right! This swinging needle, it is right!" They hurried to the table where Janine was polishing off the last bites of her burrito.

"Ok, Paulo, give it to us," Madison announced.

"I call my mother and ask her when is my birth date. She says April 20. I am the sign of *Toro* and my birth was 7:30 in the morning. She remembers because the doctors were changing at that time. One who had been with her since morning left, a new one came to work at that time, exactly."

"Well, I'll be doggoned!" Janine slapped the table and the margaritas sloshed. "I knew that baby was right. He's never let me down."

"How do you know it's a male?" asked Madison.

"I don't know, I guess I automatically always saw him that way. Maybe that's what makes our relationship so fruitful!"

"Hmm, does he have a British accent too?" Madison teased and grabbed for her drink as she dropped into her chair. Paulo stood, still staring at the board.

"Don't know. But now that you mention it, sounds like a lovely idea!" Janine clapped her hands and woke Paulo back to reality. He shook is head. "This is a very amazing thing, my friends. You have very special powers."

"Well, you want to know what our secret is?" Madison leaned forward conspiratorially.

"What?" Paulo took a step closer.

"The margaritas!" Above them the light strands bounced and jiggled. "Thanks, Paulo, that was fun. We've got to get to work now." She gave him a wave. "We'll call you when our glasses get low."

"Of course, ladies." Paulo gave a quick bow and backed away.

"So, back to the list," said Janine.

"Here are the things I'm wondering. Did she remarry? She's never shown me another husband except for Cecil and I don't think that marriage lasted more than twelve or thirteen years."

"Okay." Janine took the tablet from her friend. "Last names," she wrote.

"Also, are her sons still alive?"

"Got it." Janine finished writing the questions. "Let's do it!" She pulled out another cardboard chart that had the letters of the alphabet in a ring inside a square. Within that circle was another loop divided into quarters. On each section, a word or phrase was written—YES, ASK AGAIN, NO, DON'T KNOW. "Let's start with this: Did Helen have two husbands?"

Madison watched carefully as Janine held the pendulum steady and quiet over the board. Within seconds, the brass weight quivered at the end of the string. It started a long, slow path around the outside circle. It moved faster and faster until it made a gentle whirring sound. Then, as quickly as it had sped up, it began swinging back and forth from the middle to the band with the word NO. "Hmm, interesting," Madison murmured.

"Let's keep going." Janine set her elbow on the table and held the string again. She asked the question, "Are the sons alive?" The weight shivered and rocked to the quadrant of ASK AGAIN, so she did. She politely implored the mystical piece of brass to clarify the answer.

Madison watched the pointer swing back and forth until it settled on NO. "Well that answers that question. Jeez," she shook her head. "I can never get over how amazing these things are."

"Yup, just think. These things have been around since the scientific revolution. You know, he was invented by Galileo."

"Hmm." Madison stared at the needle. "So both sons are dead. Wonder why Helen comes through but they don't?"

"If you can answer that 'random messenger' question, you'd take our art to the next level!"

Madison smiled in agreement. "I guess there are some things we'll never know as we try to put these cosmic puzzles together. Well, I've had enough," Madison continued as she stood up. "I'm going to find Paulo and the bathroom, not exactly in that order, and when I get back, I want Galileo's little buddy back in bed. Tell him thanks for his help."

Madison walked away from the table wondering how in the hell she was going to put this information together. She made a mental note to talk with William about it when she got back. The thought of him gave her stomach a little flip. Suddenly, she was looking very forward to getting back to Sedona. She looked at Janine carefully tucking away her kit. *Nothing like a little competition to heat up the pot and make life interesting,* she thought.

THAT NIGHT, THE VIBRATING fan on the ceiling hummed soothingly. Madison's snore mingled with an occasional snuffle. She was lights out to the world. The day had started traumatically with the vision, and then continued into a haze with the Bloody Marys giving way to the margaritas, which had melted into tequila shots. It was a good thing, Madison had said to Janine over their last plate of nachos, that they had written the pendulum information down, otherwise, where would they be? Janine had toasted her and they had both downed their final shot.

Paulo had escorted them back to their hotel rooms after that and tucked them in. He had worked the whole day, a double shift, and it was completely worth it. It had been a good day for him.

Madison shifted on the bed, her sleep deep and heavy. There was no room for a ghost tonight. Maybe tomorrow the ethereal partnership between Madison's inner self, primed and perked to receive messages and the woman desperately trying to connect from the other side, would resume. But for now on this languid, Mexican evening, any signals from beyond were silenced.

The sabbatical to Algodones had done what Madison hoped. It had changed the landscape, taking Madison's quest a new step forward. She'd been re-energized by Ben's discovery of Helen's true identity. She was one piece closer to completing the puzzle the ghost had dropped her into.

Just as importantly, the heated desert day had transported Madison away from the suffocating Sedona bubble. Tomorrow morning she and Janine would sojourn home. They would launch back into the red, roasted valley. They would slide back into days of appointments and readings with thousands of forgettable faces and stories. But for now Madison rested unfettered by the treadmill of clients and expectations. In the sultry Algodones night, Madison finally slept free of other people's lives inside her head. She laid in the darkness unencumbered by visions, memories, or the ghost.

THE NEXT MORNING started hazily. Madison's ten-hour sleep had been nice, but the accompanying hangover caused the world to move in slow motion. Her mouth was dry, her vision a bit blurry. She took one look at herself in the mirror and shook her head sadly. "God, when are you ever going to listen? You are too old for this." Her reflection looked back at her dully.

She tried to do whatever she could to clean up her face, but short of a long shower and a longer makeup session, the world was in for a sorry sight as she made her way back out of Mexico.

Madison gathered her things and took one last look around the room. The bed looked uninviting in its rumpled state. It always seemed as though once the intention to enjoy a place was gone, the place itself lost its luster. This was probably a good thing, she decided. It helped her move forward.

One hour later, Madison and an equally bleary-eyed Janine were headed east on the sun-baked highway.

CHAPTER
THIRTY-FOUR

W HERE A FEW WEEKS before, the days had begun to spin by in rapid succession, now the days slowed to a stumbling gait. Katherine woke in the morning and counted the hours until the last day. She'd been so proud of herself for keeping her spirits up since her temper tantrum at the clinic. But today, despite its desperately blue sky and comfortable warmth, was a day that ticked by almost in reverse.

Katherine roused herself and forced her body downstairs to the kitchen to have her requisite glass of orange juice and army of pills. Vitamins, fish oil, calcium, magnesium, foliate . . . the list went on and on. She was never really sure if all these supplements did anything for her. Was she less tired than she might have been? Would she heal faster than otherwise? But she had taken the advice of well-meaning friends who swore by the various elements. Dr. Monyag had just shrugged when she asked him if these would make a difference. "Whatever makes you feel more comfortable," he had said nasally.

Once loaded with the various pills and gel caps, Katherine prepared to join Barb on the court for a three-hour session. Tryouts for the girls would begin in two weeks. She was nearly done teaching all the teenagers before the blackout time when coaches could no longer work with their athletes until the season began. She could only work with them until July 31, another reason this week was dragging, she figured. She would get two weights off of her shoulders (temporarily, anyway) in two days—last day of teenage drama for a while on the thirty-first, last day of treatment forever on August 1.

She began to think of the past several months and how much had transpired. She thought back to her original visit to Madison the psychic and the subsequent phone call. The memory of that call reminded Katherine of the post-it notes she had kept. She went searching for them and found them in her nightstand drawer. Katherine sat down on the bed and glanced at the clock. She had a ten-minute window. She pulled the notes apart. She had written:

"Look ahead. Don't keep your head down. You can't see what the Universe has to offer when you are fixed on the ground!"

"Find the good in every day."

"The only one who can get you unstuck is you."

"Find five things to be grateful for, every day." This one reminded her of Lorraine's quiet words of strength and encouragement.

"Redeem yourself."

And then the last phrase, with so many important words crammed in, spoke to her the loudest, as if someone very important had written them down on a napkin just for her:

"You are not perfect. Live with your back to the past. Have a worthwhile goal. Learn the will of God and do it. Go for broke."

Katherine considered the words. She realized that these days she felt a greater strength, a deeper peace than before. It was strange. Engaging in this battle for her life had stripped away the layer of worries that she had wrapped herself in for so long. Getting to this place in her head had been hard work but now learning to live here seemed like no work at all. Katherine put the notes back in the drawer and left for the courts.

CHAPTER THIRTY-FIVE

MADISON WALKED THROUGH the mini-mall toward the manicure shop. She glanced down at her nails and was appalled at how long she'd let them go. She really didn't have all that much time today, what with a list of errands, two readings from 4-6 p.m. and then her women's group at the Center. She hoped the shop wasn't going to be full. That would really mess with her schedule.

But she really needed this manicure. Two days from now was her birthday and she had to look nice for the party. Although it would be a late one, she was looking forward to it. She couldn't believe she was going to be forty-one. With that thought she walked through the mall doors and found the nail shop.

She got to the glass door and peeked in. Perfect! Only three clients and they were getting pedicures. Two Vietnamese workers sat idly, and when they saw Madison enter they perked up immediately. She was able to sit down right away and present her hands to a pretty young woman who wore an awkward smile. The girl tried to make conversation, but Madison was in no mood to do the immediate translation of broken English into some semblance of language and pleasantries. She politely shook her head, saying apologetically. "Sorry, I don't understand." The girl finally gave up and proceeded to refurbish Madison's French manicure in silence.

This gave Madison a chance to quietly zone out and let her thoughts wander. It had been a few days since Los Algodones and she was just starting to get back into the Sedona swing again. Once back home, her mind reverted to its exhausted state from the months of channeling Helen's energy, added with her own obsession about the missing facts. She tipped her head to the side to stretch out her neck and looked at herself in the mirror. She did look tired. She did look like she needed another break. She did look overwhelmed. She . . . "What the hell?!"

The nail girl clearly understood this English and jumped with shock. Madison quickly apologized and tried to laugh it off, all the while staring worriedly in the mirror at the reflection of the image just behind her right shoulder. In it, a foggy, blurry Helen slide show began to form. Madison looked carefully at the girl, who had returned to dipping her hand into the small bowl of warm water. Could she sense anything strange? Her disinterested stare convinced Madison that yet again, she was the only audience the ghost wanted.

The shape turned out to be a perfect mini-Helen wavering in the mirror. She pointed to her left and waved her chalky white hand. Slowly, individual images appeared. Madison was able to see solitary pictures of John in various stages of his life, rather like snapshots; but the really odd thing was that Madison could not only see the image, she could instantaneously feel the underlying emotional history of the moment.

"Jesus," Madison mumbled under her breath. "This show is getting curioser and curiouser."

The nail girl looked up at Madison, curious herself. Madison ignored her and kept her stare on the mirror.

The first snapshot was John as a teenager. He was clearly older than she'd seen him in his parents' room. He was lanky and fairly tall. His hair was still a light blond and despite the leanness of his frame, his face was still a bit rounded from childhood, though his cheekbones were beginning to grow more prominent under those ice-blue eyes. He was leaning against a lawn mower, taking a break, no doubt. He stood surveying the lawn and maybe even the lake beyond. Madison sensed a huge feeling of resentment. She closed her eyes . . . yes, the negativity hovered around him like a swarm of gnats.

The next image showed John in the tree house with the boys she'd seen before. But they weren't little boys anymore. Now they were big teenagers and they sprawled around the aging wood structure smoking cigarettes and sitting next to open beers. There was a small paper bag with a Woolworth's label on it. The boy who held it looked to be an older version of Clay, but Madison couldn't be sure. She shut her eyes again and felt a youthful bravado mixed with rebellion. *Figures,* she said to herself. *All this testosterone and nothin' to do but show off to your buddies.* She opened her eyes and looked again. John had a glazed, disconnected look in his eyes.

Another shot materialized and showed John as a young man, wearing a nice dress shirt and slacks. He had a stack of books in his arms and looked serious. Madison delved into the feelings swirling there and felt a sense of anticipation and grim focus. This was obviously a kid who was on a mission to grow up—perhaps to get away from home and his mother?

Finally, an image of John, Helen and Sam crystallized. John wore graduation garb and a forced half-smile. Sam had his arm slung over his brother's shoulder in an obvious pose of pride. Helen stood slightly apart, looking up wistfully at her younger son. The mixed feelings surrounding this scene spoke of pride, relief, remorse, fear and a poignant sadness. Madison picked up the ghost's deep sense of loss. It was as if Helen realized this would be the last time she'd be in a photo with both of her sons.

As had happened many times in the past few months, Madison's heart ached empathetically with Helen's. No sooner did Madison tap into that place in Helen's soul, than the last picture shrunk, faded and disappeared.

"Wow," Madison looked at the nail girl and began to analyze. "There is so much pain there, you know?" The girl looked at her quizzically, unsure how to respond. "I mean, I get that every family has its problems but these are so deep. It's like I could drop down into their souls and see the depth of the emotions that drive them. Such a shame," she shook her head slowly.

"What you say, lady?" The petite manicurist asked hesitantly. "You need something?"

"Oh, no, no. No, sweetheart, don't mind me. I'm just a little bit, you know, wacky. You know what wacky is? Like," she took both hands and whirled them on either side of her head, "like crazy? Nutty? Out to lunch?"

"Oh no, lady! It no time for lunch yet!" The nail lady looked relieved. Now she knew what this strange woman was talking about!

Madison shook her head. It definitely wasn't worth trying to clear this one up. She just nodded. "That's right, silly me . . ." She pointed to the clock. "What was I thinking? Too early." *Such a shame,* she thought again. She felt so strongly that Helen and John were stuck in the same emotional quicksand but physically were going in opposite directions. She glanced at her watch. She still had forty-five minutes. "You know, I might just go for a quick pedicure. Do you have time?" She watched to see if her nail girl understood.

"Pedicure? Good." The girl stood up and immediately went to one of the large chairs perched over a sink. She turned on the spigots, added a blue powder, checked the temperature with her fingers and waved Madison over. "Come now, here."

Madison looked again at her watch. "We'd better make this fast, okay? Quick?"

The nail girl nodded again and steered Madison into the chair. Within seconds, Madison realized what a good idea this had been. Her feet reveled in the warm, blue bubbles.

The girl worked efficiently. She cleaned Madison's feet and tidied her toenails. She began a long, slow massage of each foot. Madison felt like she could just close her eyes for a quick nap, when she heard a slam.

She sat up startled and looked at the other occupants in the salon. No one registered any acknowledgement of the noise. She looked into the mirror behind the nail girl's bent head and watched an undulating group of images order themselves into a scene.

JOHN STORMED OUT of the house, the front door still vibrating from the slam. He marched down the walk and opened his car door angrily.

206

Behind him, Helen pushed the door open. "John! Come back here! I'm not finished with you."

John stopped and looked back at his mother. Madison remembered Jerome Park's eyes the first day Helen had met him. His son had those exact eyes. "No, Mom. I'm finished with you."

Helen gasped and took a step closer. "Let's talk some more. I know you don't appreciate my opinion but—"

"But what, Mom?" He shook his head. "You're right. I don't appreciate your opinion. I know you are unhappy that my girlfriend is pregnant. I heard you. Nothing is going to change that now. We're going to have this baby. There's nothing you can say about it."

"John, you can't be so quick to decide. There are so many issues you haven't thought of. What if you don't even marry this girl?"

"I happen to love her, Mom, which is something I know you understand very little about."

Helen ignored her son. "You haven't considered all the parts of this that are yet to come. Having a baby out of wedlock is a terrible, terrible thing."

"I know, mother." John's voice dropped to a whisper. "You've reminded me of that just about every day of my life." He slid into the seat and closed the door. He rolled down the window and leaned toward her. "Listen, I get that I made your life miserable. You'd probably still be married to Dad if it wasn't for me. But I'm not going to treat my child that way. I refuse," he said pointedly, "to ruin his or her life that way."

"John, that's not what I meant—"

"C'mon, Mom, that's exactly what you meant. We both know I completely destroyed your life. There's nothing I can do about it, so I'm going to move on. I'm going to have my own child and my own life. Good luck with yours."

He turned on the car. His mother took two more steps closer.

"John," she pled with him. "Come inside, honey. We can fix this. You don't have to do this."

"That's where you're wrong, Mom. I absolutely do."

John backed his car down the driveway, onto the street. Helen lurched forward as he steered the car away. "John, *please*, please don't leave!" The engine's roar drowned out her voice as her son gunned the car away. Helen followed him into the street and watched him disappear around the corner.

Madison watched Helen's face as she turned back. Helen looked devastated. Her body broke into sobs, gut-wrenching moans and wails. She stumbled up the cement walkway and into the house.

With the slam of the front door, the vision faded away, leaving Madison's shocked reflection in the mirror.

The nail girl kneaded her feet, oblivious to the scene. She looked up and caught Madison's gaze. Madison looked down and saw her brightly painted toenails. How long had this taken? This ghost seemed to be piling on the emotion with each new visit. She remembered the Los Algodones vision. Did Helen's son die in a terrible car crash? The thoughts tumbled inside her brain. Madison felt an overwhelming need for order. She wondered how numbers could sort all this information out. Numbers were what she knew best. Numbers would calm her and help her find answers. If a calm methodical approach wouldn't work, what did she have to rely upon? The thought of additional visits like the last few caused her to shiver.

"God," she said absently out loud again. "I gotta look again at this broad's dates so I can read her cards."

The idea of going back over all this again left her with a sinking sensation. This was all getting to be too much . . . but just then she had a thought. Who was the most adept at cards and life periods? It was William. He would be a huge help to her. Plus, it wouldn't be bad to see him again. He hadn't been around since she'd returned from Los Algodones.

She decided to call him as soon as her nails were dry. Maybe she could talk him into meeting with her after her women's psychics-in-training session that night.

Finally the dark-haired girl finished. Madison held her hands and feet out, fingers and toes stretched forward gracefully. "Hmm, pretty good work."

The girl was evidently familiar with these English words. She got up and trotted to the cash register to write out the bill. Madison paid quickly and stood up. She took one last look at the now-tranquil mirror. Despite the fact that the images had faded, Madison was confident. She knew Helen would come again. The story was nowhere near being completely told and she'd get William to help her understand it. She grabbed her purse quickly and headed out the door.

CHAPTER
THIRTY-SIX

S HE WAS IN the produce section when the thought hit her. Katherine stood still holding an avocado and she realized that today, July 31, 2007, was the ten-year anniversary of her father's death.

She felt a quick flash of sadness but then, just as suddenly, the pain was gone, replaced by a familiar loneliness.

She couldn't believe it had already been ten years. She couldn't believe she'd nearly forgotten.

Along with the reminder of her father came a heightening of all sorts of senses. She could smell his aftershave in the soft drinks section. She could hear his voice amongst the butcher's banter with his customers. She remembered a handful of things that brought her an inner smile, but the handful was quite small.

Her father's suicide hadn't come as such a surprise. He'd always been a bitter man. Katherine never really understood why. He was prone to rages and during her youth, she was chosen to placate the man who would hibernate in his bedroom after a bad day at work. Her mother would send Katherine in to sit with him. She was the only one he would tolerate during one of his moods. Katherine might have been proud of her unique position in the family as not just the oldest child but also the one who could bring her father back to a happy reality, but she wasn't. She felt like she was a prisoner being sent to the lions . . . a lamb being led to slaughter.

So a large part of Katherine's childhood was to serve as a sort of emotional companion to her father. She grew to resent the role and her mother's abdication as a result. She became masterful at hiding her emotions. She had decided, early on, that she would be the exact opposite of her father.

After her mother had died in 1993, of brain cancer, her father fell more and more regularly into his black moods. In the beginning, when he first lived alone in the assisted living facility nearby, she would go to visit him regularly. She would work whatever angle she could to get him out of his dark place but his need for her to help him stay afloat in the real world was too much for her to shoulder. Her brother and sister lived in California and Oregon. She was the only one to carry him and it exhausted her. With her own life constantly calling for attention, she became less willing to save him from his emotions. She still visited him regularly, but didn't buy into his rants. The more withdrawn he became, the more she withdrew herself.

It was no surprise then, when on July 31, 1997, his home health care aid came early in the morning to find him dead in his chair by the television. The coroner ruled the suicide the cause of a pill overdose. He'd taken his rainbow collection of medicines, popped the handful and made himself a C.C. on the rocks with a twist to wash it all down.

Between the three of them, Katherine and her siblings decided not to have a service, or even to publish any notifications. The handful of their parents' friends had all long since passed. He was the last of the crowd.

Katherine moved woodenly through the store. She found herself making the rounds again and tried to shake the somber feelings. She forced herself to recall something good about him and remembered instantly, one more thing—her father's favorite dinner.

He called it the Mighty Man's Meal. He loved the modest menu above all else. It fit with his personality—simple and no-fuss. His favorite consisted of a steak, salad, and baked potato with all the fixings. Katherine suddenly put herself to work gathering all the ingredients he would have loved.

AT 6:00 P.M., KATHERINE, Grant and the boys sat down to this dinner. The boys dug in, carving their steaks and loading sour cream onto their potatoes. After a moment of remembrance for the grandfather they barely knew, they fell back into their chattering patterns. Underneath the table, Katherine squeezed Grant's hand. Leave it to the young ones to bring her out of the shadow of death.

They all set to eating and the discussion turned to Katherine's last appointment the next day. Grant had a job interview and arranged to meet the three of them at Annie's Parlor, just across the street from the University of Minnesota campus at around 6:30 p.m. Annie's was known for its famous burgers. After all she had been through, Katherine believed she deserved the biggest one they made. Her family said so, too.

CHAPTER THIRTY-SEVEN

MADISON GOT INTO HER CAR, careful not to spoil her nails. Before she started the engine, she gingerly explored her purse and fished out her cell phone. Her fingers tapped out William's number and she carefully held it to her ear.

"William here." His melodic voice gave her a pleasurable shiver.

"Hi, honey. It's Madison. What are you up to?"

"Hello, love." Williams sounded as if he was in positive mood today. "Just finished mediation and I have a packed schedule of readings to do in Cottonwood after I'm done at the office. How about you?"

Madison felt instantly deflated. She was hoping he'd be open most of the day to help her deal with Helen. How could she forget that he had a life, too? "Well, I was just going to ask you for some help with my ghost. I think I've put it mostly together, all this information. I just would like to have your affirmation."

She could hear William pause but then he powered on with his cheery voice. "No problem, old girl. Can it wait 'til later tonight? Say 9:30?"

Guilt crept into her head but she shook it off. She'd make sure to make it worth his while. "That would be so great, sweets. I'll get a bunch of sandwiches and snacks and I'll have your favorite ale ready for you."

"How can a bloke turn that down? I am at your disposal, my dear miss."

"Good," Madison exulted. "See you tonight."

NINE HOURS LATER, Madison sat in her living room waiting for either the phone to ring or William's lights to illuminate her driveway. She had gone a little overboard at the deli. The table held a mound of sandwiches (she could easily have fed an army), turkey, ham, and corned beef. There were plenty of chips and dips, and of course the requisite bottles of ale. She had also carefully laid out all the information she had on Helen's life, including the background check Ben had provided. She methodically gathered her notes and details of Helen's visits, as well as the unopened envelope of additional information Ben had sent.

She'd placed all her details in chronological order and filled out a profile of Helen's marriage and subsequent life with her sons. All she needed now was an outside opinion, a set of fresh eyes and an unsullied spirit. She got up and checked on Corriander. The clock ticked to 10:15 p.m.

AT 10:25, WILLIAM ARRIVED, exhausted but cheery. Madison greeted him with a quick hug. "How about a snack?" she asked.

"Sounds fantastic," he said. Within minutes he fell to polishing off two sandwiches and washed them down with a couple of quick beers. Madison wanted to let him decompress so she chatted with him and allowed him to share about his various clients. She was always so impressed by his ability to connect with positive energies within and around the customers. It seemed as though everyone came away from a reading with William with a renewed sense of self-worth and purpose. Madison wondered how many people she had affected that way.

After fifteen minutes, William was ready to turn his attention to Madison and Helen.

Madison went over every piece of information. She started with the afternoon of December 15 the year before, when she had first seen Helen.

"I remember that," he nodded his head. "You first talked to me about her, when, in late February, early March?"

"That's what I figure."

"Go on," he urged.

"The visits have come in spurts. It seems like they were longer in the beginning. I got big chunks of information, especially in my sleep. I was at her wake, I saw her children, and I was transported back to the time in her life before she had her younger son. She was employed at this wealthy man's home, his name was . . ."she leafed through her notes. "Ah, here—Louis Park. I don't know how long she worked there, but she ended up having an affair with his grandson."

"Wow," exclaimed William. He took a bite of a chip and shook his head.

"She gave me some really disturbing images today."

"Like the vision you had in Mexico?"

"No, haven't had that one again, thank God. That one scared the hell out of me, but I feel uncomfortable. I know it's connected and I'm just freaked out by it. Today was really strange. Flash after flash of images all of her youngest son." Madison shook her head. "What's the significance of that? Who am I supposed to be following, here? If her son is the subject, why doesn't he talk to me?"

"Are you sure she was the one that initiated the visit?"

Madison paused and considered. "Yeah, it was definitely her agenda."

"Well, go on, perhaps we'll figure it out as we move forward in the time span."

Madison went on to describe the lengthy portions of Helen's life that the ghost had invited, or rather inserted, her into. She told him of the segment in John's childhood. "At first, I didn't get why she took such a detour from her life and threw me into his."

"Why did she?" he asked.

"I think this was as much about him as her. Funny," she added. "Every time I think about him these last few weeks I get a strong pain in my stomach."

"Hmm, you know I interpret stomach pains to mean either cancer or—"

"Suicide. I know," she sighed. "I thought about that, too." She dropped from the couch down to the floor and stretched out her legs. She sat very near him and was suddenly distracted. His presence was magnetizing. She tingled from head to toe.

He leaned down into her face and gave her a beautiful sideways smile. "Yes, madam? Your thoughts?"

"Let's get back to that later," she smiled back into those deep translucent eyes. They reminded her of the ocean at high tide, holding so much life within them in the shallows of the pools.

"After she kind of introduced me to her son, she showed me the day he found out he was a bastard."

"A bastard!"

"Yes, William. He was the result of—"

"Ah, the playful grandson, Park. What was his name?"

She walked her fingers down the page. "Jerome."

"Pretty tidy name for such a naughty child." William ran a finger across his lips.

"Well he wasn't a child at this point, William. He was a young man, probably a bit younger than you. How old are you anyway?" Part of Madison scolded herself for this detour. Her sensibilities told her to press on with the investigation but she subconsciously begged her brain, *just one little diversion?*

"Really, Madison! You know it's not polite to—"

"Oh, c'mon William, we've known each other for what, four years?" She smiled at him coyly (or at least as coyly as she could—it had been a long time since she'd been on this kind of shopping trip).

"All right, first off, how old do you think I am?"

Was he being coy back? Madison decided he was. This was beginning to become fun. "I'd say . . ." She looked at his smooth skin and longish wavy hair. Not too many wrinkles, maybe one or two grays. His eyes (*oh, those eyes!*) were clear and full of sparkle. His frame was longish and lean. "I'd say thirty-five,"

He cocked an eyebrow back at her. "Right on the money, love. How'd you do that? Might you be some sort of psychic?"

She laughed back at him. "Now, your turn."

"I don't know," he hesitated, "this puts us into dangerous waters."

"Don't worry, I'm not age-phobic."

"Okay, then." He slid down from the couch and settled next to her. He turned and faced her as his eyes ranged all over her. She watched him consider her for maybe the first time in this new way. His eyes roamed her face and hair, he took care not to spend too long on her body, and his eyes came back to hers. "Ah, those eyes, Madison. The present time body may be anywhere from forty to forty-five, but those eyes are ageless."

Madison felt the melt immediately. Wow, did this guy have a way with words. She reached over and kissed him on the top of his head.

He gave her a responding kiss on her forehead and looked at her in a lengthening moment.

Somewhere inside, it felt like Helen was knocking at her with a big "get back to work," *thump thump*. "Okay, now that we have that out of the way, back to work we go."

"Hmm, if you insist," he replied obediently. He settled himself back on the couch and stretched his stocking feet.

"So we return to Helen's world." He took on a mock television announcer's voice, "When we last visited Helen, she was behaving quite the hussy," he declared. "What shall we find this time in the newest episode of, hmm . . . what would one call this?" He muddled over it for a minute.

Madison set her head against the couch and closed her eyes, waiting for his proclamation.

"I know, the newest episode of *As the Ghost Appears*."

"Oh great, I can see it now. Every afternoon at four."

"Do not mock, my friend," said William gravely. "For this is serious spiritual stuff."

Madison couldn't tell whether he was serious or kidding. She decided on the latter. "Love it, William. Maybe we've found our new profession—writing ghost tales."

"Well, let's move on so we can finish the story before I'm forty, all right, love?"

"Okay, okay," Madison turned back to her notes. "So, she goes on and gets pregnant. I don't know if she kept it a secret from her husband or not. I just remember she inserted me into her younger son's life one afternoon and gave me a quick snapshot of an eleven- or twelve-year-old boy growing up in the Midwest somewhere. Shortly after that, I became party to the night this boy John learned he was a bastard. It was terrible." Madison shuddered. The father just screamed the word at the dinner table. I don't think I'll ever forget the look of horror on that boy's face.

"Wait a second." Madison searched for a small post-it note, "Ah, here. Helen showed me this particular incident coming from a small photograph. She had written on it, '1936, Cecil's birthday.' It was the first thing I wrote down after the vision.

"You are sure the boy was around that age at that time?"

"Yes, I was able to live with him during it. I just felt like he was that age. It may not make sense but I trust it, anyway. Let's see, how old would that make him now?"

"2007," William mused. "Let's say he was eleven then, he would likely be between seventy and seventy-five this year."

"Yeah," she agreed, "but I don't get the feeling he's still with us, you know, my stomachache and all, and Janine and I used a pendulum to find out if he or his brother were still alive but we got 'no' for an answer."

William lay quiet, considering.

"Anyway, I'm rooted there in this space return continuum. And the father, Cecil, just goes off. He screams at Helen, and never even addresses John directly. It was so awful. The poor kid was basically held hostage to this man's drunken temper tantrum. Afterwards, the guy storms out and this John is left to live with something that will poison his life forever." Madison looked up at William. She wiggled her toes. "It was so strange to find myself inside the photograph, pushed back more than fifty years. Have you ever encountered that?"

"What?" he asked, "Experiencing an event along the space return continuum? Really only once, that time in Durango, remember, I shared with you?"

"Oh, yeah. Weird, both of those situations were so similar."

"Well, maybe it's that even though those who've passed have more astral and spiritual tools to move with, they only have a few ways to effectively communicate with us." He paused. "That would be our failing, not theirs. Wouldn't you agree?"

"I do." Madison said quietly. "That's why I always feel like this gift has me treading on hallowed ground, in some way."

"Wait a sec, old girl!" William scooted onto the couch. "You've been pretty vociferous about what a pain in the ass this has all been! Where is the 'hallowed ground' in all of that?"

Madison smiled at his crystal-gray eyes, "All right, you've got me. I do really know it's a special ability but then my crazy personality gets in the way. Imagine what a stronger clairvoyant I would be if I could erase myself from the whole scenario."

"Then, my girl, we would have none of the delightful presence that you bring to your clients and your friends. Plus," William arched one eyebrow. "I do believe the spirits show themselves to you precisely because of who you are. They know that you will be true to their message and that they shouldn't try to mislead you. Would you say that's true?"

"I sure as hell hope so, because if this broad's been bullshitting me, I'm going to find her on the other side and let her have it!"

"So I'm curious, when the father, what's his name, Cecil . . . had his outburst, was it because he'd just learned the truth, do you think?" William perched himself up on his arm.

"Well, he just blew up. He yelled at her that he was so sick of her and her son. But John and his older brother were sitting at the table. It was clearly meant for John, not his brother. I got the strong feeling that Cecil had absolutely known before. But this night, for whatever reason, was the straw that broke the camel's back. And boy, did it."

"Okay," William traced the information in the air with his finger. "We know that Helen was a mid-western housewife who worked for a wealthy family. She went and got knocked up, she had this illegitimate child and her husband left her . . . around the time of this incident?"

"No, I saw the day he left. The boys were just a few years older. He stormed out of the house after he said the most hurtful things. He must have been a truly tormented soul."

"No doubt."

"After that, I only saw a few more individual pictures again, just like today. I saw all these different moments of John growing up just as if I'd been looking at a photo album. You'll never guess where she showed them to me."

"Where?" William yawned, slowly starting to fall prey to a long day.

"In the mirror at the nail place today. I'm sure those little Vietnamese gals thought I'd been dropped off from planet loony!"

William snorted. "Well, you've got to hand it to this ghost, she certainly is creative."

"She is. But the thing, that really shook me up was the last vision I got. This one wasn't a simple photograph like the others. This was another scene. I was there again, in the background. I watched her whole world fall apart."

"What happened?"

"She and her son were in a hell of a fight. I was standing next to the driveway. John came blazing out of the house and practically jumped into his car. She came out behind him. She was screaming at him. He looked so despondent and at the same time so filled with hate. I think all those years of being a bastard to his mother were bubbling over."

"What was the fight about?"

"She was forbidding him to do something."

"To do what?"

"To have a child. To have an illegitimate child."

"Oh, God."

"Yeah, it was so heartbreaking, William. She was filled with disgust and she just poured it out onto this young man. But he held his own. It was if the dam broke open and he became his own person right then.

"It was scary and beautiful at the same time. He came into his own. He met himself, in a way, but they lost each other. I really don't think she ever saw him again."

"What a true, true shame," William said. He sat up now and slid down again beside her. She began to cry. He put his arm around her shoulder and held her head close to his.

"Jesus," Madison sobbed. "How did I let this spirit get to me?" She sniffled. "Why does she want to torment me so much?"

He said nothing and continued to hold her while she let out her frustration in a rant of words and tears.

"She's been torturing me for almost a year, William. What if this is more like a haunting? What if I never lose her? I may need a fucking exorcist to get on with my life!"

William touched her chin and lifted it. He gazed into her eyes and leaned closer. Madison drew her breath in quickly but before the air was in her lungs, he covered her lips with his. The kiss was soft and quick, too quick for Madison's liking, but it brought her back to the present.

William pulled away slightly, still looking into her eyes. "Ah," he said. "Even when I leave you, I can never get over the color of your eyes, love. They seem to put a spell over me."

Madison sat quietly, holding her breath. She wanted this moment to extend forever. She felt his strong arm around her and breathed his ale-laced breath. That aroma, mixed with the last lingering whiff of cologne, smelled like the loveliest fragrance in the world. She tipped her head back against his arm.

"Madison, this is a spot I'm happy to find myself in but I have a strong feeling I can't ignore."

Madison tensed suddenly. "What is it?" She wondered if he was going to say the kiss was a mistake.

"We've got to get back to work on this woman." He shifted his weight and sat up straighter. Madison sat up straight, too. The spell between them was broken, yet not broken, rather, but altered.

"I feel something is about to happen," he said. "I don't think she is going to be around you forever. She's building to something."

"Oh perfect, probably just in time for my birthday." She glanced at the clock on the mantel.

He looked at her in surprise. "Why didn't you tell me?"

"I was going to get around to it, but I haven't seen you." She answered, chagrined. She didn't want to move away from the hopeful magic of the kiss. "The gang is throwing me a little shindig at the Full Moon Saloon Thursday night at ten. I know it's a little late . . ."

"Woman, why am I always finding you a little late?"

She felt a tug of relief. He didn't seem to feel that the kiss was a mistake.

"Well, buddy, I hope you could get some sleep tonight or tomorrow and join us. It should be fun. I always love the sense that I'm starting my new fifty-two-day phase."

"Ah yes, the beginning of the first phase, six more to go and you've survived a whole new year. I've always found the cards fascinating that way." William said. "Fifty-two cards in a deck, fifty-two weeks in a year, twelve royal cards, twelve months."

"Four suits, four weeks in a month, four seasons, four elements: earth, fire, water, air," added Madison.

"The phases always bring us something." He said. "I feel at the beginning of mine a huge shift—like a giant 'out with the old, in with the new.' Sometimes it's the first day that shakes me in a whole new direction." William hesitated then turned toward her quickly. "What about . . . ?"

"Oh, my God," she answered. "You're right. We have her birthday. We can count her cycles." Madison eagerly dug through her pile of information. She opened the envelope and found two obituaries that Ben had sent her. Helen's birthdate was September 22, 1905.

They arrived at the beginning of the seventh period at the same time. Helen's last fifty-two day period had just begun. The clock read 12:45 a.m. Madison realized the date was August 1.

"This is really getting eerie," Madison whispered. "My first phase begins nearly at the same time as her last phase starts."

"Do you think that's why she found you specifically?"

Madison almost answered "yes," then remembered the first day she'd seen Helen. She rifled through her pages with William watching interestedly. "Wow," she said.

"What?"

"I left my tablets at the office. My notes on the first time I saw her are there. "I don't think she's come because of me, William." She shook her head adamantly. "I think that it has something to do with one of the women I read that day."

"But that was back in December. Do you even remember them? How many were there?"

"There were four that day." Madison remembered that much from her notes. "Two came in together." Suddenly the details crystalized. "They wanted to be read together. I read them separately. One of them made an impact on me. She was my Venus card! Yes! After *she* left is the first time Helen appeared."

"So Helen is attached to this woman?"

"I wish I knew for sure. I have a strong feeling it's this one lady from Minnesota. The Minnesota aspect didn't really hit me until I had another client who came in right before J and I went to Mexico. She was so nasty. She really pissed me off and then she told me she was from Winona, Minnesota. Something inside me lit up like a Christmas tree. Then Ben tells me Helen died in a town next to Winona.

"So, all things being equal, if I've got a strong feeling about this woman then I'll have to go with it. I don't know how Helen is attached. Maybe she's her grandmother or aunt."

"Wouldn't her obituary say?"

Madison grabbed it and scanned the first. It noted only that Helen was survived by five grandchildren. But when she opened the second obituary she found it more specific. She read it aloud. "Survived by . . . Here it is—'son Samuel Rhames, wife Caroline, (grandchildren Trent, Julia), son Jonathon Parkson, wife Doreen, (grandchildren Katherine, Carla, Christopher)'."

"Hey," William took it from her and pointed to John's last name. Didn't you say the young man who she dallied with had the last name of Park?

"Yeah, Jerome Park." Madison said.

"That would make sense," William replied. "You say he left his mother the day of their fight. Possibly never spoke to her again? Couldn't he have foreseeably created his own new last name to go with his new beginning without his mother?"

"Yes, yes, William. That's it exactly! I can feel it!"

"So, that means that perhaps this woman is, well, let's see if she's here." He ran his long finger down the names. "Jonathon and Doreen Parkson," he read. "Here, Katherine, Carla and Christopher."

"Oh my God," Madison couldn't believe it. "It's Katherine! All this time, the connection has been there under my nose!"

"Yes, but it seems as if you wouldn't have gotten to it if your ghost hadn't led you down this complicated path. She's a smart one, this lass!"

"So," Madison looked from the paper to William. "That's it. Helen has to be Katherine's grandmother. I bet Katherine doesn't even know it."

"Probably not, but we do now and we can watch for any more information, keeping in mind it falls in the context of a relationship that never occurred." William continued. "Maybe there is something Helen wants this particular grandchild to know, about herself, about life? I don't know but this is really becoming fascinating."

Madison stared at William as all the pieces fell neatly into place.

"Darling Mads, I think we should celebrate with one more ale. Then, I need to be marching home." William went to the kitchen to retrieve a beer for Madison and himself.

They sat on the floor side by side. The minutes lapsed into hours as they talked about everything except being psychics. They spoke of their childhoods, their histories up until they'd moved to Sedona. Madison felt as if she'd known William for so much longer than the four years since they'd met. She connected with him on a level that surprised her. They'd been causal friends for so long. What sparked this change? She remembered Janine's interest in William in Los Algodones. That was the turning point. She silently thanked Janine for the nudge.

After a brief foray into more kisses, William finally rubbed his eyes. "I can't say that I don't love this but I am really a bit toasted," he said.

"Okay, you're right. I'm sorry for the distraction."

He kissed her again. "Apology duly noted. I just want to make sure that we've got this ghost business as ironed out as possible. This old woman is on a mission. I just want to help her."

"Me too. Can you imagine how quiet my life would be without this spirit?"

"Perhaps the cause is to help her granddaughter in the coming days. You must be especially sensitive, love, to what she shows and tells you." William suddenly squinted as the morning sun shone in his eyes. They both looked at the clock—9:00 a.m.

"That's it, I'm over and out." He got up and found his shoes. He opened the front door and the promise of the day's heat came creeping into the living room.

"Thank you so much, William . . . for everything," Madison stood next to him and stretched on tiptoe to give him a brief kiss. "Will you be there tomorrow night?" she asked timidly.

"Wouldn't be anywhere else," he smiled. "Now," he swatted her on the rear and walked out the door. "Let me out of here, you lovely psychic hero, you!"

Madison stood on the front porch. The pleasant aroma of Manzanita bushes floated in the air. She watched him pull out of the driveway with a wave. She went inside, found her bed and promptly fell asleep.

CHAPTER
THIRTY-EIGHT

THE MORNING SUN lit the kitchen and spread a cheery ambiance. Katherine moved about busily. She had a whole day, actually a whole new life, to celebrate and she wanted the house to look just right.

The slight dimming of the light inside her from yesterday's memory of her father had completely gone. Now all she saw was a clean slate. She was so excited about how this day would turn out, how it would launch new dreams and new revelations that she didn't mind doing the laundry or wading through the boys' rooms to dust.

Everything, absolutely everything, was going to be perfect today.

It was so liberating not to have to go to the courts after spending so many summer hours in the sun. The cool air-conditioning felt invigorating. She barely noticed how the hours flew by until she saw her bedroom clock tick to 3:30 p.m. She exulted again at how great this day felt. No worries of the future, no agony over the past. She remembered a quote she'd seen somewhere, "I woke up today clothed in a right mind." She was truly fitted well today.

As soon as she finished making the bed, she went to take a leisurely bath. Then, she figured, she'd take a shower, dry her hair, put on her makeup and clothes in a slow, relaxed time frame. By the time 5:00 rolled around, she'd be ready to go with the boys.

AT 5:00, KATHERINE CALLED the boys for a second time. She'd rung Wes at 4:45 to remind them. With both of them at work, calling one was killing two birds with one stone. Wes hadn't answered at the time but this time after a couple of tries, he picked up.

"Hey, you guys coming?" She tried not to sound anxious.

"Yup. Wayne just has to find Marliss to finish his time sheet. So stupid, we have to go up to the office and turn in our time cards because the time clock in the kitchen is broken."

"Okay, well get here as fast as you can. I have a feeling traffic is going to be bad today. There's a Twins game tonight. You know that 394 is going to be packed going into the city and then with the construction on the bridge, it might just be a nightmare."

"Yeah, I know. Oh, here he is now. Wayne!" Wes yelled to his little brother. "C'mon, we gotta go. Okay, Mom, we're on our way. Be there in ten."

"Thanks, see ya sweetie." Katherine hung up the phone and looked around the kitchen. Was there anything she needed to do that would take ten minutes?

Her stomach was now growing a big knot. *Remember,* she admonished herself. *This day provides a jumping-off point.* She was a different person now. The radiation had acted like a psychological knife and cut out all the negativity she'd been carting around for the last three years. Three years! Could it have possibly been that long that this cloud had hovered over her spirit and in kind, her family?

As she'd lain in bed the night before, she'd gone over all the major ups and downs she'd had in the last few months. But she realized the funk had actually started far before then. Funny, she'd never considered that her slide into depression had been such a long one. Ironic that just yesterday it took her dad's presence in her mind to make her think bigger picture. If only he had been able to do that, himself.

Just then, the boys burst in the door. "C'mon, Mom," Wes crowed. "Are you ready yet?"

Katherine's bubble of anxiety broke. She grabbed her purse and went out to the car.

CHAPTER THIRTY-NINE

MADISON SNORED, so deep was her sleep. It was dreamless and rejuvenating. Only blackness and warmth enveloped her, until she woke with a start.

Helen stood at the foot of her bed, wringing her hands. She mouthed words that Madison couldn't understand. Helen's lips pushed out letters with no sound. Madison stared at the woman's face. She concentrated on the currents of energy creating the muscles to move and then the voice to speak.

"Help me stop them . . ." The words came out in a sliding, hollow groan.

Then in a flash as brilliant as a camera's, Madison was underwater looking up at a pile of cars and concrete falling onto her. She tried to close her eyes, to look away, to stop the crashing and pounding. She tried to roll this way and that to escape the cars falling. At the same time, huge chunks of rocks or cement plummeted past her. Helen was with her. Madison could feel her presence and hear the repeated whisper. "Help me stop them . . ."

Instantly, Madison stood alone, in front of a bridge. No one was near it. Only yellow construction tape showed any signs of movement, flapping lazily in the breeze. She saw ahead a sign with a 35 on it. She wondered, *is that the speed limit?*

Madison walked onto the bridge, noticing the complete stillness. She continued to the center of the bridge. Instantly, Helen stood in front of her, putting her hand out to stop her. The structure wavered as if it were a carpet being shaken to rid a layer of dust.

Beneath her the bridge fell away with a heavy drop.

Suddenly, there were cars around her, everywhere. Some had rear-ended others. Some, it seemed, were hanging over the edge of the bridge. Over the edge? That couldn't be right. She was still in the middle and could see the span on the other side. Then abruptly that section too jolted and sent cars careening. Horrified, she bolted to the edge and looked down. Below her, cars were smashed and sliced. They were perched upon and stuck beneath huge boulders of cement. Large portions of new blacktop lay everywhere like slices of chocolate from a fractured frosted cake.

Everywhere around her she saw people in the throes of death and panic. Some people in their cars were helplessly trapped. Her eyes roamed the faces.

Again, Helen was beside her. She grabbed Madison's hand and pointed her finger to a car below. Madison caught her breath. There, maybe fifty feet beneath her, was a car with three people inside, a woman and two young men. They were frantically trying to claw their way out of two half-lowered front windows as the water rushed in. She could see their panicked faces clearly. She didn't recognize the boys but she absolutely knew the woman.

Katherine Simon was screaming and banging on the window trying to break it. The two boys, who looked as though they could have been her sons, were trying to smash the glass of the windshield with their hands. It was hopeless.

Then Madison stood next to the three on top of the bridge, as they all gasped in horror as they watched the car sink. Katherine sobbed as she saw herself and the two boys fading beneath the rushing black currents.

Madison was so confused. Obviously, this was a terrible disaster. This bridge collapse felt so real! She realized she was standing next to a small sedan with Helen sitting calmly inside. Madison leaned in to look at her and Helen's somber eyes returned her gaze. She turned her head and pointed to the clock on the dashboard. It read 6:01. She looked back at Madison and mouthed the word *"Now!"*

Madison looked up and found herself standing in a stream of traffic creeping toward the once again intact bridge. She realized she'd been warned and started screaming at all the drivers to stop and turn back. As she wandered through the line of automobiles, she came to a car holding Katherine and her sons. They were intent in their conversation. Madison screamed and shrieked but Katherine and the boys didn't see or hear her. They continued to snake through the traffic toward the bridge. Madison banged on the side of the door but they drove on, passed her, and entered onto the bridge.

MADISON WAS FRANTIC. She bolted out the door and threw herself into the car. As she turned onto the highway toward her office, she wanted to speed but there was a cop right behind her. She couldn't believe she'd slept the whole day away until the images had assaulted her. She glanced at her dashboard clock. 4:20 p.m. That meant it was 5:20 p.m. central time. Jesus, this crazy scenario had better be right (of course, she didn't really want it to be) or the possible speeding ticket would add more than what she wanted by which to remember her ghost.

Her ghost. Madison surprised herself by labeling Helen in that way. For the past seven months, she'd called Helen practically every name in the book but what she'd seen in the last day had so connected her, she had become attached to Helen and her cause.

At least, "cause" is what William had labeled it. She thought of the night spent talking, researching, investigating together. It had all come together in the perfect painting. Helen had given her all the colors but one. That element had been saved for half an hour ago.

Madison had no idea what time she finally fell asleep. She had been so engrossed in finding out what Helen needed her to know that what seemed like seconds had actually lasted hours.

But she didn't have hours now. She had only minutes to share Helen's warning.

CHAPTER FORTY

WES SWUNG THE CAR onto I-394 and headed east toward the city. "Wow," he said, "you were right, Mom. This traffic is gonna take forever."

"Good thing we can go in the carpool lane," volunteered Wayne from the back seat.

"I just want to get there in time," Katherine worried. "Do you think we're going to be late?"

Wes glanced at the dashboard. "I don't think so. It's only 5:20 and we're almost to downtown."

"How does it feel, Mom? Your last day and all?" Wayne asked.

"It feels weird—like I've lived a lifetime in the past seven weeks. Doesn't it seem like forever since I found out?"

"It kinda feels like you just started and at the same time, like it was so long ago," Wayne answered.

"I know what you mean," agreed Wes. "Well, now it's the end and then we get to celebrate!"

"I can't wait!" Katherine exulted.

"Me, too!" Wayne drummed his hands on the back of her seat in anticipation.

The traffic snaked slowly into downtown. The line of cars going east on 94 stretched back at least a mile. Katherine glanced at the dashboard—5:45 p.m. She sighed and ran her hand along the partially open window. Inside her purse, her phone began to vibrate. She grabbed for it and found it at the bottom of her bag. "Darn," she said. "Missed it."

"Who was it?" Wayne asked.

"I don't know. What city has an area code of 928?" Both boys shook their heads.

"Never heard of that one before, maybe northern Minnesota?" Wes offered.

Wayne shook his head again. "Don't think so, I bet it's out of state."

"Oh, well," Katherine dismissed it. "They'll call back or leave a message if it's important," she said.

As if on cue, the cell phone vibrated again in her hand. The same number flashed on the screen. Katherine answered it on the second ring. "Hello?"

CHAPTER
FORTY-ONE

MADISON PULLED INTO the lot as quickly as possible. She burst in the door and galloped up the stairs. She nearly broke her office door down in her panic. Once it was open, she dashed to her desk. Her huge pile of tablets sat neatly stacked. There were easily a year's worth of readings in them. She plunged into them with growing hysteria, examining each volume as fast she could.

A sinking feeling began to overtake her. She looked up at the clock and saw it was 4:35. If she was right, she didn't have much time. Each tablet seemed to hold more and more information. At this rate, she knew she'd never find the number. But she went on, her fingers flying through the pages to look for that one day, December 15, 2006.

Five long minutes later she found December 20 and backed up five pages to the end of December 15. The last client had come in at 5:00. The client before, 4:00, and then there she was, Katherine Simon, 1:30 p.m. Madison's hands shook so violently she could barely run her fingertip through the notes. Finally, she found the woman's number and prayed it hadn't changed. The clock ticked to 4:45 and she dialed the number sloppily. She pushed END by accident before it connected. With trembling fingers, she slowed herself enough to carefully enter the numbers again.

The dial tone rang and rang. She then was pushed into the woman's voicemail. The panic set in. What if? What if all Helen's time and energy was wasted? What if it was too late? *No,* she scolded herself. *You keep trying.* She implored Helen to help. "C'mon lady. This is your grandkid. This is what you've been trying to tell me for almost a year. Do something!"

She dialed again and this time heard a connecting sound—a woman's voice came over the line, answering in a clear voice.

"Hello?"

CHAPTER
FORTY-TWO

Hello?" KATHERINE REPEATED. She noticed the number again. It seemed vaguely familiar. She stared at the traffic on I-94 packed in front of them.

"Hi, Katherine Simon?" The brusque voice asked.

"Yes, who's this?" Katherine looked at Wes and scrunched her brow.

"Katherine, this is Madison Morgan. Do you remember me? I was—"

"Wow, yeah. I remember you. We talked on the phone last spring. I met you last December?"

"Uh huh, that's me." Madison's voice sounded really stressed now. "Listen, I know you aren't going to believe this but I have a message for you. Don't worry about where it came from right now."

"Message?" Both boys were staring at her now, interested.

"There is going to be a terrible disaster on a bridge you might be taking in the next few minutes. I don't know where you are but you and your kids must not take the bridge. It's going to fall. I've seen what happens and you don't want to be on it."

"You gotta be kidding me." Katherine whispered.

"Honey, I wish I was." Madison rushed on. "Are you any-where near a bridge? Does the number 35 mean anything to you?"

"Well, we're pretty close but we're stuck in traffic and—"

Madison cut her off abruptly. "Listen to *me*! Stay away from this bridge with the *35* around it or on it. At 6:01 this thing is going to collapse."

"Collapse! That's terrible!" Katherine screeched. "What do you mean 'collapse'? How do you know this?"

"I told you, I'm not going to get into it now." Madison's voice jumped an octave in her hysteria. "You've just got to believe me, please."

KATHERINE'S FACE WENT WHITE. Wayne leaned up to her. "Mom, what is it? What's wrong?"

Katherine shook her head and spoke slowly into the phone. "How do I know this is real?"

Madison wanted to reach through the phone and shake this woman. She clearly didn't understand the gravity of the situation. The retorts for why she would never do this if it weren't true started to form in her head but she got a sudden shake and saw, in the corner, Helen's slight shimmering presence. This was accompanied by a sharp pain in her head. Knowing there was no time to waste, she added two more pieces of information for good measure. "Your grandmother told me. She is your father's mother. Don't you and your kids go over that bridge. How do you know I'm for real? I also know how your father died."

Katherine sat stunned, and then she formed the word, "How?"

Madison's voice filled with urgency took on a darker tone. "He killed himself. But we don't have time for this. Stay away from the Goddamned bridge. *Please!*"

In that moment, both Madison and Katherine were connected again, like that very first afternoon in icy Sedona. Katherine gathered herself and tried to erase the growing panic.

"Look, I gotta go," she said quickly.

"Please, please do what I said, don't get on that—"

Katherine cut Madison off. "I've got to go. I've got your number now. I'll call you back later." She pressed END and looked at her boys.

"You won't believe this." She said. "That was the psychic I saw in Arizona, last December. She's telling me I'm not supposed to go over this bridge. Jesus, she says it's going to collapse at 6:01!"

"What?" snorted Wes, "that's the craziest thing I ever heard! I hope she's not charging you. Why did you call her in the first place?"

"I didn't call her. She called me."

"Out of the blue?" asked Wayne incredulously.

"Yeah. She said the bridge with the 35 on or around it was going to fall. She said she'd seen it and it was terrible. The other weird thing she said was that my dad's mom told her about this. How could this be? I never even met her." Katherine sat forward quickly. She looked at Wes. "She also told me that she knew my dad was dead. And . . . she knew how he died. How would she know that? We didn't have a funeral for him. There was no announcement in the paper . . . How did she know that?"

"Mom, you can't believe this freak. She's not a psychic, she's a psycho!" Wes started laughing and Wayne joined in. Clearly the boys didn't take this seriously at all.

And then, it hit her. The boys. That Madison woman had said, "Don't you and your boys take the bridge."

"Oh my God," Katherine gasped. "She told me something else."

"Can't wait to hear it." Wayne smirked.

Katherine felt her fear swell. "She said specifically 'don't you and your boys go over that bridge.'" She turned and looked into Wayne's eyes. "How," she said in a desperate whisper, "would she know I was with you two?"

Wayne looked back at her, clearly perplexed. He and his brother shared a glance and then he shook his head. "I dunno, Mom, this just sounds so crazy. Doesn't it?"

"Sure as hell does," Wes agreed.

"It's absolutely the craziest thing I've ever heard," admitted Katherine. "But . . ." she sat back. Ahead of them, the traffic was starting to break up. "I don't know. Something inside of me is saying listen to her. I'm really feeling a sense that something is terribly wrong."

Katherine immediately turned to Wes. "Let's go the other way today." She said urgently. They were coming to the on-ramp to I-35W. "Yes," she said again. "Let's just do it today. What will it hurt?"

"It might make us late," warned Wes. But despite his caution, Katherine noticed a change of tone. Wes was considering the validity of this crazy woman, too.

"C'mon, honey. Let's take the other route. You have to get over now."

Wes pulled the car to the right and exited underneath the University of Minnesota sign. He followed the road around until he could turn left onto Washington Avenue. It seemed as if all three of them were holding their breaths. The clock said 5:57.

As Wes steered the car onto Nineteenth Avenue, Katherine felt a bit of doubt creep in. She hadn't heard from this woman since their phone consultation, (*when was that, late April?*) and she felt so odd and upset about this phone call. The information was all correct and that's what really freaked her out. How could this woman get all these things right? Who was this grandmother figure, anyway? Why would she be so concerned about a granddaughter who she'd never known?

Still, the reference to the boys was the trump card. How did this woman know the boys would be with her just now, and that they would indeed be heading toward the I-35W Bridge? She knew she hadn't mentioned where she was or whom she was with. So how could Madison possibly know?

CHAPTER
FORTY-THREE

MADISON SAT ON the floor of her office, head in her hands. She kept trying to bring back Helen's energy but the ghost was clearly gone. Madison wanted to call William in the worst way. She needed his calm affirmation that she'd done the right thing, but she didn't dare get hung up on the phone in case Katherine called back.

When she looked up at the clock a chill rifled through her. The hands stood at stiff attention—5:00 precisely—6:00 central time. Madison appealed to the Universe and begged on behalf of a woman she barely knew to keep her safe.

THE DRIVE ALONG NINETEENTH Avenue was quiet. Despite the immense traffic on 94, this street seemed a best-kept secret. The road widened a bit and then transitioned into Tenth Avenue. Katherine and the boys were silent, all sitting a bit forward in their seats as they maneuvered onto the Tenth Avenue Bridge. Katherine had always loved this beautiful old structure. Its lovely stone construction had graced the Mississippi River since the early 1920s, and it was a well-known historical landmark to everyone who traveled back and forth across the river.

Now they finally entered onto the bridge and found traffic again. "Wow, I thought we'd escaped the rest of it," Katherine said, calmly enough despite the sharpened knot in her belly.

"Me too," said Wes. "You never can tell how—"

A huge explosion stopped his words. Underneath them, the bridge shook gently. The dashboard clock read 6:01.

"Oh, my God," Katherine shrieked. "It's true, it's true!" She set her trembling hand on the door release and gripped it. "Oh my God," she screamed again. "She's put us on the wrong bridge!"

That realization propelled her and the boys into action. They leapt out of the car and started a sprint past the cars stopped behind them. Katherine then noticed something strange. She and the boys were the only ones running off of the bridge, which still stood solidly. All the people had left their cars and hurried over to the north side. She stopped.

"Wes!" She shouted to her older son, who looked around. "Mom, you've got to stay with us!" he panted as he ran back to her. "This is too dangerous. Wayne!" he yelled frantically. "Wayne, get back here. I've got Mom!"

"Look, Wes!" She grabbed his arm and pointed at the people leaning over the railing. There were dozens pointing and screaming. They held their hands over their mouths. They groaned and shrieked.

Katherine and the boys sprinted to the guardrail. The three of them joined the ever-growing mass of people huddled at the edge.

Katherine got to the cement-and-steel barrier first. She instinctively looked below her to assess for any damage but the bridge seemed normal. Quickly her scan rose from the bottom of the huge pilings beneath her to the river only yards upstream.

The I-35W Bridge was disconnected from bank to bank. It had pancaked onto the shore and into the fierce river. Everywhere, in the water, on the bridge center section—which sat in the middle of the rushing currents—people were screaming for help.

"Oh my God," shouted Wayne. He pointed to the water. "There must be at least fifteen cars in the water! Look at those people! Look at the red car going under! Wes, let's go. We've got to help!" Wayne looked at his mother worriedly before he grabbed his brother. "Mom, will you be okay?"

Katherine stood in a state of shock. She put her hand out to stop Wayne but was interrupted by a man who stood next to them. He forcefully took hold of Wayne's arm.

"Nothing any one of us can do, young man. See all the people on the banks? There are plenty there. Now the rescue squads are coming. Amazing," the stranger marveled. "How did they get here so fast?"

Wayne and Wes stood staring across the river at the devastation. Wayne looked at the man and nodded his head reluctantly.

"Yeah, look, Wayne," Wes pointed to the east bank of the river. "Look at all the rescue people. They're pushing the bystanders back."

Katherine, Wes, and Wayne perched paralyzed above the black, fast-moving water. Katherine began to cry. "Oh, those poor people! I can't stand it. How are they going to get them out of the water?"

They stood in horrified silence as the crowd behind them pushed and crowded to the side of the bridge. The structure, just yards upriver from them, was divided into three parts. The opposite river banks' sections teetered at steep angles above the water. Police and firemen desperately lowered ropes into the water and tried to get access onto the middle span, where survivors still sat in their cars. Above that shattered newly paved segment, cars still halfway on the east side clung on the shore's span. A yellow school bus sat perilously near a burning semi-trailer. Katherine could see a young man trying to get a group of children off the bus and away to safety.

Everywhere, there were flashing lights and sirens but Katherine could only see the people. One man crawled to the roof of his car as it floated in a tangle of cement and steel. He kneeled precipitously, one hand frantically waving in the air, the other gripping the top of the broken out window. Two others nearby had climbed out of their car only enough to hold on to the door amidst the rushing currents.

Other cars were stuck in the river's grasp. They bobbed, floated and sank as they moved with the flow. Some cars stayed stuck amidst the debris covered in as much as thirty feet of water.

"Mom," Wes grabbed her shoulder. "We should get off this bridge. You never know if it's been damaged somehow by the force of the other one falling."

Wayne took her other arm and between her two boys, Katherine joined the crowds migrating slowly.

CHAPTER
FORTY-FOUR

MADISON LOOKED at the clock. It read a calm, impersonal 6:15. She couldn't believe fifteen minutes had passed so quickly as she sat rocking back and forth on the carpet. She got up stiffly and stumbled to her desk.

Madison quickly turned on her computer. She found CNN's website and watched as the site loaded. On the front page under the BREAKING NEWS banner was the thing she hated to see. The bridge looked like a fractured leg. It was broken into three pieces: two on either side of the river and the third stuck in the middle. Everywhere it looked like controlled pandemonium. Workers and ordinary people worked together to pull people from cars in the river and on the hanging spans.

A feeling of despair mixed with hysteria and panic rushed through her. She also got a very strong sense of death and it rattled her. She scanned the video, looking for Katherine among the people on the bridge, but all the camera showed were hordes of people roaming like a frantically chaotic stream of ants.

CHAPTER
FORTY-FIVE

A S THEY MADE their way toward their car, Katherine was struck by the size of the crowd all around them. She and the boys found their car, grabbed their cell phones, locked the vehicle, and joined the line of people moving slowly off the bridge. The evening air howled with the shriek of sirens.

Katherine dialed Grant but kept getting the busy circuit message. She tried three more times and finally connected with his voicemail. *He must still be in his meeting,* she thought frantically. She waved at Wes and pointed to his cell phone and then to her wrist. "What time is it?" she mouthed.

"6:15" he mouthed back.

Katherine tried to keep her voice steady. "Hi, honey." She could hear the anxious cadence to her words. How could she not sound that way, after what she'd seen? "I'm with the boys and I want you to know we are all okay." She licked her lips. They felt parched.

"We're heading off of the Tenth Avenue Bridge and Grant—" she broke down now, sobbing. Wayne put his arm around her shoulder and gave his brother a concerned look. "It was so awful! The 35W Bridge just collapsed and there are so many people in the water and in smashed cars and—"

Wes grabbed the phone from her. "And we're all okay, Dad. We're walking back to the west side. We'll walk 'til we can find a place where we can call a cab. We locked the car and left it."

Just then, in the middle of the voicemail, the phone rang with a call-waiting signal. Katherine took the phone back and peered at the screen. "Oh, thank God," she said shakily. "It's your father." She stopped and stepped aside from the moving crowd. "Grant, honey. Something terrible has happened."

"What, Kath? What happened?" He sounded panicked. "Are you okay?"

"Yes," she answered. "The boys and I are okay. We're on the Tenth Avenue Bridge. Oh, Grant," her sobs began again. "The 35W Bridge is down. We saw it. There are injured people everywhere, in the water, on the bridge."

"Kath, are you sure you're okay? Give the phone to one of the boys."

She held the phone away from her ear and Wayne took it. He looked at his brother and tilted his head toward the exiting on-lookers. Wes immediately got the message and led his shaking mother away.

"Dad? It's Wayne."

"Oh my God, honey, are you guys okay?"

"We're fine. You won't believe what happened," Wayne's voice shook. "We decided to take the Tenth Avenue Bridge and the 35W just collapsed right as we would have been on it. It's so surreal, Dad. It's so horrible."

"Okay, buddy, stay calm. Which direction are you walking?"

Wayne described where they would end up once off the bridge. Grant knew it would take him an hour to get there even though he was close on the Mississippi's east bank. He gave directions for Wayne to find a place where a cab would be able to pick them up. He told his son to hurry. Most people didn't know about the collapse yet. They could get lucky and get a ride if they got away from the bridge quickly.

Wayne hung up and trotted to keep up with his mother and brother. As he handed the phone to Katherine, the phone rang again.

"Hello?" Katherine's voice trembled.

"Katherine, oh Lord. Are you okay?" Madison stumbled over her words. "Where are, I mean, did you—Oh crap," was all she could get out.

Katherine sounded weary. "We're okay, Madison. We listened to you. My God, we listened to you—" She began sobbing once again. "It was terrible. Just like you said. It happened just like you said. There are people in the water, still on the bridge. It collapsed in one huge explosion."

"I see it." She turned the volume down on her computer. The images looked even more surreal with no sound behind them.

"There are people everywhere. There must be a hundred people on this bridge. We're all walking together. We left our car in the middle of the bridge. They are making us get off now."

Madison was immediately panicked. "Which bridge?"

"Don't worry," Katherine's voice grew stronger, the initial shock wearing off. "We're on the Tenth Avenue Bridge. It's just a few yards downstream—wait, is this bridge okay?"

"I don't get a feeling that it's not, but I'd really rather you guys get the hell off the damn thing and get out of there."

"I will. We are. I don't even know what to say to you. I don't understand how you knew all this but I'll never be able to thank you. You don't know how scary this is. We would have been right in the middle of it."

Madison had never been so thankful. She felt her heart nearly explode out of her chest with relief. "I'm so glad."

Katherine went on, "I'm looking all around and it seems like rescue people are coming from everywhere." She paused. "Look, I'm gonna go now. I'll call you back."

Then, just before Katherine pushed the END button, Madison could hear five brief words: "Hey, guys, look at that."

Madison started to respond but was cut off. She got a sudden familiar shiver and closed her eyes expecting to see Helen. She saw nothing at all, but realized intuitively what Katherine was looking at.

KATHERINE POINTED BACK behind them. About fifty feet away an older woman stood next to the guardrail. Katherine had to shield her eyes from the sun to see her. It wasn't easy to tell what her face looked like. The reflection of the sun bounced off the pavement and blocked her features. She looked strangely displaced standing in front of the railing looking down into the river below. The woman turned toward Katherine and held her hand up as if in greeting. Her image shimmered in the heat.

Katherine rubbed her eyes again and blinked. "Boys," she said more forcefully this time. "See that lady over there? Let's go help her. She looks lost."

Wes and Wayne looked back in their mother's direction to see the woman behind her. Both saw only an empty expanse of railing stretching across the river.

CHAPTER
FORTY-SIX

THE EARLY EVENING STORM had cleared away from Sedona's cliffs with a steady wind from the east. The remaining clouds on the horizon looked like a collection of cotton candy treats. They lingered above the red rocks, the wispy puffs glowing ruby on the bottom and silver on top.

Madison thought they looked absolutely delightful and told Coriander so. He only opened one eye slightly in response. He was perched on Madison's belly. The minute Madison sat down with a cold beer in hand, the cat jumped up and draped himself across her, comfortably yet precariously rocking back and forth with her slow breaths.

She took a sip of her beer and rolled the word "psychic" around in her brain. The word felt good. It fit now, and she knew it in a way she'd never experienced it before. This was her destiny. Madison was gifted, insightful, and qualified. She was Madison Morgan, Extraordinaire, no doubt about that and despite whatever misgivings she had about this life, it was one she was destined to inhabit. The thought of returning to this existence felt comforting, like putting on a familiar pair of shoes.

She laid her head back against the lounge chair and reveled in the rare coolness of the evening. The storm had broken the oppressive 100 degree heat with a swat of cool air and a downpour of rain. The plants in her backyard looked revived. The fragrances of her creosote bushes and Mexican and autumn sage shrubs gave the backyard the aroma of paradise. Even the piñon tree looked perkier as it waved its branches at her.

"Well," she told herself sleepily. "It's over and done. Everybody's been put away . . . right? Everybody?" She called into the twilight. She neither heard nor felt anything. She was alone . . . for now, at least. Madison toasted the quiet energy of the yard and took another swig.

She yawned and allowed all the events of the last eight months to settle in her. Despite the chaos of the process, the days and weeks when she'd been certain she was crazy, her instinctive belief in her own abilities had given her a clearer view. She was finally at peace, knowing who she really was. It was if she were standing on the top of Airport Mesa and seeing Sedona for the first time in all its clear, crystalline, ethereal beauty.

Madison gazed up at the sky. She should have known better than to question the Universe, even when it communicated in the most veiled and circuitous ways. The Universe was always right and always in its right time.

Her cell phone's ring punctuated the crepuscular silence. "Hello?"

"Madison? That you?"

She adjusted herself in the chair. "Yesss? Speaking. Who may I ask is calling?"

Ben's voice echoed his eternally joyful bellow. "Your biggest fan, of course. Well, gal, you seemed to have survived the experience none the worse for wear," Ben beamed on the other end of the phone. "Had any visitors lately?"

"Nope, the last couple of weeks have been quiet."

"Okay, so tell this old man, is your Helen ordinary now?"

"Oh, her," Madison snorted. "Can't even remember what she looks like. Maybe it was all a dream."

"Some dream, the way it turned out, huh?"

"Yeah, that's for sure. I don't know all the ins and outs of it, Ben. Maybe I never will. But I sure get a sense of closure, of peace. This ghost is done chasing me. Thanks to her work, she got the job done. I think she feels she made up for some of the mess she spread into the Universe. Thank God she followed me around. She saved three people's lives." Madison said a quick prayer for those thirteen who had not been so lucky.

"It's really something," Ben said, "when you see a full circle experience happen. But it's really something else when you are a part of it. Madison, I'm really proud of you."

Madison grinned. "Thanks, Ben. Couldn't have done it without you."

Ben answered in his cheery cadence. "Don't thank me. I think there's a certain astral celebrity who needs some applause. I, for one, have to offer my own thanks to our spirit. No accident, our reconnection. Maybe we should invite her to join us every now and then."

"Don't give her any ideas. All I need is a never-ending traveling Helen road show. You could really lock me up if that happened!"

"Well, Madison, I don't think you'll hear or see her any more. She's completed her destiny." Ben sounded quiet, more contemplative. "Amazing, really, to come back to this realm, to work this hard—"

"To choose me!" Madison shifted accidentally, knocking Coriander to the ground. "Such a smart ghost."

"I'm off now, Miss Extraordinaire. Look forward to seeing you next month for our symposium. I think you'll blow the socks of this crop of new students."

"Sounds great," Madison answered. "See you soon." She clicked the OFF button and settled back into the lounge. Coriander quickly reclaimed his sleeping spot. The yard settled into sweet silence again. The energy was clear in the air and in her head. She was so relieved, so complete in this moment. This had been a destiny-changing year, for her, the ghost and her granddaughter two thousand miles away. Who knew what the coming years would bring?

She glanced quickly at her watch. 7:00 p.m. She had at least an hour before she had to get up and get ready to meet William for dinner. Madison closed her eyes and drifted off to sleep. Above her in the sweeping piñon tree, the wind chime jingled softly.